NOOGIE'S TIME TO SHINE

Other books by Jim Knipfel

The Buzzing
Quitting the Nairobi Trio
Ruining It for Everybody
Slackjaw

JIM KNIPFEL

NOOGIE'S TIME TO SHINE

A NOVEL

Distributed by Holtzbrinck Publishers

This is a work of fiction although it was inspired in part by a real ATM caper. All of the characters, companies, organizations, and events portrayed in this novel are either the products of the author's imagination or used fictitiously and are not to be understood as real.

Portions of this book, in different form, appeared previously in *Mezzomint*.

FIRST EDITION

Designed by Laura Lindgren

Library of Congress Cataloging-in-Publication Data
Knipfel, Jim.
  Noogie's time to shine : a novel / Jim Knipfel. — 1st ed.
    p. cm.
  ISBN-13: 978-0-7535-1283-8
  ISBN-10: 0-7535-1283-1
  1. Fugitives from justice—Fiction. 2. Life change events—Fiction.
I. Title.
  PS3611.N574N66 2007
  813'.6—dc22   2007025175

10 9 8 7 6 5 4 3 2 1

For Morgan, with my deepest love and gratitude

"First is first and second is nobody."
—Mr. Brown, *The Big Combo*

PROLOGUE

December 25
9:30 a.m.

He averted his eyes. He always tried to avert his eyes when he was near a mirror. These days he did, anyway. He just didn't want to know.

No, that's a lie. He knew well enough. Just say he didn't want to be reminded. He'd watched the softness grow and spread, from his ass to his belly, then upward toward his face. Somehow seeing himself that way while he was brushing his teeth only made things worse.

It wasn't always this way. He used to love mirrors. They confirmed everything he wanted to believe. He may not have had much else going for him when he was a kid but he did have his looks—the hair, the dark eyes, the winning smile. He was sure they'd do something for him. But that was another life, and one that was long gone. Somebody else. Now, God—he shouldn't feel this way. With what he had? Stupid. But he couldn't help it.

Removing the toothbrush from his mouth, he forced himself to look in the mirror, if only for a second. He squinted hard, his eyebrows crawling close together, his white-smeared lips tight. Then he stopped. Even that didn't work anymore. There wasn't anything there. Now he just looked queasy.

He opened the cabinet over the sink with his right hand as he continued brushing with the left, just to turn the mirror aside. As he worked the plastic brush, his eyes drifted idly over the shelves.

Shaving cream, antacid, toothpaste, razors. All those plastic amber bottles, most of the printing worn off the labels. Deodorant. Band-Aids.

He bent and spit the foamy toothpaste into the sink, watching it swirl down the drain. He replaced the toothbrush in the small rack under the cabinet. Then, cupping his hands under the open faucet, he sipped what he could, swished it around his tongue, and spit that out, too.

He shook the cool water off his hands, rubbed them on his T-shirt, closed the cabinet door, and headed for the kitchen.

It was too warm outside. For Christmas it was. Unnatural. That was something else that used to be different. The earlier life again. But with the air on at least he could ignore it. Keep the shades pulled. Forget all about the sun and the heat.

In the kitchen, the heavy gray cat buffed against his bare shin. He reached down with a grunt and scritched it behind the ears. The cat tilted his head back, his blue eyes half closed, the mouth cracking open just enough to bare the points of his lower fangs. That, at least, was something that hadn't changed. He smiled slightly at the creature.

With another small grunt, he pushed himself straight again and opened the fridge, reached in, and pulled out a beer. It was about all that was left in there now, beer. Looked like enough for the day. Good. It meant he wouldn't have to go out. It was all he needed at this point. If he ran out, there was that half bottle of Harveys out there. That'd carry him through.

He popped the can, returned to the living room, and lowered himself slowly onto the black leather couch. So much grunting these days. These past few months anyway. Fuck it. He tipped the beer can back. A few empties from the night before still cluttered the coffee table in front of him. He noticed that there wasn't as much left in the Harveys Bristol Cream bottle as he'd figured. Maybe the cat got into it when he'd let his eyes close.

He picked up the remote and started clicking through the channels. Seven different stations were showing that fucking *It's a Wonderful Life*. He hated that movie so goddamn much. Lies. He always wanted to take the film, cut it right at the point when Jimmy Stewart jumps in the river, then roll the closing credits. He'd rerelease it as *It's a Horrible Life*.

Five other stations were showing the original *Miracle on 34th Street*. A couple dozen were showing religious crap.

He kept flipping, thinking it was hopeless. Nobody was going to be showing *Christmas Evil* or *Black Christmas*, he'd bet. Not at nine on Christmas morning. Maybe he could find something with the great Whit Bissell in it. Shouldn't be too hard—Whit Bissell was in damn near everything.

Then on the screen he saw Lee Van Cleef's face, and he stopped there. He punched up the volume a few notches.

Lee Van Cleef was telling Karen Black how she should go about removing the bullet that was lodged in his belly.

Thank God for cable, he thought. Hell, he probably *could* find *Christmas Evil* if he kept looking. This was fine for now, though. He took another swallow.

Weird that *The Squeeze* would be shown twice around the holidays. There were other things that made much more sense, most of them crap. There wasn't a sleigh bell or group of stupid carolers anywhere in the movie. But who cares? Cast like that.

He was suddenly very glad it was being shown again. Just to thumb their noses, maybe. He remembered that the first time around, in the hotel room, the ending confused the hell out of him. So many contrived twists. Too many, he thought. Too clever for its own good. At least the director thought so—or maybe the writer. That's the impression he had. He'd been drunk at the time, so maybe that got in the way a little bit. Now at least he knew what he was headed toward. Never understood people who couldn't see movies if they knew the end. Knowing the ending helps you pay more attention to the rest of the film. 'Course that generally reveals how sloppy most directors are. Lazy bastards.

He took another drink. The cat had curled up tight at the far end of the sofa, paws covering his eyes.

He set the can of beer on the table in front of him, then stretched out on the sofa, careful not to kick the cat. He pulled the throw pillow from beneath his head and clutched it against his belly. His eyes stared at the screen.

Yeah, Merry fucking Christmas, he thought.

PART ONE

1

There was a gnat in the room. More than one. From where Ned lay, it sounded like there were hundreds of them, one or two making a shrill, hard dive toward his ear every few minutes. Just enough to keep him awake.

He rolled over in the narrow bed. His back, chest, and ample belly were sticky with sweat. The gritty sheets didn't make things any more comfortable.

A few hours earlier—what he guessed to be a few hours, at least—his brain had begun to swirl with half phrases and old injustices. Memories he'd rather not remember. Like that time when he was a kid and the bees had chased him. He'd hid in the garage, but they seemed to have known he was there and waited for him to come out. Nobody believed him when he told them about it. What was that line from the Bible again?

It happened without warning once a month or so, this not being able to sleep. He'd be sleeping as fine as he normally did when his eyes would abruptly snap open in the darkness and his brain would start marching in tight, jagged circles.

And sometimes, like tonight, there were the gnats to contend with.

There was no breeze through the open window above his bed, and he could hear every tiny sound from the sidewalk outside. On the street, a car pulled up to the stoplight, blasting some of that salsa crap at an inhuman volume. He hated that kind of music and he hated whoever was playing it. Ned was tempted to scream something at them, tell them to turn it the fuck down, but he figured they'd never hear him—not over that racket—and if they did, they'd probably just shoot him with one of those zip guns they used.

He rolled up on an elbow and peered at the dusty clock radio on the bedstand. It was two-thirteen. Who the hell plays anything that loud at two-thirteen in the morning? The car turned the corner and sped away.

"Shit," he whispered, before letting his bulk flop backward onto the pillow once more. He had to do something. If he didn't he'd be a mess. If he did something now, he'd still be able to get three or four hours of sleep before he had to leave for work.

He dropped one foot to the carpeted floor, then the other, and pushed himself into a sitting position. He leaned over and felt for the thin bathrobe he'd hung on the bedpost the night before.

He stood, found the shirt on the chair next to his bedroom door, and reached into the breast pocket for the pack of cigarettes and the matches. He knew the smokes would be stale by now— he'd been carrying that same pack for a month—but he was glad to have them.

He opened the bedroom door and stepped quietly down the short hallway to the kitchen, where he dropped the cigarettes and matches on the table. Without bothering to turn on the light, he opened the cupboard above the refrigerator and felt for the half bottle of Grant's whiskey. It wasn't the best, but it was pretty cheap and came in a triangular bottle. He always liked that, for some reason. It was also the only booze he dared keep in the house, shoved to a back corner of the cupboard where she couldn't reach it.

He found a juice glass in the sink, splashed some whiskey into it, and returned to the table.

This should do the trick, he thought as he lit the stale cigarette. *Smokin' an' drinkin'.* He exhaled and immediately felt himself begin to relax.

It seemed like only a matter of seconds before he heard the shrill croak from down the hall.

"*Noogie!*"

He squeezed his eyes tight and felt all of his back muscles contract simultaneously. "Yeah?" he shouted back.

"*I think the house is on fire!*"

Eyes still shut tight, he took another pull from the cigarette and blew it in the general direction of the voice before answering. "No, Ma, the house ain't on fire."

"*I smell smoke!*"

"It's just me, Ma. I'm havin' a smoke."

"*Well, put it out—it stinks!*"

Sometimes he wished she'd at least bother to get out of bed to yell at him. It'd save an awful lot of yelling. But no, he knew she was lying there, comfortable, head on the pillow, eyes closed, and the minute she no longer smelled smoke she'd be fast asleep again. She wouldn't remember any of this in the morning.

"Sure, Ma," he said into the darkness, then stood, moved to the sink, turned on the water, and stuck the smoldering butt beneath the stream. Maybe he should think about getting a small fan or something. Something that would blow the smoke out the window before it reached her room. Or he could always go out on the front step. Only problem with that was knowing she'd hear the door open when he came back in, become convinced he was a burglar, and call the cops before he had a chance to convince her otherwise.

Ned loved his mother. He really did. She'd taken very good care of both him and his dad all the while his dad was sick, and she still took very good care of him after his dad died. But *Christ* she could grate on his ass sometimes.

He downed the whiskey, nearly gagged, screwed up his face, shook it off. Then he poured himself another splash and downed that too, with the same reaction. He shoved the bottle to the back of the cupboard again and returned to his room. As he tried to crawl back into bed, however, he heard a deep growl from near the pillow. Or, more specifically, a growl from the pillow itself.

He flicked on the small lamp next to the clock radio and found Dillinger, his aging and overweight Siamese cat, staring at him with enormous blue eyes. The cat appeared to have no interest in moving.

"C'mon, scat," Ned said, gesturing. But Dillinger had already closed his eyes again. Ned waited a moment, sighed, then reached out with both hands, scooped the cat off the pillow, and dropped it to the floor.

"You're rushin' toward death, swear to God," he said as it marched out of the room with a series of complaining meeps and indignant slaps of the tail.

Finally, Ned lowered himself back onto the pillow, thinking that it had all been an exercise in futility. Thinking also, as he had once or twice a day for the past thirty-some years, that he really, really hated being called "Noogie."

Within ten minutes he was asleep again, in spite of everything, until the radio went off at six-thirty.

Noogie felt a small flash of pride every time he buttoned his gray, short-sleeved work shirt. It wasn't the red-and-white PIGGYBANK, INC. patch sewn over his right breast pocket so much as it was the epaulets on his shoulders. He wasn't exactly sure what they were for, but he knew they gave the whole ensemble that added touch of class. That and the silver shield pinned to his left breast pocket. The badge didn't really say much of anything if you looked at it closely, but that didn't matter. What mattered is that it was a uniform. An official uniform with a badge and epaulets. That's what impressed people. That's what earned him respect.

He pulled on the black pants with the gray stripe down each leg, then—this was the really important part—he reached over to the hook on the back of his bedroom door where the holster belt hung.

He always got a flutter in his stomach when he strapped on the gun. That was worth a hell of a lot more than even the epaulets and the badge. After it was buckled and secure around his soft and growing midsection, he stood in front of the mirror and admired himself. He lowered his head and glared up from beneath his eyebrows. He scowled slightly. Yeah.

Despite what he knew in his heart to be the God's honest truth, Ned Krapczak, at thirty-five, did not inspire confidence and respect in those members of the public he encountered every day. His weight had quietly inched up well past two hundred pounds in the past few years, which was pretty hefty for a guy who was only five-foot-nine. His dark hair grew over the tops of his ears and hung in straight bangs across his forehead. And though he thought the thin mustache that arced low across his upper lip made him look suave, sort of like Robert Taylor or Clark Gable, it only left him looking a little sleazy. If anything, those who knew such things thought he looked much more like Joe Spinell than Clark Gable.

Still standing in front of the mirror, he unsnapped the holster, slipped out the .22 pistol, and aimed it at his reflection.

"It's your move," he whispered at himself. He paused, checked to make sure the safety was on, pointed the gun again, and pulled the trigger.

With a private smile, he returned the gun to the holster and headed to the kitchen for a quick cup of coffee and piece of toast—and, with luck, very few complaints from his mom—before grabbing his clipboard and heading out.

. . .

It wasn't a bad job, as jobs go. Not at all. Not like the others he'd had since he got out of school—busboy, convenience store clerk, janitor. Here he got to wear a real uniform, not just some stupid costume. More than that, he got to wear the gun. Hell, he was almost a cop. Even if it wasn't his dream job, it was something he'd be able to draw on later.

Plus, the job kept him moving. He liked that. "Always gotta keep moving," he'd tell people. "That's real important." The hours weren't bad, and it paid okay, if not great, for being pretty easy work. The thing he liked most about it (apart from the gun-toting part) was the fact that it brought him into the city almost every day. Noogie had grown up in Jersey City, and while he was fine with that—still lived there, after all—he always saw New York in the distance, like Oz, or Rome, or one of those magical cities from his Dungeons and Dragons days.

A lot of his work took place in northern Jersey—Jersey City, Newark, Hoboken. But when he'd been assigned to handle a few places in Manhattan as well, he was thrilled. Some of the guys he knew from around the neighborhood were actually afraid to go into New York, but not Noogie. He always knew it was where he belonged. Ever since high school, he'd gone into town every chance he got. That's where the action was.

Ten minutes after pulling out of the driveway of the tired, cramped two-bedroom house he shared with his mother (that's the way he preferred to think of it—he shared it with her; he didn't live with her), he pulled his battered black van into Happy Jack's Secure Parking Lot. The sign out front announcing the name also sported a big picture of a lobster. Noogie never really knew why, and he never bothered to ask.

The eighteen-year-old Puerto Rican kid who was working the lot that morning waved him in. He drove to the back corner, as always, and parked in his regular spot. He grabbed his clipboard and climbed out of the van, then strolled over to the booth, where the kid was reading the *Post* and smoking a cigarette.

"Anybody win?" Noogie asked him, sliding the keys to his van across the small counter, not bothering to notice what section of the paper the kid was reading.

"Teamsters, it looks like," the kid replied.

Not knowing much of anything about sports, Noogie assumed this was some new expansion baseball team. "Well that's good," he said as he accepted the second set of keys the kid handed him.

As he walked away, he didn't hear the kid mutter "stupid ass" under his breath while turning the page.

Noogie returned to the far corner of the parking lot, unlocked the small armored van parked next to his own 1985 Ford Econoline, tossed the clipboard on the front seat, and climbed in.

PiggyBank might have been a fairly low-rent operation so far as ATM businesses were concerned, but the bosses did shell out for two permanent parking places, which Noogie thought was pretty swell.

He checked his watch as he pulled up alongside the back doors of the Greenstreet Bank, six blocks away from the parking lot, on Manila Avenue. For a small independent bank, it handled an unusually large volume of transactions every business day. One of those was the business account PiggyBank had set up to supply the 115 cash machines it maintained in the New York area. So long as he was the company's man out here, Noogie was the only one in town who had access to that account, which at any given time might contain well over two million dollars.

To say he had "access" to it is a bit of an overstatement, though. Each one of those 115 cash machines was connected to a computer system in Fort Lauderdale, Florida, where PiggyBank was headquartered. Every time someone withdrew some money from one of its machines, that amount was registered on the central computer. Every two weeks, the total amount of money removed from those machines was tallied, then redeposited into the Greenstreet account. Every day, Noogie stopped at the bank and received a canvas bag full of cash. On a normal day, the bag might contain between thirty-five thousand and fifty thousand dollars (depending upon the stops he had to make), all of it in tightly bound stacks of twenty-dollar bills.

Noogie's job then was to drive the bag of cash around to the convenience stores, bodegas, greengrocers, bars, and large grocery stores that featured PiggyBank machines and refill the ones that needed refilling.

He didn't hit all 115 every day. It was a question of volume. Some machines doled out only a couple hundred bucks a day, others—especially the ones in the big grocery stores—several thousand. Some places, Noogie had to stop by only once a week, while others he hit every day. Everything was all mapped out for him on the checklist he carried on the clipboard.

Before he had even killed the engine, the back door to the bank opened, and Roy, the aging, too-thin security guard, waved at him.

"Hey, Noogie," he said, without much enthusiasm.

"Hey, Roy," Noogie said, climbing from the van. "This is a stickup."

It was a joke Noogie made every single goddamn day, and one Roy had never found all that funny. It sure made Noogie laugh, though. Every day.

As Noogie walked to the back of the armored car sorting through his keys, he asked, "Got it all set for me?"

"Yeah," Roy told him, again without much enthusiasm.

The armored car was not exactly a top-of-the-line Purolator model, though it shared the same basic design. Noogie unlocked the three padlocks on the double doors, slid back the three iron bars they'd held in place, and pulled open the first set of doors. Inside was a second set of doors, with another padlock and two internal deadbolts, which he also unlocked. The second set of doors, once opened, revealed an interior that was much smaller than you'd expect.

"Okay, we're all set here," Noogie said. Though he did it every day, unlocking the armored car was something else that gave him a kick. He reached inside and pulled out the empty gray canvas sack from the previous day, which he tossed to Roy.

Roy then stepped back inside the bank for a moment, tossed the empty sack to the floor, and returned with another canvas sack, this one full. He checked the yellow tag on the top of the bag and made a small notation on his own clipboard.

"Great," Noogie said, taking it from him and tossing it into the back of the armored car. He turned back to Roy, who was holding the clipboard and pen out to him. Noogie initialed the form where he always did. Then Roy put his initials on the proper form on Noogie's clipboard. They were all set.

"Now," Noogie told him, "I want you to lie on the ground, facedown with your hands on your head, and count to five hundred. You get up before that, believe me I'll know—and I'll come back and gitcha!" Noogie broke into a high-pitched giggle as he slammed and relocked the doors.

"Yeah, whatever," Roy said, going back inside the bank and letting the door close and lock behind him.

At eight-forty-five on the money, it was time for Noogie's day to begin.

. . .

He couldn't say exactly when he had acquired the name "Noogie," but he could narrow it down. All the local kids had nicknames when he was growing up. They were named after either something they did, something they were, or something that had been done to them. If you were to take a stroll through his grade-school playground during recess, you'd swear you had stumbled, somehow, into a convention of rejected dwarfs. There was Shorty, of course, but there was also Stinky, and Nimrod, and Crybaby, and Dumbhead. There was also a Cripple and a Rusty (so named because he had an unfortunate red birthmark that covered the lower half of his face), who was alternately known as Oil Can.

Little Neddie Krapczak—who was a very handsome young man but who, unfortunately, had none of the social or athletic skills to back it up—had become the subject of an inordinate amount of schoolyard bullying. As a result, once the other kids got tired of calling him Crap Sack, he'd been designated Noogie.

That much he understood. He also understood that was the reason why he started seeking refuge in movie theaters when he was ten. What puzzled him was why everybody, to this day, still called him that. His mother, the neighbors, the few friends he had—as well as people he'd never met before. He never told anybody about the nickname, yet upon meeting him for the first time everyone—regardless of race, creed, age, tax bracket, color, or area of residence—started calling him Noogie almost immediately. People who spoke no English whatsoever called him Noogie. It was almost innate in some way. Something people seemed to sense instinctively. It bugged the hell out of him, but there was nothing he could do about it, because he simply didn't understand it.

He'd tried telling people not to call him that, to call him Ned instead, as that was his name. Sometimes this worked for a few minutes, but the effort it apparently required not to call him Noogie eventually proved too much for them, and they gave up. By the time he reached thirty-one, he'd given up, too.

In a way, it was like this business of living with his mother. Whenever he told people he lived with his mother, they always looked at him cross-eyed, like he was some kind of retarded freak loser. But that wasn't the case at all.

He'd planned to move out a long time ago, right after he graduated college. He was going to head to LA, where he knew he belonged. But then his dad got sick with the cancer, so he had to stay home and help out. Granted, it was Noogie's mom who went out to get the job and support them, while Noogie mostly watched the television, but that's beside the point. Way he saw it, he was an emotional support.

Then a few years after his dad died, after all the paperwork and accounts were settled, he planned to move out again. But before he could do that he had to save up some money so he could afford a place. Before that, even, he had to buy a van so he could get around, right? Buying a van ate up most of everything he'd saved, so he had to start over again.

Although he was still setting some aside, well, his mom was getting old, see, and needed someone to look after her, and he didn't trust those nurses who come to the house. They're just out to rob you blind. He could do just as good a job himself.

Besides, working for PiggyBank had given him an idea.

In the late 1990s, there had been an explosion in the private ATM business. Before that, you could find them only at banks. Then banks and casinos. Then banks and casinos and racetracks. Then grocery stores. Then the independent companies started popping up, and in a matter of months, it seemed, it was impossible to go into a store that didn't have one. PiggyBank was partly responsible for that.

Along with installing and running the machines, PiggyBank

also leased and sold ATMs to individuals. A guy who ran a bagel shop could buy his own ATM and keep it stocked himself. Every time someone used it, the two-dollar service charge went straight to the bagel guy. As things stood now, the owners of the places who allowed PiggyBank to install and maintain an ATM got only twenty-five cents out of every two-dollar service charge.

It was easy. He'd buy himself a whole bunch of these machines, place them in stores himself. Every time someone used one, it was money in his pocket.

Only problem was, those machines cost a bundle. And if you have as many out there as PiggyBank did, well, you'd need at least half a million in the bank at all times to keep them stocked.

After a while, sure, that thing would just start supporting itself, but you needed money there at the beginning, before you did anything at all.

That's what Noogie was saving for now. And that's why sharing a house with his mom made sense. She charged him only three hundred a month for rent.

2

If Noogie had known the Korean equivalent of "lard ass," he would have understood what the smiling guy behind the counter at the Green Many Products Grocery was saying to him every week when he showed up to refill the machine. The proprietor's English was quite good, actually—better than most of the customers he dealt with here at his Lower East Side location—but there was something about this Noogie character that made him want to use his native tongue.

"Hey, Nyang," Noogie said in response, as he carried the canvas bag to the machine at the back of the store.

He'd seen other ATM guys tossing the money bag around like it was a football or a chicken, but that was too cavalier for him. It showed a real lack of respect. Noogie always carried the bag gingerly, as if it could explode at any second.

When he reached the machine—parked in a corner back by the cat food and the charcoal briquettes—he lowered the bag gently to the floor, placed a foot on it to make sure it didn't mysteriously vanish, and reached for his key ring.

The MicroBank 4000 was a snazzy little device. Four feet tall, two feet deep, and about a foot and a half across, it was one of the most space-efficient ATMs on the market. It came with enough features to make anyone happy, and though it weighed only about three hundred pounds it was bolted into the floor, making it almost impossible to steal without some heavy-duty equipment.

Best of all, in Noogie's mind, it was a front loader. That made his job much easier.

He inserted the first key into the slot below the keypad and turned it. It slid easily. He removed the key, found the crease along the sides of the machine, and lifted. The entire top flipped up like a car hood.

Inside, he took a cursory glance at all the gadgetry at work. He didn't know the first thing about the computer components, really, and it certainly wasn't his job to fix them, but he always looked anyway, to make sure there was no gum or anything stuck in there. He checked the receipt roll to make sure there was enough paper for a while and that it hadn't jammed. He then checked the reject box, where any bills that were too wrinkled or torn or unreadable for any reason got shunted, and found it empty. Then he moved on to the cassette.

It was called a "cassette" in the business, though it was really a miniature vault. It was small, it was tough, its walls were made of several layers of steel, and it had a locking mechanism much more complex than the one on that thing he was driving.

He bent down with a grunt and punched his four-digit code into the small keypad above the lock. A green light told him it had been accepted. Then he found the small electronic key card on his chain and dragged it through the slot next to the keypad. For the final step, he slid yet another key into the lock on the front of the box, turned it, and slowly slid the door open.

There was between four and five hundred dollars left. By now he could tell just by looking.

This particular cassette was designed to hold two thousand bills. But that was maximum and Noogie never liked filling the machines to the maximum, especially at slow locations like this one. If the machine got jammed, that meant it'd be down for a week while they waited for a repairman to get around to it. And who would get blamed? Not the guy who fixes it, certainly—he'd be a hero. No, it'd be all Noogie's fault.

Way he saw it, he'd give these people more than enough to hold them for the rest of the week, but no more than that. No need to go crazy and cram the bills in there like some people do. You're just asking for trouble that way.

He checked around him to make sure no suspicious-looking characters were lurking about, reached into the bag, and pulled out two bundles. He tore open the paper bands with the Greenstreet logo on them and put the two stacks together. He gave the new stack a quick flip-through to make sure no bills were sticking, then inserted the money into the cassette and made sure everything was smooth and lined up properly. He did the same thing with two more bundles from his sack. Eight thousand bucks was more than enough to hold this place for a week. He closed the door and turned the key again.

Inserting less than the maximum capacity wasn't a problem to the PiggyBank people. They were interested only in what came out of it, not into it. As long as the machine was pumping twenties whenever anybody wanted them, they were happy.

After Noogie started working for PiggyBank, a lot of people asked him what it was like to be handling all that cash all day long. Wasn't he tempted to just take it all and run away?

That sort of thing, oddly enough, had never occurred to Noogie. That only happened in the movies—and even then, people in the movies rarely got away with it. To him, the cash he handled every day—all those thousands of bills—was nothing more than what the gasoline is to a gas station attendant, or the chips to a Vegas blackjack dealer. Just part of the job, another bit of hardware.

Two minutes after closing and relocking the cassette and lowering the top of the MicroBank 4000, he was on his way to the next stop, a gourmet health food store on Park and Twenty-fifth, where he'd do exactly the same thing.

. . .

By four o'clock Noogie was beat. He didn't know why. Maybe the incessant July heat was finally getting to him (it hadn't been below ninety in three weeks). Maybe it was the traffic. It didn't seem unusually heavy, but trying to think back now he wasn't sure.

Whatever the reason, he was exhausted and finding it hard to focus. At least he had only one more stop to make before the long trip back to Jersey City.

He double-parked in front of Fast Eddie's Drug Hut over on Hudson. He always liked stopping at Fast Eddie's, primarily because he enjoyed talking to a guy he could call "Fast Eddie." Moreover, he could actually understand what the hell Fast Eddie was saying—not like that damn Korean or those trust-fund hippies at the health food store. If they thought capitalism was so damn evil, why the hell'd they have an ATM machine in their store anyway?

Fast Eddie was also the only person he knew who didn't call him "Noogie," and for that he was grateful.

He sat in the truck a moment, trying to come up with a question. Tired as he was, no good ones came to him, so he settled on what he considered a gimme, climbed down from the truck, and grabbed his bag.

"Hey Fast Eddie," he said, waving, as he walked into the store. Eddie, a solid but weary character in his early sixties, looked over the top of his reading glasses. "Hey Crap Sack," he said, then returned to his paper.

The Drug Hut was a small, brightly lit neighborhood shop. Nothing fancy, not the biggest selection of cold medicine and vitamins you'd find in the city, but from what Noogie could tell it always did a pretty brisk business.

"Here's one for you," Noogie said. Every time he came in, he asked Eddie a movie trivia question. It was a thing they had. As long as his mom wasn't around, Noogie thought, what was the harm? "This one's almost too easy. What sissy turned down the role of Ben-Hur because he didn't like all the violence?"

Eddie looked over the top of his reading glasses again and gave Noogie a silent, uninterested shrug.

"Burt Lancaster!" Noogie announced, a bit too loudly for a store this size. "Didja know that?"

"Well obviously not," Eddie told him, before raising the paper in front of his face.

Still smiling at having stumped the old man again (he always did), he carried the by now almost empty canvas bag over to the machine, set it down, and placed his foot on it.

Confronted with the twenty-third machine of the day, Noogie felt the weariness flood back through him. He'd forgotten about it there for a second while chatting with Fast Eddie, but now that he was back to work he remembered. Sometimes he had to remind himself that it really wasn't that bad a job, even if he wasn't completely convinced of it. Not as convinced as he used to be, certainly. Even if you're paying only three hundred a month in rent, twenty-seven-five a year doesn't leave much to set aside.

He shook the thought out of his head and got down to work, unlocking the front of the machine and flipping it up.

After getting the cassette open and gauging the situation, Noogie sighed, reached into the sack, and pulled out the last two bundles. He snapped the bands, dropped them toward the bag, and placed the two stacks together. Man, his hands were moving slow. He gave the stack a cursory flip-through and moved to slide them into the cass—

"*BANG!*" Noogie's muscles jumped, his hands clapped together involuntarily, and he watched in helpless horror as four thousand dollars in twenties flew into the air in front of him, then fluttered like dead leaves slowly to the floor of Fast Eddie's Drug Hut.

"*Shit!*" he yelled before the last bills twirled to the linoleum. He spun around, eyes blazing, hand reaching toward the holster, to find a kid—probably eight or nine years old—standing directly behind him, finger pointed like a gun, grinning.

"This is a stickup!" the boy said, giggling.

"What in the *fuck* are you thinking?" Noogie demanded. "What's *wrong* with you?" He stopped himself just short of grabbing the child by the throat and squeezing. "Where the fuck is your mother?"

"I'm right here," a stern voice said. "And I'll thank you kindly not to use that sort of language around my child."

Noogie looked up and saw her. She was in her mid-thirties, with an expensive hairdo, lots of jewelry, and a skirt and blazer getup that probably cost more than he'd just dropped all over the floor. He immediately recognized what he was dealing with. One of those affluent, self-satisfied, indulgent "nurturing parent" types. No matter what the hell her kid did, regardless of how snotty or bratty, she always thought it was "cute" and "empowering." Parents like that were everywhere in New York, and in Noogie's mind they were raising an entire generation of obnoxious, spoiled rotten little sonsabitches.

"Did you see what he did?"

"He was just playing," she said with a *tsk*. "We think that play is very important."

"Yeah, lady," Noogie said, glancing at the child, "you're doing a real bang-up job. I'm sure the kid's headed toward a wonderful career." He turned away from her and began, slowly, to scoop up the bills.

"Better than yours," she said. "Come along, Justin." She smiled coldly and held out a gentle hand to the child, who pointed his finger at Noogie's back again, wishing he had a real gun.

"Dummies," Noogie whispered under his breath. He didn't

like getting so mad at people. It usually did nothing but leave him feeling bad in the end. But jeeze, that awful fucking kid.

It took a few long minutes for Noogie to gather the twenties together again. All the while he was keenly aware of the fact that the cassette door was still standing open. That was a bad move. He was also aware of the car horns coming from outside. Car horns, he assumed, that were directed at his double-parked van. Well, screw 'em, they could wait a few minutes. Just long enough for him to tie that little monster—and maybe his mother—to the rear bumper before speeding back to Jersey.

He tapped the money together neatly, gave it a quick, cursory count, slid it into the cassette, and closed the door, giving the key a sharp, almost savage twist before removing it.

He flipped the lid of the machine back down and locked it, still fuming over the encounter. When he reached for the bag, he noticed the green and white triangle sticking out from beneath his shoe.

"Aww, *crap*," he hissed as he moved his shoe, leaned down, and picked up the stray twenty. He looked at the bill, then at the machine. He was in no mood whatsoever to reopen the whole thing. He sighed heavily, considering his options.

He could just shove it back in the bag, use it later. But this was his last stop. *Shit*. On the bright side, PiggyBank counted only what came out of the machine, not what went into it, so he wouldn't catch any hell for shorting Fast Eddie. He could always hang on to it and slip it in with one of tomorrow's stops. So long as everything came out even at the end of the month when the accountants went to work, it didn't really matter which machine the bills ended up in. Fine, then. That's what he'd do.

He slipped the bill into his pocket and grabbed the bag.

What a day, he thought, heading toward the door.

"See you next week, Crap Sack," Fast Eddie said as Noogie pulled the door open.

"Some kids should be kept on a noose," Noogie offered in response with a small wave.

It was after six-thirty when he pulled his own van back into the driveway of the small, shabby, prefab house. Even though the place had aluminum siding, it struck Noogie every night when he came home that it looked as if it was in desperate need of a paint job. In that way, though, it wasn't much different from the rest of the houses on the block. Most of his neighbors were blue-collar lower middle class, if that. They had more to worry about than getting new siding on the house or putting weed killer on the lawn. Though for some of them, it seemed, the lawn was all they had to care about.

Noogie slumped through the front door. All he wanted was to eat some dinner and go to bed. He still had no idea why he was so worn out. Apart from the heat and that kid, it hadn't been that bad a day. Maybe he was catching cold or something. Hope not. Well, he'd sleep it away tonight.

"Hey, Ma," he said as he closed the door. "Just me." He paused and sniffed the air but smelled nothing. Maybe he *was* catching cold. "What's for dinner?"

Mildred Krapczak appeared in the kitchen doorway, across the tiny living room. She was sixty-seven years old but carried herself like she was seventy-five. She was wearing a bathrobe and slippers—her usual ensemble. She only bothered to change into anything else if she had to go out somewhere. And without Noogie there to drive her where would she go? So why bother getting all gussied up for nothing?

"Oooh, anything you want," she said. "Steak, potatoes, a nice stew…"

Noogie stared at her, feeling his face sag even farther toward the scratchy brown carpet beneath his feet. He knew what was coming next. It was her Marie Windsor routine, even if she didn't realize it.

"...and it's all waiting for you down at the supermarket."

"Oh, *Ma*—"

"Don't 'oh, Ma' me. You want me to cook something for you? You go down to the supermarket and get me something to cook. Unless you want crackers again."

After so many years of complaining about pretty much everything, the corners of her mouth had been dragged into a permanent frown. Noogie couldn't remember the last time he'd seen her smile, or even make the effort.

She's been through a lot, he had to remind himself sometimes. *It's all she knows.*

"Okay," he said, scooping up Dillinger, who had been rubbing against his legs from the moment he walked in. He dropped himself on the old couch, careful to avoid the broken spring. "Whaddya want?" He stared at the small, blank television in front of him. No use in turning it on—it got only three out of a possible six channels as it was. And ever since she'd made him throw out the VCR, there wasn't much point. A standing fan in the corner moved the thick air around, which was about as much entertainment as he ever found in that place.

"I told you—steak, potatoes, stew..."

"A couple tv dinners, then?"

"Whatever." She turned and went back into the kitchen. To do what, he had no idea. Sometimes he thought she was getting a touch of the Alzheimer's. And sometimes he thought she was much more clever than he could ever hope to be.

He prodded Dillinger off his lap, heaved himself back to his feet, and headed out.

. . .

The woman behind the register rang up the tv dinners, the quart of milk, the loaf of bread, and the six-pack. They were always running out of milk and bread and he didn't want to have to make another run later that night. The sixer was for him. He'd leave it in the van when he got home, then sneak it into the house later and hide it in the cooler he kept in his closet.

"That'll be fourteen seventy-eight," the middle-aged cashier told him as she started cramming everything into a plastic bag.

She looks like she's more tired than me, Noogie thought, reaching for his wallet. *Maybe she's getting a cold too.* He flipped open the wallet and reached inside, pulling out two singles.

He looked at the bills in his hand in disbelief, then inside the empty wallet, as if looking would make more bills materialize.

"Aw, crap," he said quietly, feeling his stomach tighten and the blood rush to his face. He hated when this happened, especially with people lining up behind him. He considered for a moment zipping over to their ATM (not a PiggyBank), but reconsidered. Payday wasn't until next week, and he knew there wasn't much there.

"Problem?" the cashier asked, pausing with the thawing Salisbury steak tv dinner in her hand.

"Ummm," he said. Then he remembered, and he felt his stomach relax again. "No, not at all. Everything's fine." He replaced the two singles in his wallet and put the wallet back in his pocket. Then he reached into his other pocket and pulled out the twenty, handing it to the woman.

On the way home he worked it all out. As soon as he got his check, first thing he'd do is take a twenty off the top and put it back in Fast Eddie's machine—or, hell, anybody's machine. *They won't notice, so long as I take care of it before the next accounting period. Worse comes to worse, I'll tell them it was a rejected bill. There are always a few of those in every machine every month. No problem. I'll take care of it.*

Noogie fell asleep quickly that night, and he slept hard until five o'clock the next morning, when his eyes snapped open and he whispered, "No, they won't notice, *ever.*"

He wouldn't take much, he told himself as he went about his rounds later that day. That wasn't the idea. Just a little something here and there. Hell, bosses expect their employees to snag a little. That's why they didn't pay them anything to begin with.

No, he'd just snag a twenty now and again when he needed it. Just to help with the necessities at home. Groceries and all that. Maybe sometimes he and Ma could even have a nice dinner.

These machines are such cheap pieces of crap anyway, he argued to himself. *They're always screwing up somehow.*

None of the people he dealt with that rainy afternoon noticed much of a difference in Noogie. They didn't notice that he was going about his business with a newfound vigor and enthusiasm. Most of them found him to be kind of a jackass blowhard anyway and paid as little attention to him as possible. But Noogie himself felt different. He was slick and suave. He was the essence of cool, just like Steve McQ.

Thursday was Noogie's heaviest day of the week with some thirty-five stops to make, but the hours flew by. Every job was smooth and easy. Traffic was snarl free. He was able to find a convenient parking spot for nearly every location. The smile never left his face. And he went home that night with an extra sixty dollars in his pocket.

Before she could even tell him to, he'd stopped at the store after dropping the armored van off at the lot and picked up a chicken and a box of stuffing mix. His mother didn't even ask why or how. She just cooked the chicken.

After a few weeks of chickens and briskets and even a new pair of slippers to replace the ratty pair she'd been wearing for the past twelve years, Mildred started to grow suspicious. Not only was her son suddenly able to afford all these extravagances—he was *happy* all the goddamn time, too, and it was starting to get on her nerves.

Finally one night, over a turkey casserole she'd thrown together from the leftovers of the previous week's meals, she asked him bluntly, "So what the hell's going on?"

"Hmm?" he said around a mouthful of casserole.

"You know what I mean."

Noogie's eyes darted to the right. "I'm— I really ain't sure what you mean, Ma."

She pursed her thin lips and stared at him. "The *money*, Noogie. You suddenly got a lot more than you should. You're buyin' nice groceries without me tellin' you to go get them. You're talking about getting a new couch. I thought you were saving your money to buy some of them bank things for yourself."

"Aww, Ma. I'm always talking about getting a new couch. And I'm still saving my money for the ATMs some day. But"—his brain was working mighty fast—"I just thought it would be nice to, you know, have a few nice dinners. I was tired of eatin' that other crap all the time. The heat-and-serve stuff. I got you some nice slippers, too. You like those, don'cha?"

"They're fine. A little small for me, but fine. An extravagance, though. You shouldn't have done that."

"Ma, didn't I tell you I got a raise?" It wasn't exactly a lie.

She stopped, looked over her shoulder, then back at him. Now she *knew* he was up to something. "No you didn't."

"Sure I did, Ma. First of August it started. An extra hundred a week...I'm sure I musta told you."

She continued staring at him. "Noogie," she said, "you don't *get* raises."

Noogie shrugged and dug his fork into the pile of casserole on his plate (his third). "Fine," he told her. "You don't like me getting these necessities for us, I'll stop. Whatever. Put everything in the bank."

Mildred Krapczak considered this for a minute—the same minute she considered doubling his rent—and said, "That's not what I'm saying. I just want to know where you're getting it, is all." Then she considered something else. "You're selling drugs, aren't you? That's why you're happy all the time."

"Ma, are you nuts? I'm happy because I like my work and I got a raise. Besides, if I were selling drugs, I'd be able to buy us a hell of a lot more than I am. We'd be eatin' out every night, and I'd trade in my van for some fancy sports car. If I were selling drugs I could probably buy us a whole new house, get us out of this thing."

She had to admit he had a point. What's more, she knew her boy wasn't bright enough to sell drugs without getting himself killed or arrested. He'd never been bright enough to learn to keep his mouth shut.

"Fine," she said, then returned to her own dinner.

Noogie smiled quietly to himself. He'd figured she'd bring it up at some point, and he thought he'd been pretty smooth. One less thing to worry about down the line.

It was a good thing she wasn't allowed in his room. He knew she didn't go in there while he was out either, because if she did he'd've heard it all up and down about the beer in the closet and the magazines under the bed. He'd laid out a few obvious traps for her, just to make sure. There was a bra hanging on his chair that she'd never said a word about. And he even put one magazine with naked men in it in his nightstand drawer. Nothing. That's why he knew his shoe box was safe.

In the closet, behind the cooler where he stashed the beer, was an old shoe box. At present, it contained six hundred and forty dollars. When he emptied his wallet tonight before going to bed, it would contain seven hundred and sixty. All neatly stacked, all of it in unmarked, nonsequential twenties.

3

He knew better than to start making regular cash deposits into the bank. A few times, sure, but after a while they'd start to look at him funny, just like his mom had after only a couple weeks. He also knew better than to spend too much of it. Not at once, anyway. Little things were fine, especially if he got them at different places. But no cars or anything like that. Not that he could afford a car yet. He wouldn't be able to afford a new car for a long time. Not a good one at least. But that time would come. And by the time it did, he'd have figured out a way to launder all this cash, so he wouldn't end up paying for a thirty-five-thousand-dollar automobile with a stack of twenties. That wouldn't fly at all—not if he wasn't famous.

First thing, though, was figuring out exactly how one goes about laundering money.

Noogie had stumbled upon the perfect slow-motion heist. He didn't even need a box man to pull it off, or a wheel man. No team at all, no potential rats. All he needed was himself. So long as the people could still withdraw whatever they wanted from the machines (up to and including their daily limit), and so long as those clowns in Florida were getting a cool dollar seventy-five every time they did, Noogie could pretty much snag what he wanted. Everyone was happy, and no one was the wiser. He'd never heard of anyone pulling a heist like this one before, except in that Johnny Cash song about the Cadillac, but that was different. Yeah, he had to admit it, if only to himself: he was a genius.

. . .

It was a cold winter that year, so for Christmas Noogie bought his mother a very expensive long suede overcoat. Not that she would ever wear it, not in a million years (especially given that she never left the house), but he still thought it was a nice thing for her to have. In return, after hanging the coat in the front closet, she allowed him to have a beer and a cigarette at the kitchen table, promising she wouldn't say a word. She also promised that he shouldn't plan on making a habit out of it. It was a onetime deal, it being Christmas and all.

Her eyes watered and she coughed dramatically as he enjoyed his smoke, but she was true to her word and said nothing.

Although in general she was still on his case about nearly everything he did, and certainly everything he was and wasn't, she never said a word about the money after that first night in early September. Noogie guessed that she was likely still as suspicious as ever but in the end was happier having it around than not.

Noogie had been at the "job," as he liked to think of it, for six months now, and so far he'd been right. He hadn't heard a word from PiggyBank. No more than the usual, that is—emergency holiday-season refills, confirming that certain machines were on the fritz, and the like.

The Christmas season was always an extraordinarily busy one for him, hitting as many as fifty machines a day. Locations he normally visited once a week, he now hit three times a week. Places he serviced three times a week he now hit every day.

During November and December, his own take diminished dramatically, as he thought it best to pack each machine in order to save himself the effort of making an emergency refill a few days down the line.

That was okay, though. He was a patient man. Now with the season about over and done with, he could start thinking about getting back to it.

Not that he'd exactly been starving the past two months. The shoe box in his closet was still there, but he hadn't bothered to open it since the end of September. It was as packed as it was going to get. Next to the shoe box, there now sat a blue laundry bag, which he had also started to fill with twenties.

In the early days, he would count what he had amassed before going to bed every night. It was a confirmation and a comfort. He was well beyond that point now, however. It took too long, and he always lost count halfway through. He knew he was into the tens of thousands (he'd gotten a little cocky in mid-October). Exactly where in the tens of thousands, he wasn't quite sure anymore.

In the early days, he had made a point of keeping the bills neatly stacked when he placed them in the shoe box, all the heads pointing the same way. Now when he cleaned his wallet out at night, he simply opened the laundry bag and tossed the cash in there. He had another laundry bag up on the shelf when this one was full.

When he started back to the job in earnest the second week in January (after he was pretty sure all the post-holiday sales and clearances had ended), he started slowly. No more than a hundred a day. Soon, though, he was leaving himself a bundle or two at the bottom of the canvas bag every evening when he headed back to Jersey City. Instead of returning the bag to the back of the armored van after his last stop, he shoved it under the driver's seat, grabbing the bundles before locking things up at the parking lot.

By late March the second laundry bag in his closet was already a quarter full. He hadn't yet spent any serious time considering what he was going to do with the cash—how he was going to get it into a bank account or whatever without raising suspicions. Hell, maybe he didn't *need* to. People always seem much happier when you paid in cash, right? Nobody took checks anymore and credit cards were a pain in the ass. That's why there were so many ATM machines out there in the first place. Why not buy a car with a couple bundles of twenties?

But what would he do if the house burned down? That was something to keep in mind. He wasn't worried about burglars much. One look inside their house (if they bothered to consider the crummy old place at all) would show any would-be robber that there wasn't anything worth stealing. What, he's gonna grab a couple bags of dirty laundry? Unless he knew they were there. No matter how tempted Noogie sometimes was to tell people what he was doing, he knew it was best to keep his mouth shut.

When he heard people like Fast Eddie, the hippies, and especially his neighbors start complaining about taxes, all Noogie could do was smile and agree with them.

"Yeah, taxes sure do suck," he'd say, trying to contain his laughter.

4

It was seven-forty-five p.m. on Thursday, November eighth. A small, bespectacled man with only the slightest fringe of brown hair sat in front of his computer terminal, a puzzled look on his face.

"Hey, Jer," a voice behind him asked. "You going home or what?"

Jerry Curlan glanced over his shoulder to see Harry Craighton—a rotund, red-faced man who'd never really been able to get that whole "necktie" thing mastered. Both men were mid-level accountants at Jarrett & Earle, one of the largest accounting firms in the Fort Lauderdale area. They were one of the largest because they advertised on television and on the sides of buses. They weren't, however, the best. More than anything, they were a layover, a weigh station, a first step for young CPAs just out of business school. A way to get their feet wet before moving on to a real firm.

Curlan, however, was both a good accountant and a company man, who'd been with the firm for eight years now. He didn't complain about the fact that he was still working in a cubicle, or that people who had been hired after him and weren't nearly so good—such as Harry—had already ended up in their own offices and were getting three times the pay. No, he didn't say a word. Those kinds of things weren't important to him, he kept telling himself. What was important to him was that he do a thorough job, and do it right.

"Oh, I'll be along soon enough," he offered amiably. "I've got a real stickler here."

"You still working on that PiggyBank account?"

"Yes," Curlan said, nodding slowly at the screen. "A real *stickler.*"

"You got that right," Craighton told him, coughing out a thick laugh. "That thing damn near destroyed the last three people who tried to straighten it out. Real mess, I hear... How long you been at it?" Harry pulled a chair out from a nearby desk and sat down. He had trouble standing for very long. Weak ankles.

"Oh, just this past week," Curlan told Craighton. "And I think I've got most of it ironed out." He looked back at the screen. "The company's been around for six or seven years now, and it looks as if they've never run a careful audit. Every two months, there's an automatic computer check, but apparently nobody's taken a close look at the results. So long as they have more coming in than they have going out, they're perfectly happy. It's crazy. But like I said, I think I got most of it."

"I don't have any doubts," Craighton said as he made a move to stand again.

"All except for one thing that I can't quite figure," Curlan continued. "There's something screwy going on around their New York accounts."

"Well," Craighton said, a bit dizzy from the effort of standing but still managing a hearty smile, "that's no surprise, crazy place like that, huh? I bet if no one else's been able to figure it out, you will. But don't knock yourself out tonight. It'll still be here in the morning. Go home, have a drink, relax."

"I will," Curlan said, relieved to see that big lummox finally heading for the door.

"You first notice the discrepancies if you go back over a year ago," Curlan said. "Back to early August of last year. Before that, everything was clear." He was sitting in an uncomfortable, straight-backed chair in the office of Len Martinez, one of Jarrett & Earle's chief accountants, as well as Curlan's supervisor. The office was not what you'd call lavish. The walls were bare, the floor was linoleum, and there were no windows. Martinez's small desk was cluttered with papers, a computer monitor, a small framed picture of his wife, and one of those little occupation-themed statuettes you see at cheap gift shops. They're supposed to be funny, these statues. The one on Martinez's desk was wearing a green visor and black patches on the elbows. Curlan hoped it was a gift from his children and not something he'd picked up for himself.

"Mm-hmm?" Martinez offered. Martinez was about forty-five, with a lean, angular face, dark eyes, and a heavy mustache. The thing that Curlan always found funny, almost charming, about Martinez was the fact that one of the elbows had been worn out of every single shirt he owned. Usually the left one, but not always. Nobody ever mentioned this, of course, figuring their supervisor knew all about this already.

"It didn't amount to very much, and at first I didn't think much of it. Twenty dollars here, forty dollars there. I thought it could be put down to simple machine error. You see it all the time with these stand-alone ATM operations. Less so with the major banks. These small companies though? Cheap equipment. It could be nothing more than the server blinking."

"Yeah," Martinez said, stifling a yawn.

"But it kept happening. And it kept happening in the same area. Just the hundred or so machines the company has in the New York area. A few in Jersey, but mostly in New York. The machines they have elsewhere are mostly okay."

"Mm-hmm?"

"Like I said, in August, everything was almost understandable." He was nervous. He didn't like being in here or trying to explain things to a man who didn't seem to care very much.

Curlan felt, for reasons he couldn't explain, as if he was the one who was being judged here. "But in September and October of last year, the discrepancies kept—well—*growing*."

Martinez sighed. "Yes?"

"Then in November and December," Curlan said, glancing back at the printout he was holding, "things are back to normal— no problems beyond what's to be expected... But then in January it starts again. All these shortages. And over the course of the year, they've grown larger by the month."

Martinez nodded and leaned back in his chair. "Okay..." he said, thinking a moment. "Bottom line—all told—what sort of final discrepancy are we talking about?"

"Well, sir," Curlan said. "I admit there is some guesswork involved here. But measuring what's coming out of the bank every day against what's actually coming out of the ATMs, factoring in when certain machines—according to the figures PiggyBank has provided us—have come up empty..."

"How much?"

Curlan cleared his throat and fidgeted, then straightened his glasses nervously. He glanced at the printout he held. "Well, sir, if we begin in August of last year, when this all began...we're talking about something along the order of...something between four-point-six and five million dollars."

Martinez's eyes opened a little wider.

Presley Buckitt, the dapper, thirty-two-year-old founder, president, and CEO of PiggyBank, Inc., hung up the telephone.

It had been a good morning. The sun was shining. The hangover he'd been expecting wasn't nearly as bad as he'd been prepared for. When he got dressed that morning, he even found an unexpected glassine envelope of coke in the inside pocket of his Armani suit. He'd forgotten all about that.

But now he had this shit to deal with.

Ever since he was a kid, Buckitt knew he was going to be rich, with nice clothes, a nice house, a beautiful wife, and a fleet of fast cars. Only thing was, he had no idea how he was going to get there. Lord knows his dad (that loser fireman) was no help. He had thought of going into banking, like his cousin Earl. Then he learned that this would require a little more school than he was prepared to deal with, so that was out.

No one—including Buckitt—could've guessed back then that he'd make a fortune on these cheap ATMs. By falling into the market at the right instant, by the time he was thirty he made his stupid fancy-ass banker cousin Earl look like a fucking deadbeat. Hell, bankers worked for *him* now.

This shit he didn't need, though. He'd be goddamned if he didn't get every last penny he deserved out of these machines. He picked up the phone and punched two buttons, waited a second, then said, "Could you come in here, please?"

A moment later there was a brief knock before the door opened and his funny-looking personal assistant Floyd—"Count Floyd" to most everyone in the office—walked in.

"You rang?" Floyd asked through one side of his mouth. One hand still clutched the doorknob, while the other dangled dangerously close to the ground. Buckitt would have much preferred having some young hottie as a personal assistant, but his wife had insisted upon, as she put it, "some funny-looking creep." So here was Floyd.

"Yeah, uh, Floyd, I just got off the phone with Jarrett and Earle and I may have a small problem to contend with."

"Heaventh!" Floyd exclaimed, his arms in the air, copious amounts of spittle spraying from his mouth in the process.

Buckitt closed his eyes and raised his eyebrows. "Umm...yeah, Floyd. So here's what I need from you. I need you to find out for me who handles our New York–New Jersey route. Or routes, though I think there's only the one."

Floyd tried to say "on the q.t." without much success, but his salute told Buckitt that he understood.

"Oh, and Floyd," he said, before the misshapen young man was out the door. "I'm also expecting an important fax from Jarrett and Earle. If you could keep an eye out for that as well?"

Floyd sneezed loudly before closing the door behind him.

5

November twenty-seventh had been a light day for that time of year. The whole season had been light so far. Christmas seemed the last thing on people's minds. Noogie could understand that, given what had happened. And hell, it made his job easier, so he wasn't complaining. He had only twenty stops, most of them clustered in Hoboken and Jersey City, and was home by four-fifteen.

"*Ma!*" he yelled as he walked in and headed for the kitchen. "Hey! I'm home early again!"

"Yeah, bully," she said from behind the bathroom door just off the kitchen.

He set the bag of groceries down on the small counter next to the refrigerator, went into his room, kicked off his shoes, and opened his closet door.

The third laundry bag was nearly three-quarters full. He pulled three more bound stacks of twenties out of his pants and added them to the pile. Another six thousand. He closed the closet door, returned to the kitchen, and began unpacking the groceries.

"Hey Ma, you okay?" he shouted toward the closed door.

"Yeah," a croak came back.

"I got us a couple chops for tonight," he said. "I thought we might broil them up or something."

"Oh good, ya remembered," his mother said.

Noogie squinted toward the door. "Remembered what, Ma?"

"Eh, you remember. Before you left this morning, I told you to bring home something for dinner that'll bind me up even more. Now *shut up* and let me concentrate."

"Sure thing, Ma."

He'd unpacked most of the groceries when the phone rang. He closed the refrigerator door, strolled across the kitchen, and picked up the receiver in the middle of the third ring.

"Yeah?" he said. Telephone etiquette was never a top priority in the Krapczak household.

"Uhh...Mr. Crap Sack?" The voice was echoed, almost metallic.

"Yeah?" Noogie asked suspiciously.

"You're home early, aren't you?"

"It was a light day today," Noogie answered, confused. "Tuesdays are always pretty light, and this season— Who is this?"

"Oh forgive me," the voice said again. "This is Mr. Buckitt. From PiggyBank?"

"Oh, hi," Noogie said. "Got another emergency refill? Just give me the locale and I'm on it."

"No, it's not that—"

"Say, where's John? John's usually the guy who calls."

"John's right here with me."

"What, are you being trained or something? Is John quitting?"

"No, Mr. Crap Sack, John's not quitting. This is a conference call."

"Hey Noogie," said something that approximated John's voice.

Mildred Krapczak's voice hollered, *"Noogie! Who is it on the phone?"*

"Ma!" he yelled back. *"Don't worry, I got it! You just concentrate in there."* He turned his attentions back to the phone. "So...who are you again?"

"My name," the voice on the other end repeated slowly, "is Presley Buckitt...I'm the president of PiggyBank, Inc."

"Oh," Noogie said, as he felt the first flutters of doom in his belly.

"And I'm here with John from Security, whom you know, as well as Mr. Len Martinez, an accountant from Jarrett and Earle."

"Hey," Noogie said quietly. "How's it, um, goin'?"

"Now, Mr. Crap Sack—"

"Krapczak," Noogie corrected. "It's pronounced Krap*czak*."

"Okay, I'm sorry about that," Buckitt offered. "Anyway, we're calling you this afternoon—and I'm glad to have caught you at home—because we've run into a small problem... Well, it's not all that small a problem actually, and we were hoping you might be able to help us out."

Noogie felt the blood drain from his head. Suddenly he felt very warm, and very woozy. He reached for a kitchen chair, pulled it over, and lowered himself into it.

"Yeah?" he said, his voice still quiet.

"Well, the accountants here, they've been encountering some...what they call 'discrepancies' in some of our records. That in itself isn't surprising. But the reason we're calling you about this is the fact that these discrepancies can, in nearly every instance, be traced back to—"

"Hey," Noogie interrupted, perhaps a touch too sharply, glad they couldn't see how badly he was sweating all of a sudden. "I'm more than happy to help you out in any way I can. Any way at all."

"That's great," Buckitt said. "We appreciate that."

"But I need to ask a favor."

There was a pause on the other end, some unintelligible, metallic chatterings. "What's that?"

"Ummm...do you suppose you could give me about, oh, fifteen minutes? Call me back in fifteen minutes, I mean? I just walked in when you called, and...my mom...she lives here with me and she's pretty sick. And now's the time I usually hafta give her her medicine—"

As if on cue, a voice from inside the bathroom screamed, *"Noogie! What's going on?"*

"—and I'd just be able to concentrate better on what you were saying if I, you know, had that out of the way first. She's...not well."

There was another pause. "I'm sorry to hear that," Buckitt said, sounding almost sincere. "Fifteen minutes?"

"Noogie!" Mildred bellowed.

"Yeah... No, you better make it twenty. She's pretty cranky today. It might take some doing."

"Okay, then," Buckitt said. "Twenty minutes. That's fine. But it's very important. I think it would best for everyone involved if we got this matter cleared up as quickly as possible. If it's just a machine error we're looking at, we need to get to work on fixing it."

"I'm, uh, sure that's all it'll be in the end," Noogie offered, though he had gone completely numb. "I'll hear from you, uh... in...uh, twenty then. Sure thing."

6

Hardly aware that he was moving at all, Noogie went into his bedroom after hanging up the phone and pulled the three laundry bags out of his closet, cinched the third one shut tight, and dragged them down the hall to the living room. He then returned to his room, pulled a small brown plastic suitcase from under the bed, and tossed in a handful of shirts, underwear, and socks before closing and latching it. That, too, he carried to the living room.

He returned once more to his room, sat down on the bed, and put on his shoes. He stole a glance at his watch. It had been nearly five minutes since he'd hung up the phone. He still had fifteen minutes.

Trying not to whimper too loudly, he took one last look in the closet and spied the well-packed shoe box, which, over the months, had been nudged into a corner along with the cooler. He snatched it up and, holding it under his arm like a football, headed for the kitchen.

"*Noogie!*" his mother screamed from the bathroom. "*What's going on? Why are you running back and forth like that?*"

"Ma," he said, trying to keep his voice from cracking. "Ma, there's something I gotta do now. That was just a call about an emergency refill they want me to take care of right away... It's—it's in Manhattan...again...um...so I'll be a while. You—you just go ahead and eat, okay?"

"*Did you get any vegetables?*" she shouted through the door.

. . .

He stared at the shoe box for a moment, then placed it on the kitchen table. *It should be enough to hold her for a while at least,* he thought. He wished he had time to leave her a note to explain things, explain the money, but he didn't.

He propped open the front door and then, one by one, he dragged the three laundry bags out to the van in the driveway and wrestled them in the back. They were much heavier than the money bags he was used to handling.

Christ, these things must weigh three hundred pounds each, he thought while heaving the second one in the back of the van. It was about as close to a coherent thought as he was capable of at that particular moment.

He looked at his watch again as he returned to the house to grab the suitcase. Seven minutes left. He'd still have some sort of head start. Not much, maybe, but it was something.

His suitcase lay on the floor, and Dillinger lay on top of it, staring at him with those enormous blue eyes, daring Noogie to make the first move.

"Okay," Noogie said. He reached down and scooped up the cat, swinging him under his right arm before reaching again for the suitcase. The cat didn't make a sound as Noogie turned for the door. Then he stopped again and set the suitcase down.

"Can't," Noogie said quietly.

He held Dillinger up in front of him and stared the cat in the eye. "You know what's goin' on here, John," he said. "You're the only one who does." Over the past months, the cat had taken to nesting on top of the laundry bags in the closet during the day.

"And you know I'd love to take you along." Noogie could feel a small lump growing in his throat. He swallowed it. He had enough on his mind, and he couldn't waste precious minutes negotiating with a cat. "But it's gonna be dangerous out there. *Real* dangerous. And I would never want to put you in harm's way. When they start shooting, they don't care who they hit. You know that."

The cat emitted a low, slow—almost understanding—growl. Then he reached out a paw and planted it firmly on Noogie's mouth.

Fact is, the decision to leave Dillinger behind had nothing to do with flying bullets. If he took the cat along, that would mean grabbing the litter box, and litter, and the food dish and food as well. Plus he'd have to keep an eye on him all the time. He just couldn't afford that kind of ball and chain. He'd have to go it alone, unencumbered.

"I'm sorry, kid," he said, "but you'd just get in the way."

He gave Dillinger a quick kiss on the nose, dropped him to the floor, and headed outside, pulling the front door shut behind him.

For a moment the cat sat staring at the closed door. Then the door flew open again. Noogie ran past him into the kitchen and returned carrying a food dish, a box of cat food, and a bag of litter under one arm. He scooped up a cool and waiting Dillinger with his free hand and headed for the van again. Two minutes to spare. Two lousy minutes. It would have to be enough.

Seconds later, the sound of victorious whooping sprang from behind the bathroom door, followed by a flush.

The telephone rang in the Krapczak kitchen. Mildred, who had been at the refrigerator scanning what sort of crap Noogie had brought home that night, closed the fridge door and shuffled around the table to the phone.

"Yeah?" she said when she picked it up. She'd grown up without a phone in the house, and never much liked the idea of having one of the damn things around now. Nothing but an intrusion.

"Mr.... Crap Sack?" Buckitt's metallic voice asked.

"This is *Mrs.* Crap Sack," Mildred snapped. "What's wrong with your voice?"

"This is a...a speaker phone, Mrs. Crap Sack. Um...my name's Presley Buckitt? From PiggyBank? Is your son available please? He's expecting my call."

"I can barely understand a thing you're saying."

"I *said,*" he yelled into the phone, *"Is...your...son... around?"*

"Christ," Mildred spat back, holding the phone away from her ear. "I didn't say I couldn't *hear* you. I said I could barely *understand* you. *Dummy.*"

"Okay," he sighed. She heard a small click, and when he spoke again his voice sounded normal. "How's this? I took you off speaker phone."

"Better."

"I'm sorry, Mrs.—"

"And no, you just missed him."

There was a silence on the other end of the line. "Missed him?"

"Yeah. You sent him on that emergency job, remember? It was just, Christ, ten minutes ago. So he took off right away."

"Emergency job?"

"Yeah, *dummy,* don't you remember? Emergency job in Manhattan. That's what he said. Then he headed right out to take care of it. Sped right the hell away. Didn't even wait for dinner."

"I...oh."

"I'm thinking he should be back here pretty soon, though."

"Really?" Buckitt asked, almost hopeful.

"Yeah," Mildred said. "He said it was an emergency refill, right?"

"Uh...sure."

"Well, he left his box full of money on the kitchen table here. I'm sure he'll be back for it."

· · ·

Whaddo I do whaddo I do whaddo I do whaddo I do...

First thing, gotta calm down calm down calm down—stop it. Essence of cool. Remember. Essence of cool...

He tried to take a deep breath and force his hands to stop shaking. Behind him, Dillinger was screaming, his claws dug fiercely into one of the laundry bags.

"I *know!* All *right?*" Noogie screamed over his shoulder. "I'll take care of it! Now just *shut up* for a minute, will ya?"

He had no idea where he was going. Just driving by reflex alone. *Gotta get away. Don't care where—so long as it's the hell away from here.* He'd just let his body do the driving while he came up with a plan. He should've come up with a plan earlier. Long time ago. Always meant to. *But why? Who would've figured it would come to this? That the dummies would ever catch on?*

They did, though. They did catch on. Took them a while but they caught on. Maybe they weren't so dumb after all.

He didn't even know how much he had in those bags. He knew that there was nine thousand seven hundred and sixty dollars in the shoe box. *That should hold her, yeah. She can get groceries delivered, pay for them then. You can get anything delivered today. Anything at all— God whaddo I do whaddo I do whaddo I do...*

First thing he had to do was come up with a plan. Get out of the city. That was a plan. That's what he was doing. Getting out of town, yeah. Good. Right. Outta Dodge. He was doing that. He was driving, he was getting away. He wasn't speeding, either, no sir. No reason to stop him. *Just driving like everyone else. Stopping at stoplights, signaling turns. Just driving, driving, driving. Gotta get out of town—*

He glanced at the gray storefronts he was passing, the gray houses, the gray sky, the gray people.

Maybe it'll snow. Snow hard. Snow'll bury my tracks. Doesn't smell like snow, though... Smells like shit... Jersey City's a stinkhole. Hate this fuckin' place. But where else to go? Get somewhere, anywhere, make a plan. Got all that money, can do whatever the hell I want. All that money. Can't take it on a plane. They'd stop me for sure. Like Sterling Hayden. Shoulda eaten something. No time. Help me think straight. Not now, not yet. Do that later. Get something. Stop and get something once I'm away. Litter box, too. Can't have him pissing on everything. And more cat food. Gotta drive now, just drive, drive, drive... Think and drive. More thinking. Think straight, dammit...

In Fort Lauderdale, Presley Buckitt was still holding the receiver, his eyes empty, his face ashen, his mouth half open.

"What's the deal there, chief?" John from Security asked. He got no response, apart from a quick twitch of Buckitt's left eye.

"Mr. Buckitt?" Martinez said.

There was more silence, as John from Security and Martinez looked at each other and shrugged.

Then, with what appeared to be great effort, Buckitt replaced the receiver in its cradle, though the expression on his face didn't change much. The two other men in the room, while quite curious, were starting to get a little bored with the melodramatics. They were relieved when Buckitt finally blinked and closed his mouth.

"Okay," Buckitt said. "Clearly we've got a major problem here."

Well, Noogie hadn't run into any telephone poles. Almost hit a few cars, maybe, but didn't. And then there was that brief detour into lower Manhattan, but nothing had slowed him down. He was on his way.

On my way, he thought. *On the lam. Jesus—I'm on the lam!* He smiled to himself again. He'd been smiling a lot that evening, in spite of everything that was happening. *Yup, on the lam. Just like Steve McQueen. Van full of money, cops on my tail, trying to stay three steps ahead. Yeah, just like Steve fuckin' McQueen.*

He noticed two things after coming through the Jersey end of the tunnel, and he began to calm down. First, there wasn't a massive police roadblock waiting for him, all flashing red lights and drawn guns.

Shit—the gun—

He dropped his right hand from the wheel to his hip. Sure enough, he was still wearing his uniform and his gun. When he'd gotten home, he'd taken his shoes off but hadn't changed.

Well, good. If I'm on the lam, I'm gonna be on the lam proper. I may well need it.

The other thing he was happy to notice was the fact that the sun had dipped below the horizon, and it was now completely dark. That would certainly slow his pursuers down a bit. He wouldn't be on the news for another couple hours, and wouldn't be in the papers until the morning.

Behind him, Dillinger had finally stopped screaming and had curled himself up atop one of the bags. He was sleeping soundly.

Instead of following Highway 78 back toward Jersey City the way he did automatically most every night—his house was probably surrounded by now—he took the Skyway, then cut south toward Newark. After that, who knows? Maybe south was the way to go. Yeah. It's warmer down there, and he hadn't brought any winter clothes or sweaters or anything.

'Course he could buy some if he needed, but no. South was the way to go.

Or maybe the way to go is anywhere at all. Just away, so long as he could avoid the toll roads. He'd be a dead duck for sure on

the toll roads—all those toll collectors in their little booths giving
you the once-over. He'd end up getting it just like that Sonny.

"Dinkelton, two miles," Noogie snorted as he passed the sign.
Then he added, *"Dingleberry."*

Well, I guess that means I must be heading south, he thought
and began laughing much too hard. Then he realized he'd better
get himself something to eat, and soon. Stuff for Dillinger too.
Why had he brought the cat along? Christ, he knew the answer
to that—because he couldn't trust anyone else, especially not Ma,
to take care of him. It was the two of them now, the two of them
on the run.

Luck was with him as much as it had been so far that day, and
a mile down the road he saw the bright lights and unmistakable
rotating sign of a fast-food chain. He pulled the van into the parking lot, swung around to the back, and stopped. He looked behind
him, where the three laundry bags and Dillinger lay, decided
everything would be fine for fifteen minutes, then went inside
and got himself a burger and a large root beer.

"Say," he asked the overly madeup sixteen-year-old who took
his money, "do you happen to know where I could find a pet food
store and a motel around here?"

She eyed him suspiciously, and he noticed. Had there been
something on the television already? A special bulletin? He looked
around but didn't see any television sets. Maybe her shift started
after she saw the evening news and they'd flashed his picture all
over the place. He couldn't ask her what time she came on, that
would just be creepy, and he was in it deep enough as it was.
Damn, he should've asked the retard with the mop over there.
Best thing to do now is just carry on as normal as possible.

"I've been driving for a long time," he told the cashier. "With
my dog. All the way from Canada, nonstop. And I figured I'd bet-

ter get some shut-eye before going any farther. And, y'know—
feed the dog."

She seemed to buy it and he relaxed. She pointed out the window to the road he'd just been on. "Just follow that," she told him,
"for like, I dunno, another ten miles? There's a Motel Six. They
got some stores there, too, I think."

"Really," Noogie said, lifting his tray from the counter. "That's
great. Thanks."

"Uh-huh."

"Oh," he said before he turned. "And your bathrooms?"

"Right around there," she said, pointing again.

"Thanks."

The restaurant was empty, which was a relief—except that
it would be pretty hard to hide, or even blend in, should any
cops stop by. But he'd worry about that when the time came. He
unwrapped the sandwich and started eating.

Dingleberry, he thought again as he took a sip of his root beer.
Dingleberry R.F.D.

Noogie had never seen much of the country, outside of New
Jersey and New York. When you grow up there, you figure that's
all the country there is. All that's worth anything, anyway. You
hear about other places, other cities, but it's like hearing about
Paris, or Morocco, or Venus. They're just pictures, they're just
stories is all.

Once when he was four, his folks took him to Disney World,
but that was it, really, so far as getting out of Jersey goes. They
weren't real big into vacations, the Krapczaks. Not the way other
families were. He had friends in school whose families went all
over the place. Some drove way out to California. Others went
camping. Some went to Texas. He knew a bunch of kids who did
the Disney World thing not just once but three or four times, when
they were old enough to appreciate what was going on down there.

Mickey and that shit. What does a four-year-old know? Mickey was just some deformed guy with a huge, misshapen head, like the Elephant Man.

Most of Noogie's "family vacations" revolved around staying home alone with his dad while his mom went to work. And his dad spent most of those days drunk in the backyard, screaming at neighbors and ghosts. When he could get away, Noogie had hid in one of the two movie theaters that were within walking distance from his house.

He had friends in school, but he had to tell them that his dad was sick with the cancer to keep them away from the house. After a while—after his father died in that drunk-driving accident when Noogie was twenty—he even came to believe it himself sometimes. It made everything easier.

Now he could remember with clear eyes, and know that it just didn't matter. He was free now. Everyone was free. He had the law on his back, sure, but he was free. Free from his dad, free from the job, and, most important, free from his mother.

God bless her for what she did, he loved her for it and all that, but criminey she was a pain. Made him throw out the VCR and all his tapes. Hundreds and hundreds of tapes. Wouldn't even let him sell them, out of fear he'd end up meeting more people who were into movies the way he was. She told him he was "wasting his life" and "crazy." Hell with that. She not only forbade him from going out to the theaters (he still snuck out when he could, telling her he had to work late), she even forbade him from *talking* about them. What kind of insane crap is that?

Well not anymore. Fuck her. Now he could talk about whatever the fuck he wanted to talk about. He could smoke, too, as much as he wanted. And have a beer without trying to hide it. As many as he wanted. Even smoke pot and do drugs if he wanted to.

He was a wanted man already, so why not take it all the way? He could do and say whatever he damn well pleased.

Plus he had a whole shitload of money. He was Steve fuckin' McQueen, and it was his greatest role.

I'm in it now, though.

So where to go? He'd get some rest, but tomorrow?

The first thing that came to mind was Mexico, but that was mostly because everybody in the movies was always headed for Mexico. He could sort of understand that, across the border and everything, but in the end he had no real interest in Mexico. He didn't know the language, the food did awful things to his stomach, and in all the movies and cartoons he'd ever seen it always looked so damn dusty.

Why not Canada? Canada—what he'd heard of it, at least— always struck him as so much nicer. Closer, too. But colder. It was winter, for godsakes. And what about the border patrol? He didn't exactly remember to bring his passport. Okay, so forget that.

Given that he was headed south anyway, maybe he could head for Florida. Lots of people end up in Florida. Florida doesn't seem nearly as dusty as Mexico—he would've remembered that from the time he was there. It's closer than Mexico, and he wouldn't need a passport. They got alligators there, too. Sounds good. Lots of people. Easy to hide.

Even better, that's where PiggyBank's headquarters were. Bet they'd never expect him to come hide right under their noses like that. *Dummies.*

It was settled, then. He crumpled up all the papers on his tray, crammed them into the now-empty soda cup, and headed for the bathroom. Then he'd start looking for this supposed motel down the road.

7

Noogie found the motel without any trouble, though it was closer to twenty-five miles down the road than the promised ten, leading him to conclude that the little hussy at the burger joint was, like, totally on drugs or whatever.

No matter. He'd found it. It was a motel, too, which was necessary. He wasn't about to leave Dillinger in the van overnight. Not when it was this cold. Better still, it was next door to a massive Drug-O-Rama, where he was sure he'd be able to get some pet supplies.

Once again he pulled the van around back, out of sight of the highway. Before going inside to check in, Noogie squeezed himself with some tremendous effort over the front seat into the back of the van, where he opened his suitcase. Sweating and grunting in the cramped space, with a very curious and possibly amused Dillinger watching him, he changed out of his uniform and into civilian clothes. He'd almost forgotten what he was wearing. The badge and the gun would have drawn far too much attention. It wasn't the smartest move wearing them into the burger joint either, but it was too late to worry about that now.

He packed the uniform and the gun neatly into the suitcase, then closed it once again. He then pulled open the nearest laundry bag in order to pad his wallet with a few extra twenties, just so he wouldn't be caught short. There was no way he dared use a credit card at this point. He should get rid of it, he reminded himself. Not yet, though. Once he was farther away. Once he got to Florida, he could cut it up and sprinkle the pieces in the ocean or feed them to an alligator.

He decided to leave the bags—all except the suitcase—in the van. Trying to drag them all to his room one at a time would attract even more attention than wearing the uniform would have. Lonely as it was out here, he figured he didn't have much to worry about. They'd be safe. He'd grab Dillinger later.

He squeezed himself back over the front seats, dragged the suitcase behind him, and went looking for the check-in desk.

"I hope you enjoy your stay here, Mr.—" the crisp, neatly coiffed man behind the counter said, spinning the registration card around in order to read the name, "Hilts."

"Call me Virgil," Noogie said with a friendly grin, as he took the key and headed back outside to find the room. Pay for a hotel room in cash, nobody says a word, he found.

The room was on the first floor, which was perfect in case he needed to make a quick getaway.

After dropping off his suitcase and turning on a few lights, he went outside again and through the parking lot to the drugstore. Pet supplies were easy—they even had small litter boxes. He grabbed one of those and filled it with as many cans of cat food as it would hold. He also grabbed another bag of litter. No telling how long he was going to be on the road.

That night he slept the sleep of the extremely guilty, awaking refreshed at seven sharp, Dillinger stretched out against his wide back. He took a long, hot shower. The water pressure left a little to be desired, but he wasn't complaining. In fact, he couldn't imagine complaining about much of anything at this point. Everything had gone almost perfectly. He tried to stop himself from thinking, *Yes, almost too perfectly.*

He left his shirt untucked when he dressed, shoved the .22 pistol into his waistband the way he figured he was supposed to despite how uncomfortable it was, dropped the room key at the front desk, and was on his way again.

Once out on the road he saw for the first time how barren his surroundings were. There was that motel, yeah, and the big drug-store next to it, but they were in the middle of Nowheresville. A ramshackle barn now and again, but mostly all he saw were bare trees and sickly scrub brush. Maybe it made sense, given that it was...what? December first now? Noogie couldn't remember. It was winter, though, but there was no snow. The land was dead green with broad patches of brown. Winter should be white. And if it wasn't going to be white, he wanted to be someplace where it wasn't really winter—or at least didn't feel like winter. He turned the van's heater up another notch.

He preferred driving with the windows down, but that was out of the question. It was for the best, he thought. He didn't want to have to worry about the money—couldn't have all those bills fly-ing around. But the bags were all tightly cinched. He made sure of that. And Dillinger seemed comfortable. He'd set up the litter box and food dish on a clear spot. That was something that would ensure he drove quietly and safely. For now, anyway. If he saw those flashing reds in the rearview, Dillinger would just have to hold on.

He was headed south, he was guessing. He assumed he was still in Jersey, too. At least he'd had no indications to the contrary. Didn't even know what the hell road he was on. Hadn't seen any signs to tell him that, either. He knew he should try and find I-95. That'd take him right down there. But he also knew that actually driving on I-95 would be the kiss of death. Too busy. Too many cops. If he could somehow drive parallel to it, along quieter side roads where no one would be looking, that would be ideal.

The road he was on now was a narrow, two-lane blacktop that wound its way through the spiny trees and the nothing. Noogie found it relaxing. He hadn't seen another car all morning—nothing at all to panic him. And after a lifetime in Jersey City, where the closest you could get to "nature" was going down to some grimy park with a rusted swing set and mountains of dog shit everywhere, this was okay, even if it was, y'know, half dead.

Yeah, this is probably still Jersey, he thought.

Not knowing exactly where he was wasn't so bad. If he didn't know where he was, then they didn't know where he was, either, he figured. It was probably for the best, given the circumstances, so long as he didn't end up back home. Noogie wasn't the type to ask for directions. People who give you directions on the street, without fail, always give you wrong directions, so what's the point? Way Noogie saw it, if a man can't count on himself, who can he count on? He practiced his cool face again: head down slightly, eyes peering up from beneath the brow.

He reached over and flicked on the radio. Maybe he'd catch some news about himself. That would be great. You always saw that in the movies when someone was on the lam. Every time they turned on the radio, there was a special bulletin about them, and every time they picked up a newspaper there was their picture.

As he spun up and down the dial, all he found was static, a call-in sports show, and a couple stations with that Mexican music. He knew he couldn't have gone that far already. He snapped it off. Piece of crap. He'd been telling himself for a long time that he needed to get a new radio in this thing. One with FM. Hell, he had the money now—why stop there? He could get himself one of those fancy stereo setups.

When he was in high school, he'd known kids whose cars sported stereo systems that ended up costing more than the car itself. Of course most of them were stolen within a matter of weeks, but that's not the important thing.

Then Noogie had an idea, one he was amazed he hadn't considered before. He was awfully slow sometimes.

I need to get rid of this thing.

Christ, yes. People had seen him driving it. It was registered in his name. Who knows how many people had written down his license plate number? That chick at the burger joint? The guy at the motel? He began to panic again. He had to do this, and do it fast. But he had to get out of Jersey first. No way in hell he could dump the van in Jersey. No way he could dump the van, period. He had to trade it in. Like in *Psycho,* or *Detour.*

Yeah, but look what happened there, he thought. Then he remembered that none of the troubles facing those people had anything to do with trading in their cars. So long as he had all his paperwork (which he did), and he remembered what kind of insurance he had, he'd be fine. His name was on all the papers, yeah, but so long as he got out of Jersey first and took care of it quick and easy, he'd be okay.

Hey, he thought. *I'm a dangerous wanted criminal on the lam. Why don't I just steal a damn car?*

Remembering that he had no idea how to go about stealing a car, remembering also that nobody just leaves the keys in the ignition anymore, he decided the trade-in idea was much better. But he'd have to get a cheap used one. Quicker that way, and he wouldn't have to worry about paying for a forty-thousand-dollar car with twenties.

That's it, then, as soon as he got into the next state—whatever that was, though he was guessing Pennsylvania—he'd find a used-car lot and take care of it. Get himself something with a nice stereo, too. FM at least. And air-conditioning. Maybe he could even find himself a '68 Mustang. What could be better than that?

. . .

An hour later, still on the same stretch of, well, something or other, having passed only three or four cars all day, Noogie noticed an innocuous green and white sign by the side of the road, which read "Welcome to Pennsylvania—the Keystone State."

Whatever the hell that means, he thought.

Still, he took it as a number of good signs. It meant first and foremost that he was out of Jersey at last.

Damn straight I'm crossing state lines with a van full of stolen cash. Let the feds try and catch me.

Pennsylvania, so far as he could tell, also meant that he was still on course, heading south. He should be in Florida in no time.

Things changed in Pennsylvania. Everything was a little greener. It was hillier. Winter hadn't yet struck down here, either. A lot of trees still had leaves on them. It was all mighty pleasant. For the first time, Noogie could actually feel that sense of freedom he was telling himself he should feel back in the burger joint.

Speaking of which, he was hungry. He hadn't had anything at all to eat since that burger. It had sat there like a rock for a good long time—which was fine, it kept him going—but he needed something else. The day was getting on.

In a small town called Sterling Passage, Noogie found everything he was looking for. Along a commercial strip about half a mile long, he not only found a diner where he could get a real meal—he also spied a used-car lot just down the street.

He figured he'd eat first, then take care of the vehicle business. Better that way, with a full belly.

He parked the van in front of Norm's Deli (where he'd be able to keep an eye on it). He checked on Dillinger, who still had plenty of food, then climbed out.

The air was crisp and fresh, not nearly as sharp as it had been in Jersey. There were bells above the door, which jangled when he opened it. With what he felt was a smooth, decisive gait, he stepped over to the counter and took a seat. Noogie always preferred sitting at the counter when he could, even if that sometimes meant a reasonably tricky balancing act on his part.

"Hey hon," the middle-aged waitress said as she approached. Noogie also liked it when waitresses called him "hon," even if they were obligated to do so. "Coffee?"

"You bet, sugar." Noogie gave her a big smile, which was met with a dead stare. He turned his attention to the menu board mounted on the wall behind the counter.

"I think I'll just have a cheeseburger," he told her when she returned with his coffee. "*Dee*-luxe." The waitress sighed, made a scratch on her order pad, looked over her shoulder, and shouted, "*Another one, Stu.*"

"God*damn*," came a gruff voice from inside the kitchen. "People got no *goddamn* imagination anymore." Then the voice rose to a shrill, mocking whine. "*Cheeseburger deluxe! Cheeseburger deluxe! That's all we ever want! That's all you should ever make!*" It quickly faded under the sound of meat sizzling on the griddle.

Noogie looked around. Nobody else seemed to have heard. Or if they had they were paying no attention to it.

"Don't mind him," the waitress told Noogie. "He spent eight years in culinary school, and hasn't quite, well...you know."

"It's okay," Noogie told her. Then, apropos of nothing, he offered, "I'm just down from Canada...on my way south."

"That so," she said, walking away.

There were three other men in the diner. All of them sat at the counter and all of them appeared to be well over sixty.

"Yup," Noogie said, mostly to himself. "Canada."

The man sitting two stools down from Noogie—a hawk-faced gentleman in a tattered brown fedora—finally took the bait. "Canada, you say?"

"Yes sir." Noogie held out his hand. "My name's George Fowler, and I'm mighty pleased to make your acquaintance."

"Well...y'ain't yet," the man said, without looking at him or acknowledging the outstretched hand.

Noogie stared at him, his smile wavering, his hand floating, unshaken, in midair. "*Hanngh?*" Noogie asked finally, in confusion.

"Y'ain't made my acquaintance yet, and so y'don't know yet whether or not you're pleased on account of it."

"Oh, come off your damn high horse, there, Harold," said the man two stools farther down the counter from him. "It's just a figure of speech. You know damn well enough what he means."

"The English language is very important to me," Harold explained solemnly. "And so is logic." At last he took Noogie's hand, which was still out there. "George," he said. "I'm Harold."

"I know," said Noogie.

"So let me ask you a question, George."

"Shoot," Noogie said, relieved to be talking to another human being in a diner, even if it was kind of weird.

"You say you're from Canada."

"Left there three days ago, yes sir," Noogie said, trying to remember everything he said, so he'd be able to keep it straight if called upon to do so.

"And you're heading south, you say."

"Yeah...?"

Harold scratched his chin pensively for a moment. "Well tell me this, then, George. If you're from Canada...and you're heading south..." He spoke slowly, as if he were calculating all these bits of information in his head as he uttered them. It was beginning to make Noogie nervous, like he was being called upon to solve a word problem up at the blackboard. "...then why does your vehicle sport New Jersey plates?"

There was a silence across the diner, as Noogie felt himself growing very warm. He remembered the gun and considered drawing it and blasting every one of these smug bastards straight to hell, but reconsidered. That wouldn't do any good.

Harold read the discomfort and befuddlement in Noogie's face. "Yup, I notice things," he said. "Ain't got call to do much else these days, but notice things. Fr'instance, a van pulls in right out front here," he nodded toward the front window, through which Noogie's van was clearly visible, "and I happen to notice it has New Jersey plates. That in itself is not interesting. Till you come in and start telling everyone how you're from Canada. Now *that* I find mighty peculiar."

Noogie's lips moved for a long time, but no sound came out. At last he said, "No...you misunderstood me, uh, Harold. I never said I was actually *from* Canada. Like a Canadian. I just said I was *driving* from there. I'm from Jersey. But I'm a...salesman. On the road a lot. Came from Canada, and now I'm headed south. Just like I said." *There, you old coot. You like logic, how's that for logic? Beat that.*

"Salesman, eh?" Harold said, drawing it out real slow, as if drawing back the bowstring before letting the fatal arrow fly.

"Oh, for godsakes, let the man eat his damn burger, Harold."

Noogie glanced down to see that, indeed, his cheeseburger had arrived.

"*You* let him eat his damn burger," Harold shot back. "I'm just being neighborly. Young fellah comes in from parts elsewhere, a man gets curious. Man can be curious, can't he?"

Harold was up on his feet now, facing down the other two, who also dismounted their stools.

"You know the rules, boys," the waitress told them all. "Take your beefs outside."

Without any further discussion, the three men filed out the front door and disappeared from view. As soon as they did, however, a great clamor and ruckus arose from the parking lot. Not just the voices of three old men but the smashing of glass and the *kerranng* of metal trash can lids as well.

As they went about their business, Noogie continued eating his burger, which he enjoyed considerably.

He paused a moment and asked the waitress, "Excuse me, miss? None of those men happens to run the used-car lot down the road, do they?"

After ordering a couple turkey sandwiches to go, settling his bill, and leaving a nice (but not extravagant) tip, Noogie left the diner and climbed back into his van. Outside, Harold was the only one of the three still standing. His hat had fallen to the ground and he had a small cut above his right eye but he was upright.

As he backed away, Noogie gave Harold a friendly wave, which Harold returned with an upraised middle finger.

Well fed and entertained, Noogie drove a few blocks down the road and pulled into the used-car lot.

Noogie didn't know much about automobiles, and he'd be the first to admit it. He didn't know how they worked, how they were put together, or how to fix them. He was able to buy them okay, though. That skill was especially useful now.

Although he was disappointed to learn they didn't have a '68 Mustang for sale, an hour after pulling into the lot he drove off satisfied in a Ford Econoline van nearly identical to the one he'd traded in.

There were very important differences between his old one and this new one, all of which would work to his advantage. This was a 1982 model, not a 1985. This new one was white, not black. And the new van not only came with air-conditioning and an FM radio, it even came with a working cassette deck. Noogie was absolutely thrilled to have a tape deck.

He explained the laundry bags to the dealer by saying he had just left his wife and had thrown everything he had into the bags. He'd cleaned out the bank account (hence the cash transaction), snatched the cat, and ran. The dealer—who, it turns out, was in the midst of a particularly ugly, drawn-out divorce case himself—sympathized and asked very few follow-up questions. All the papers seemed to be in order, and cash was just fine by him.

At first, Noogie had been more than a little horrified to see that the guys in the garage had transferred the old license plates to the new van, but then he remembered that the cops would be looking for a black 1985 Econoline and not a white 1982 Econoline, and he relaxed. And while he was sorry to lose his I BRAKE FOR TRIBBLES bumper sticker in the process, he hoped that maybe he'd find another one somewhere. Maybe he could even pick up some paint and alter the numbers on his plates. He'd seen that done in more than a few movies.

As he drove away the first thing Noogie did was snap on the radio. He was immediately able to find three different news stations, and as he drove he listened to each one in turn, hoping to hear something about himself.

After forty-five minutes, he'd heard plenty of news about floods in Oregon, and a volcano in Italy, and a bear that had escaped from the Lincoln Park Zoo in Chicago—and about those damn attacks, of course—but nothing about Ned Krapczak, criminal mastermind and wanted fugitive.

What the hell kind of deal was that? He was one of the most brilliant and clever bandits in American history. Shouldn't there be something? A nationwide manhunt? A dragnet? Roadblocks?

He snapped off the radio in disgust. Stupid fuckers.

Maybe he was lying too low. Maybe that was it. Maybe he'd just been too clever for them, sneaking away in the dead of night like he did.

In spite of everything, he was already getting a little bored with this "on the lam" business. That wasn't right. You weren't supposed to be bored when you were on the lam. You *can't* be bored when you're on the lam.

Look at Charlie Starkweather and Caril Ann Fugate. Look at Bonnie and Clyde. Look at Butch and Sundance, or Dirty Mary and Crazy Larry, or that guy in *Vanishing Point*. For godsakes, look at *McQueen*. They were never bored. They were always getting into little side adventures, doin' stuff and crackin' wise.

He considered for a moment that robbing a bank might be worth a try. That would sure make people sit up and pay attention.

He knew almost immediately after the thought occurred to him that it wouldn't work. What he did was different. To rob a *bank* bank, you needed a team. He would need that box man and that wheel man. And machine guns. Anyway, guys who rob banks nowadays almost always get caught within the hour because they're dumb and stupid. Nope. Not him. He was a lone wolf, wild and free.

And Christ, why was he even thinking about banks? The most he'd ever get away with is a quarter mil. If that. Chump change. He had at least five or six times that—more, even—in the back of the van right now, even as he sat there. But still, bank robberies are a real class act, when they're done right, and you don't end up having to kill all the tellers and customers. He didn't want to do anything that would hurt anybody.

He gave up on all the silly thinking, deciding the thing to think about now was where to get some rest. Tomorrow when he got up he'd see...well...what would happen tomorrow. Maybe he could buy himself some neat tapes or something.

About eight o'clock that night, Noogie saw a little motel off the side of the road in a place called Fleiskahonna (he was guessing he was still in Pennsylvania) and pulled into the gravel parking lot. He'd always wanted to stay at a place that actually called itself the "Dew Drop Inn."

8

Although the curtains in his room were open only a crack, Noogie could tell immediately upon awaking that the skies outside seemed overcast. Overcast days always made him a little sad. Unless maybe the sun hadn't come up all the way yet—there was always that possibility.

He looked at his watch, which he'd left on the rickety bed-stand before going to sleep. Seven-fifteen. If the sun was going to be coming out, it'd pretty much be there already.

He rolled out of bed, then got himself washed and dressed. Dillinger had followed him into the bathroom, meeping. For an old cat, he seemed to have grown accustomed pretty easily to this traveling business. He hopped up on the closed toilet lid and stared at the wall.

Glancing briefly at himself in the bathroom mirror, Noogie realized he'd need to shave one of these days. He was starting to look kind of seedy. Unless he just went ahead and grew a beard. It'd be an easy disguise. He never much liked the idea of having a beard, though. He smacked his lips and grimaced. He'd also need to brush his damn teeth one of these days. He knew that the way he was looking now was exactly the kind of "wanted criminal" picture they loved to print in the papers. At least he'd been able to shower enough that he didn't stink.

When he checked out, he'd make a point to ask the guy where the nearest place might be to get some—man he hated using this word—toiletries. He should've picked them up back at that place in Jersey, but he had a lot on his mind then.

There, he thought, well satisfied. *I have a plan for the day. It may not be a bank hit, but it's something useful to do.* He closed up the suitcase, leaving the gun in there for the time being. It was awfully uncomfortable trying to drive with that thing jammed against his belly and right next to his, well, you know. Plus he was worried about hitting a bump. He always checked the safety but, still, what if it went off somehow? He'd heard stories like that. Some guy bleeding to death after blowing his thing off.

He locked the room door behind him, tossed the suitcase and Dillinger in the back of the van, and walked around the corner to the office, scratching at the stubble on his cheek with his room key. Then he froze.

The state patrol cruiser was parked just to the right of the office doors. Noogie took three large steps backward around the corner and pressed his back against the wall.

"Shit, shit, shit," he whispered, his mind racing. What the hell should he do? He could get back in his van and just speed away, but that would be obvious. Too obvious, and the cruiser, being right there, would be on his tail in a heartbeat. He could go back in his room and wait until he heard it leave, but who knows how long that would be? And what if the motel guy told him what room Noogie was in? It could all be over with. He remembered the gun in the suitcase. He could just blast his way out...

No. No, that wouldn't do. Not before he knew what was going on. Maybe this cop didn't know a thing. They were looking for a black van. His wasn't black at all. It still had the old plates, but maybe he wouldn't look—he'd see a white van and let it go.

What if the cop had a picture of him, though? What if they'd put his picture out on the wires? Dammit.

He had the beard thing going now, and the most recent picture taken of him, the one for his driver's license, was four years

old. He didn't have the mustache then and he'd been about fifty
pounds lighter. Maybe things would be all right after all. Maybe
the thing to do was just play it cool. Don't give them any reason
to be suspicious. If there were any questions, he'd trot out that
"wife" story again. It had worked pretty well with that guy at the
car lot the day before.

He straightened his shirt, brushed back his hair, and stepped
around the corner again, crunching through the loose gravel to
the office. The air was warmer than he expected—or maybe it
was just him. In any case, he was already starting to sweat.

This'll only take a second, he thought. *Then I'll be gone.*

He pulled open the screen door and saw the state trooper
leaning against the check-in counter.

"Mornin'," Noogie offered.

"Mornin'," replied the trooper, a stocky, light-haired man
probably around Noogie's age. He clutched a Styrofoam cup in
his right hand.

He'll have to drop that before reaching for his gun, Noogie
noted. *That'll give me time—and he might even burn himself.*

He quickly glanced around the small, drab office, looking for
the motel guy. The door behind the desk opened and the clerk
emerged, clutching his own cup of coffee, a newspaper under his
arm. Noogie's eyes dropped to the folded paper and he forced a
nervous smile. "Hey," he said. "There you are."

"Ah, good morning, Mr. Crown," he said. "I trust you slept
well."

"Just fine," Noogie told him. "And like I said, call me Tom." He
was relieved the clerk had reminded him what name he'd used.

Despite his best efforts not to let anything show, Noogie's eyes
kept darting to the state trooper. He thought it would be weird
not to acknowledge that the man was there and staring at him, so
he said, "I hope there's not been any...um, trouble."

The clerk looked befuddled for a moment, then smiled. "Oh, you mean Chuck?" he nodded at the trooper. "Naw, Chuck just stops by every morning for the free coffee."

"Sergeant Chuck Callahan," the trooper said, setting his coffee down, taking a step toward Noogie, and extending his hand. "Pennsylvania State Patrol."

"Tom Crown," Noogie said, taking the officer's hand, half expecting to find his own hand twisted and cuffed behind his back. Then he turned to the clerk. "Free coffee, huh?" Might as well play it to the hilt, now that he could relax.

"Sure thing," the clerk said, disappearing through the door again.

"Tom Crown?" the trooper asked, after the door closed. "You mean, as in *The Thomas Crown Affair*?"

"Oh—" Noogie began, his stomach going cold. *Dammit, why didn't I go with Mike Delaney? More appropriate anyway, new car and all.* "I...I hadn't really considered that before, but I guess so, yeah."

"You mean nobody's ever mentioned that before? That's my favorite Norman Jewison film of all time."

Noogie tried to control his stammering. "Really?... I guess my...uh...my parents... It was just a coincidence."

"Pretty weird coincidence," the trooper said, "naming you after a thief."

Noogie's eyes shot to the door as it opened, and the clerk reappeared with a third Styrofoam cup. "Sometimes I think the only reason anyone stops here at all is for the free coffee," he said, holding out the cup. Noogie took it with shaking hands and thanked him.

"You know he's got a point," the trooper said, apparently having abandoned his earlier train of thought. "With the interstate, not too many people come by this way."

"And fewer stop," the clerk added.

"Don't see why that should be," Noogie said, taking a sip of the coffee. It was lukewarm and thin. He couldn't imagine anyone stopping here just for this. "You've got a nice little place here. It's quiet...and the area's quite, um, beautiful." He took another swallow to try and cover the obvious lie.

"Yeah, we like to think so. Most people don't get off the interstate, though, to find out for themselves."

"And that's a damn shame," Noogie said, regaining his nerve. "Whenever I drive, I try to make a point of avoiding the interstates when I can. Always try and find a route along the, you know, side roads and such. Wherever I'm going. You want to see what America's really all about, that's the only way to do it."

Both men nodded in agreement.

"So, Mr.... uh, Crown, where you headed?"

"Florida," he said, then added, "Fort Lauderdale."

"Really," the trooper said, then flicked his eyebrows. "Okay."

"Like I said, I like taking roundabout ways."

"Well, you're certainly doing that, huh?" the clerk noted.

Sensing that he was somehow getting in over his head here, Noogie decided it was time to finish the awful coffee, drop off the key, and get the hell out of there. He tipped the cup back, fought off the urge to gag, and placed it on the counter. Then he retrieved the room key from his pocket and laid it next to the empty cup. "Well," he said, "it's been a real pleasure gentlemen, but I think I'd best be on my way."

"What you got planned for Lauderdale?" Sergeant Callahan asked as the clerk replaced the key on the wall behind him. He said "Lauderdale" almost as if it were in quotation marks.

"Fishing," Noogie blurted. He didn't know why. He'd never been fishing in his life, but it was the first thing that came to mind.

"Really," was all Sergeant Callahan said.

Noogie just wanted to get out of there, and fast. Then he remembered something. "Hey," he said, his attention focused on the clerk, "where's the closest place, d'you suppose, where I could stop and get a new razor and some toothpaste, stuff like that? I just discovered that I'm running pretty low."

"Lauderdale," the trooper said, almost smirking.

Yeah, go back to Macon County where you belong, Noogie thought. Thankfully, the clerk jumped in before he had a chance to open his mouth and screw himself.

"Best thing I can think of," he said, "is if you get over on the interstate. Plenty of truck stops along there. I'm sure they'll have whatever you need."

"And more, eh, Rubin?" the trooper added. He barked a strange and knowing laugh and the clerk shot him a look.

Noogie thanked him, nodded to the trooper, and left.

I thought I handled myself pretty smooth in there, he was thinking ten minutes later, a few miles down the road. That's when he glimpsed the flashing red lights in his rearview mirror.

"Shitshitshitshitshit—" he began to chant. It seemed to have become his mantra this morning. There was no way he could outrun them. Not in this thing. Maybe he could get himself a faster car somewhere down the road. Finally get that Mustang. That is, if he got away from here somehow. But he wouldn't. This was gonna be it. *"Shitshitshitshitshit…"*

He pulled the van over to the side of the road and stopped. He reached behind him, grabbed the small suitcase, and placed it on the passenger seat. He wasn't gonna go down without a fight. He knew that all he'd need to do was flip up the lid. The gun was right there on top. He could say he was going for his license and registration, grab the gun, turn—

The cruiser pulled onto the shoulder and stopped some fifty feet behind the van. Noogie kept a nervous eye on the rearview mirror, trying, as subtly as possible, to flip open the two latches on the suitcase.

The cruiser door opened and Callahan got out. Noogie had seen this scene on *Cops* so many times. Nothing good ever followed. What was wrong with these fucking latches? At least Callahan was alone. Alone in the middle of nowhere. But if he has one of those cameras on his dashboard—shit.

The trooper took his time, strolling casually, looking around every which way, his right hand poised on his holster.

Man, this is all very anticlimactic, Noogie was thinking. *Fucking solo state trooper, and I can't even get the fucking latches open.*

Callahan leaned an elbow on Noogie's window. "Hello again, Mr. Thomas Crown," he said, without a trace of a smile.

"Hey, sergeant." Noogie was trying not to cry. "P-problem?"

"Just one little thing," Callahan replied, looking back down the long, empty stretch of unmarked gray pavement. There was an uncomfortable pause. Noogie felt his throat grow tighter. He knew he was going to say something about the license plate, or the money, or all the warrants. *If he asks me to step out of the car, I'm a dead man.*

"We never told you about the short cut to the interstate," a still unsmiling Callahan finally said. "It's right up ahead a piece. And if you use it, there's a rest stop right there that'll have everything you need. Plus you can get right back off it again if you like… Meander on down to do some fishing. You know, the thing about fishing is…"

Noogie was on top of the world. Not only was he able to get himself a big stack of flapjacks (slightly burned around the edges, just how he liked them) at the truck stop, it also had a store where he could get, as that cop had promised him, everything he needed. A razor, a toothbrush and toothpaste, deodorant, shampoo—even quart-sized bottles of high-octane caffeine pills. He found himself fast coming to love a country he never knew existed. In the restaurant, he'd even had a waitress named Flo, for godsakes—and what could be better than that? He left her a forty-dollar tip on a two-dollar-and-fifty-cent bill just to prove it.

As he was carrying everything to the checkout he stopped. His eyes lit up when he saw the rack of cassette tapes, only ninety-nine cents each. As he scanned the titles, he couldn't believe it: they had all the best ones. It was hard to believe they could sell them that cheap, but here they were. He was even able to find a plastic case to carry them all in so they wouldn't go flying everywhere. And a big cup holder, too. All he had to do was clip it onto the dashboard. They had everything.

The only disappointment was the bumper sticker collection. Nothing really seemed to speak to him. That was okay. He'd found plenty to keep him happy.

Standing at the checkout, he told the girl behind the counter that he thought this was the greatest store in the world.

"Yeah, obviously," she said.

He glanced down and saw the stacks of newspapers. They had the *New York Times* and the *Post* along with the local papers, and he dropped a copy of each on the counter as well.

When he got back to the van he put the bag with all his amenities on the floor of the cab, then began scanning the *Times*. He found nothing. There wasn't a peep in any of the other papers, either.

In short, there seemed to be no evidence that they were looking for him at all. He wasn't sure how to take that. Were they maybe conducting the investigation secretly, keeping it out of the papers? Or had he, in fact, pulled off the perfect crime? Although the lack of publicity was disappointing—where's the urgency?— he did kind of like the idea of having pulled the perfect heist.

Well, this calls for some tunes, he thought as he folded the papers and reached for the plastic bag.

9

Noogie knew it was a big damn country, but this was getting ridiculous. How wide could Pennsylvania possibly be?

Granted, he was staying on backroads that twisted and turned quite a bit, and because of that, and Dillinger in the back, he never pushed the van much above forty. By not relying on any maps or directions, he was just letting the roads take him where they would, and sometimes this seemed to mean "in circles." He was also making a lot of stops along the way—wherever he could, actually—to stretch his legs, get a snack, fill the tank, use the bathroom, buy another pack of cigarettes, and look to see if anyone might have some more of those cassettes for sale.

Still, getting to Florida was taking an awful long time. He figured to have been relaxing on some beach by now, not plodding along over more hills and through more farmland.

In the dying sunlight, it took him a moment to recognize what he was seeing along the side of the road some fifty yards ahead. As he drew closer, though, it became clear.

The young woman in the blue jeans, down vest, and oversized plaid shirt stood off to the side, her thumb out. At her feet was a knapsack.

"Well there's something you don't see every day," Noogie said aloud, as he hit the brake and the van ground to a halt.

The young woman picked up the knapsack and sauntered toward the van. She seemed to be in no tremendous hurry.

When she reached the passenger side, she paused, looking through the open window at Noogie.

"Where ya goin'?" he asked, grinning broadly.

"Wherever," she said.

"Hey!" Noogie exclaimed. "Me too!"

She considered this, hesitated, then opened the door anyway and climbed in. By Noogie's guess, she was in her mid-twenties, but he might have been wrong. Her face and her eyes seemed much older than that, already lined and hardened for someone so young. She was an unhealthy pale, and her eyes were set close together. Her brown hair, which reached just to her shoulders, clearly hadn't been washed in some time. It seemed she hadn't washed her hands in a while, either, the dirt packed in black beneath the nails. She stared through the windshield as Noogie beamed at her.

"Let's get moving," she said finally, rolling up her window. "And don't use the brake. Cars are made for going, not braking."

"I know that," he said.

"Then why aren't you moving?"

"Sorry." He put the van in drive, hit the gas, and pulled back onto the road. "I meant the line."

"What line?"

"What you just said—about cars are made to go."

She glanced at him out of the corner of her eye. "I have no fucking idea what you're talking about."

"It's from *Breathless*."

She stared at him, squinting.

"Not the stupid remake, I mean the original French movie." Her eyes revealed no recognition. "Jean-Luc Godard? Nineteen-sixty? The film that spawned the French New Wave? You gotta know it. You just quoted it."

"I really have no idea," she said, looking away. She sounded weary, and she was. "I don't know much about movies."

"See? There you go again!" he said, lifting one hand off the wheel to gesture. *"Taxi Driver*, right? Now I *know* you're just playing with me. Okay, okay wait, now it's my turn. Where's this from?" Noogie cleared his throat. " 'He could make a man look like a...*bulldog*,' " he said in a heavy German accent, forcing the corners of his mouth into an exaggerated frown, " 'or a *monkey!*' " Then he giggled. "Where's that from? You give up?"

"Jesus," she muttered quietly, looking out the window, thinking that maybe she should just get the hell out of the van now and take a bus. She'd about had enough of the weirdoes.

"Dark Passage," he announced. "The scene with the plastic surgeon, you remember?" He smiled again, happy to be winning the game. *"Bulldog,"* he repeated in the same accent. "Great fuckin' movie—if you'll pardon my French."

"Doesn't fuckin' bother me," she said flatly, before the two of them fell into silence.

"It's so great," Noogie said, "to be able to actually talk to someone about movies again. It's been a long time. Years. My mother, see"—keeping his eyes on the road he didn't catch the reflection of the face she was making out her window—"my mother, she...she didn't let me watch movies. Well actually at first she did, but then she made me stop. Only thing in the world that ever made me happy at all, and she went and took it away. I even went to film school, you know? NYU film school, same place as Martin Scorsese. I was gonna be better than him. Man, the movies I was gonna make. Amazing. But then my student film, the one I did at the end? They didn't like it. Know why?" He didn't wait for an answer. "They didn't like it because it had *characters* and a *plot* and a *story*. Things happened in it. All the others, those pretentious little... Their movies were artsy. Which meant they weren't about anything, you know? Two people sitting in a room, talking. Or not talking. Just sitting there. Who in the hell wants to see that? But oh, the professors just fell all over themselves..."

He knew he was talking too much. Too much and too fast. He caught his breath and tried to slow down. It's just that he hadn't had a chance to tell anyone about any of it in a long time.

"Anyway. Then after I graduated nobody gave me a chance, and I—" He stopped himself again, thinking that maybe he was getting too personal too fast with someone he'd just picked up by the side of the road in the middle of nowhere. Hell, and here he was hogging the whole conversation.

"So what's your name?" he asked. "Mine's Eric. Eric Stoner." He held out a chubby hand, while keeping his eyes on the road. "But I'm not really a stoner or anything like that…it's just a name. I don't do anything like that. I mean, nothing *against* it, and I suppose I smoke cigarettes—"

"My name's Velda," she said. She seemed reluctant to take his hand, but did.

"Velda? Really?" he said as he shook her hand. "That's great. I think so at least. You don't meet many Veldas around anymore, though I met a Flo the other day. Don't see too many hitchhikers anymore, either."

"Most people don't pick up hitchhikers nowadays, either."

"Well I guess there are a lot of weirdoes on both ends of the deal, huh? You hear enough stories, it's enough to make anyone, y'know, nervous."

"I guess," she said.

"But I'm not a weirdo," he assured her.

"Uh-huh." She looked over her shoulder into the back of the van. She'd noticed them when she first climbed in. "Then what's with all the laundry?"

His hands tightened on the wheel. "Nothing," he said. "I guess I just use those instead of regular luggage. It's easier, I think. I'm not real formal that way. Just throw everything in a bag and go. Plus it gives my cat a place to sleep."

"Cat?"

"Yeah, Dillinger. He's back there someplace. You want me to wake him up?"

"No," she said. "That's okay. I'm kind of allergic."

"Oh, that's rotten," Noogie said. "I'm sorry."

"Uh-huh."

They rode in silence for a few miles. The sun was long gone. He had no plans to stop at a motel that night anyway. Those pills he'd picked up were really doing what they promised. He felt like he could drive forever—except for occasional bathroom stops. He'd seen things in that store that seemed to handle that, too, but he wasn't quite ready to go that far yet.

"You got any music?" Velda finally asked, breaking the silence. She'd noticed the tape player.

"Music," he said. "That's a great idea. I just picked up a bunch of things at this store. They had everything there." He gestured toward the box on the floor. "You should've seen this place. It was great—*and* it was on an overpass, if you can believe that. No other store like it in the world."

"On an overpass?" she asked, not sounding as amazed as he'd hoped. "You mean it was a truck stop?"

"Well—maybe, yeah—but it wasn't like anything else I've ever seen."

"Whatever," she said. "You got any Elvis?" She pulled the cassette box into her lap and opened it.

"Well…no," he admitted, almost apologizing, "but I have all the best ones. Just look for yourself. Put in whatever you'd like."

He turned on the dome lamp so she could see better. She lifted the lid and there, neatly packed together, she found tapes by Molly Hatchet, Glen Campbell, Roy Clark, .38 Special, Black Oak Arkansas, Procol Harum, Alan Parsons Project, and ELO.

"All the best ones," he said, with some pride in his own taste.

Velda couldn't believe what she was looking at. "You have all this crap," she said, "but you don't have any Elvis?"

"It's not *crap*," Noogie protested, a little hurt. "It's all the b—"

She cut him off. "You don't have any Elvis, you don't have the best ones."

"No, but I do," he insisted, thinking that this new breed of kid simply didn't understand music. "You ever hear of Survivor? They did the songs for most of the *Rocky* movies. Three through five at least, which adds up to most of them. The movies weren't so great, but man, that music was really rockin'." As it happened, his new Survivor tape was already in the machine. He hit the PLAY button and cranked the volume. The music blasted through the van.

"*Listen to this*," he shouted, nodding his head along with the beat.

"*Maybe*," she yelled back over the near-deafening noise, "*maybe we could just play the radio?*"

Noogie frowned, shrugged, and stopped the tape. "All right," he said. "Whatever you'd like."

They settled on a classic rock station, though Noogie took issue with what the people at that station regarded as "classic," and he didn't speak for a long time. Velda dozed, relieved that this guy hadn't made any of the usual moves.

"So you really don't know much about movies, huh?" he asked.

She half opened her eyes, groggy, and said, "No."

"That's too bad," he said. "Especially since you seem to know so much about them, quoting them like that and all." He gave her a sly wink. "Naah, movies are great," he continued. "Especially if your own life hasn't been so hot. You know, boring or whatever. Gives you something to look forward to."

"Uh-huh," she said, wishing he'd just let her sleep.

"Even now, driving along here, I'm thinking that one of my favorite movies of all time is about a guy who picks up a hitchhiker."

"Really," she said, closing her eyes again anyway.

"Yeah. It's called *Detour*. Ever hear of it?"

"Mmnn," she said.

"It's great. It was directed by Edgar G. Ulmer—the *great* Edgar G. Ulmer, I might add—and he filmed it in about a week. Tom Neal plays this guy who starts out hitchhiking himself, see? He's going from New York to LA to be with his girlfriend. But then the guy who picks him up dies. Just like that"—he snapped his fingers—"so the Tom Neal character doesn't know what to do. He knows if he tells anybody, it'll look like he did it, like he killed the guy, right? So he drags the guy off to the side of the road—real lonely road like this one—takes his clothes and his wallet and everything and figures he'll just pretend to be this guy until he gets to LA. Real simple."

"Mm-hmm," Velda said, in a tone anyone else would recognize as almost terminal disinterest.

"Then he picks up a hitchhiker himself—a girl this time. Ann Savage. But it turns out that she knew the guy who died, and she knows that Tom Neal ain't him, get it?"

She didn't say anything. Noogie glanced over and saw that she looked like she was asleep. As least he hoped she was asleep and not dead, like in the movie. That would be too weird. He went on anyway.

"And this Ann Savage, see, she turns out to be one mean motor scooter. She starts screwin' with this guy, demanding all his money, crap like that. Sayin' she'll turn him in to the cops for the other guy's murder if he doesn't do everything she tells him to.

"In the end, though..." he paused and looked at Velda again. "You think you'll ever see it? 'Cause if you are, I won't tell you how it ends."

She opened her eyes slightly. "I don't think so."

"Okay. So she's doing all these things. They get to LA but the guy can't go see his girlfriend because this woman is still hanging this thing over his head. And one night, she gets real drunk, see, and says she's gonna call the cops."

Velda was actually listening by this point.

"She grabs the phone and runs into her room—they were sharing an apartment, did I mention that? Long story. Anyway, she runs into her room with the phone and locks the door behind her. Then Tom Neal panics, right? And he grabs the phone cord and starts pulling on it—"

"If the phone cord was still coming through the door, why didn't he just unplug it from the wall?"

"Because it's a *movie*, all right?" People who pointed out things like that, who were unwilling to suspend disbelief, always annoyed him. "So he's pulling on the cord, but what he doesn't know is that, drunk as she was, she'd gotten the phone cord all wrapped around her neck."

"So he strangles her."

"*Yeah!* But he didn't do it on purpose. Just like he didn't kill the other guy."

"Yeah," she said.

"I'll tell you one thing, though," Noogie said. "I would never have put up with shit like that. No sir. I mean, not saying that you would, but if you, y'know, tried to do something to me like that Ann Savage? No *sir*. None of that. Not me."

Velda had both seen and heard a transformation take place while Noogie talked about the movie. His voice had grown flat and cold, his eyes had taken on a frightening gleam she could see even in the darkness. He was no longer the doofus who'd picked her up. He seemed almost angry, but about what, she couldn't tell. Was it the movie? What had happened to the guy? Whatever it was, it made her uneasy. Then she remembered the laundry bags sitting just a few feet behind her. What did he really have in there? The last couple of hitchhikers he'd picked up, probably. This guy looked like he could do it, too.

Velda wasn't sure she wanted to stick around to find out. No, she *was* sure—and she didn't.

She looked over at him again. His face hadn't changed. It was still set, still frozen. The doofus wasn't there anymore.

"I...I think I should get out here," she said.

"What?" Noogie said, turning his head. "You're crazy. This ain't no place."

"Sure it is," she said. "It's where I want to get out."

"Middle of the night, middle of nowhere? That's crazy. Wait'll we get to the next town at least. It's freezing out there,"

"No," she said, pretending to look around at various land-marks. "This is it."

Noogie couldn't think of anything he might've done, but you never know with people. "Was it because I gave away the ending?" he asked.

"No, not at all," she insisted, not wanting to upset him in any way. "I mean it—this really is the place I want to be."

Noogie had to admit that he'd heard of stranger things.

"Oo-kay," he said. "Rider's choice." He slowed the van and pulled over. "It's been a real pleasure havin' you along here, Velda."

"Yeah," she said, pulling at the handle. "It's been great. Thanks." She opened the door and slid out, pulling her knapsack behind her.

"And hey," he said, before she closed the door. She hesitated. "If you take anything at all away from our time here together, take this..." He cleared his throat again.

She waited, aching to slam the door and disappear.

NOOGIE'S TIME TO SHINE

"That's life," he quoted. "Whichever way you turn, Fate sticks out its foot to trip you."

She slammed the door and ran.

As he put the car in drive again, Noogie thought that maybe he should've passed along something a little more upbeat and encouraging, given that she was hitchhiking and all, but that was the first thing that came to mind.

"Oh well." He reached down, punched the PLAY button on the tape machine again, and stepped on the gas.

At four-twenty that morning, less than an hour after dropping Velda off, the van's headlights caught another small green sign by the side of the road.

"Welcome to North Carolina," it read.

Noogie may not have been the most geographically literate of men, but he knew enough to realize this meant that, though he was heading south, he was making really lousy time.

"Well, damn," he said, passing the sign. He considered for a moment just hopping on I-95 when he could. Then he thought about that. Why was he in a rush? Why not take his time, meander? Especially if he didn't have the fuzz right on his tail. And the more he wandered, the more he'd throw them off. He was no dummy. Not like a lot of people he knew.

"Yeah, why the hell not? Florida's a big craphole anyway." He reached for a cigarette.

10

The hills and trees disappeared as quickly as they had first appeared upon entering Pennsylvania. As if to replace them, small towns began to pop up with a greater frequency. All in all, it seemed a much more difficult place in which to disappear.

"Bear Falls," he read off a passing sign. "Hey! Look out! *Ahh!*"

Once his laughter subsided to quiet chuckles, he shook his head and thought, *Boner.*

He'd been driving for too long, and he knew it. All night, for godsakes. He was starting to get a little funny in the head. There had been flashes of explosive anger with no discernible cause. He found himself screaming things like "No fucking way—no *fucking* way at all" out his window for no reason.

Those caffeine pills had worked, sure, but he also decided he could afford to take a break. Maybe not zip straight through every little chunk of civilization he encountered. He had the money to relax, lord knows. And they weren't even looking for him.

He'd been listening to the news and had heard nothing. Blizzards in Colorado, more flooding in Oregon, serial murder in Atlanta.

Again he thought, What if he had actually done it? Not just actually done it but gotten away with it, too? That's the real cherry—the getting away with it. It was almost unheard of, especially when you're talking about that much loot. McQueen always got away with it but real people didn't.

Then something else occurred to him.

What if that phone call wasn't about the money at all? Maybe those "discrepancies" were something else entirely—something that had nothing to do with the money in his closet? It could've been computer problems or something, like what's-his-name said. There might have been no excuse at all for him to leave his home and his mom. The fact that he did up and leave could only make them suspect something.

But no, that didn't make sense. It was the big boss calling, and he was there with John from Security and some auditor. They wouldn't have done that if it had been about a couple of broken machines. No, it had to be about the money. So where was the all-points bulletin? Where were the roadblocks? It was a little odd that he hadn't heard anything at all. Where was the massive FBI manhunt? Damned if Noogie knew. It sure wasn't like this in the movies. Certainly not the movies he would've made. This was a big deal, what he'd done.

If they were looking for him, they sure as hell weren't looking for him anyplace where he happened to be, that's for sure. *Suckers.*

He rolled down the window. The air rushing past the van was cool, not cold. Almost warm. He leaned his head out, opened his mouth, and screamed, *"Come and get me, coppers!"* Then he quickly pulled his head back inside and pretended he hadn't just done that.

Yeah, maybe I should take a break somewhere along here real soon.

It took him longer than he planned to find a place to stop, having found himself quite unexpectedly picky about where to pull over. Now that towns and villages and outposts were becoming more plentiful, he could afford to look for one that suited him. Most of them didn't. He didn't want to hang out in a place that featured the same main drag strip mall, the same chain stores and chain hotels and chain restaurants as all the other towns he'd driven through.

In a way, he thought, it might be better to hide in such a place. How would they ever find him in a burg that looked like all the others? It'd be like a shell game, with nothing on the outside to indicate that there was anything different happening inside.

He'd use that plan if he ever needed to, if the heat got too close, but for now he was interested in finding a place with a little style, a place that told him a little something about where he was. Where was the small town America he'd seen in all those movies? Where all the businesses were local and unlike any other anywhere (like that truck stop he'd been to)?

Noogie kept his eye out for road signs, following them randomly, taking lefts or rights when directed, if a town sounded interesting, or if it looked like the road would take him someplace.

At one point, he heard the unmistakable scratching from behind him. Dillinger was awake. A moment later there was a growl and a thump beside Noogie, as the cat materialized in the passenger seat. Noogie reached out a hand and scratched the purring beast behind the ears.

He'd stopped popping the pills once the sun came up, and now his stomach was starting to burn and his eyes felt scratchy. If he didn't find an interesting place soon he'd compromise, then keep looking.

He followed a sign that told him a town called North Dorchester was some seven miles away. He could do that. He'd stop there no matter what it turned out to be, crash for a bit, then move ahead on.

In North Dorchester, Noogie's calm persistence was rewarded. One of the first places he saw was called the Round at Both Ends

Motel. Sure enough, the building had been designed to be, well, round at both ends, like one of those old silver trailer homes or a septic tank.

Dillinger was asleep again on the passenger seat. Noogie parked the van, reached over into the back to grab a few more twenties, and got out. His legs were wobbly and his ass was numb from all that driving. He felt dazed and a touch loopy. He stood next to the van for a moment before going into the front office, waiting for the blood to start flowing back into his butt so he wouldn't walk funny. It took a minute.

The Round at Both Ends check-in desk was shaped like a half moon. In fact, Noogie noticed, everything in the lobby was smooth and rounded in some way. The small leatherette couch was semi-circular. The coffee table in front of it was kidney shaped. Even the landscape paintings on the wall were set in oval frames. The only things that weren't curved were the walls themselves, the doorway, and the Christmas tree, which had been set up in one corner. Round mirrors, round throw rugs, round windows. It was as lavish a place as he could ever remember being in.

"Wow," Noogie said as he approached the desk, "somebody musta been high in the middle, huh?"

The chubby, red-faced man behind the counter smirked only briefly. Like he hadn't heard that doozy at least once a day for the past four years. The only thing that really surprised him was that, for all the times he'd heard the moronic line, not one person had ever bothered to ask why a motel named after an Ohio joke was located some forty miles northwest of Raleigh. "Can I help you?" he asked.

Noogie's eyes were still filled with wonder as he scanned the room. There were round lamps and a round goldfish bowl—even a globe right there on the desk, he guessed for people who'd gotten lost. "Yeah," he said, turning his attention back to the clerk, who's name tag read "Rolf." "I'd like a room please."

Rolf sized up the stranger who stood in front of him. Disheveled clothes, unshaven, red-rimmed eyes, mildly odiferous. The stranger's hands were trembling, and even from where Rolf sat he could tell the guy had breath that could knock down a mule. He'd had worse come through. At least this guy was wearing pants. Nevertheless, he'd give him number five. It was the room they set aside for cases like this. "Of course sir," he said. "We have a very nice room." He reached behind the desk for a registration slip. "Number five. It's only twenty-seven-fifty a night."

"That's pretty good," Noogie said. "But let me ask you. The rooms down at the ends," he pointed in the general direction, "are they really round?"

"Yes sir, they are," he sighed. There was no way in hell this guy was going to get one of those, Rolf thought. It'd take forever to air it out.

"Is number five one of the round ones?"

"Well, no sir...no it's not."

"I want one of the round ones."

Rolf's eyes darted. *Why did they always have to do this?* "I'm afraid I must warn you, sir, that those are, as you can imagine, our most popular rooms, and so as a result we must charge considerably more for them."

"Yeah, fine, " Noogie said. He'd noticed only one other car in the parking lot, so they couldn't have been all *that* popular. "How much?"

"Two-twenty-five," Rolf said. That always put an end to the discussion.

"Wow, that's an awfully big jump there, don't you think?" Noogie said. "From twenty-seven-fifty to two hundred twenty-five? That's almost two hundred bucks."

"We know that, sir, but like I said, the rooms—and there are only two of them—are in very high demand by people who are willing to pay that sort of price."

"Yeah I can imagine," Noogie told him. "Okay, I'll take it." What the hell? It was about time he started living it up a little.

"Really," Rolf said. "And how do you intend to pay for the room?" He didn't believe this guy for a minute. If he tried to pay with a credit card, he'd run it through every check in the world.

Noogie could hear the suspicion in chubby's voice and wasn't much liking it. Maybe he didn't look like Montgomery Clift, but he had the cash and the room was vacant.

Everyone had been so nice to him up to this point. For the most part, at least. What the hell was this guy's problem? "Got it right here," he said, reaching for his wallet. "Cash money."

It was a good thing he'd filled his wallet before coming in here. He had just enough. He didn't want to flash too much cash around. There'd been the big tip he'd left for Flo, but that was an exception. In this case, though, he was glad he had it right here, if only to see the look on that smug bastard's face.

Noogie couldn't think of any other reason why staying in a round room had suddenly become so important to him, other than to show this guy a thing or two. That, and the fact that staying in a round room reminded him of his favorite Polish joke. Plus it was classy.

He signed in this time as "Henry Charriere," took the key to number twelve, then moved the van to a spot right outside the room. Now that there were getting to be more people around, he was becoming more nervous about leaving the money in the van. Maybe that night he'd drag it inside with him.

More than anything else, room number twelve resembled something from a high-class New Orleans cathouse, not that Noogie had ever actually been to one. Curved walls, round bed, round tub, everything done up in lacy blood reds and carnation pinks. Noogie thought it was worth every penny.

Where would Al Capone—or Rico Bandello, for that matter— have stayed if they'd come through here? Noogie reasoned. *Crappy, square room number five? Gimme a break. They woulda been right here, living in splendor, and sleeping on a round bed.*

Man, he thought a few minutes later, as he stood in the round, red tub beneath the hot spray from the ceiling-mounted shower head, *I should just build myself a place like this somewhere. The desert or the mountains or something. A big mansion, where every room is a different shape. And there'd be secret passages and shit.*

He shaved for the first time since he'd left Jersey City. He'd forgotten how good it felt to shave. He washed his hair and then just stood there under the cascading water for a long time.

When he shut off the water and pulled open the curtain, a blast of air-conditioning made him shiver.

"This is living," he said.

He brushed his teeth—also for the first time since he'd split— and that felt good, too. New toothbrush and everything. He then nudged Dillinger off the pillow and crawled into the bed, under the frilly silk comforter, and closed his eyes. A few minutes later, however, his eyes opened.

Damn. Those pills were still doing their business. He'd been popping them three at a time every half hour for a while back there. He guessed he'd maybe overdone it. His stomach was still burning and his hands, he noticed only now, were trembling slightly. He hadn't yet noticed that he'd been chewing his tongue all morning.

He decided he needed something to eat—a nice big meal. Maybe even a couple beers to bring him down a few notches, get him back on track. It was four o'clock. Maybe that dummy at the front desk could suggest something in town.

. . .

Rolf (who, after seeing the newly washed and shaved Noogie, felt only mildly ashamed of his earlier judgment) told him about a couple of places just a few miles down the road. One was a seafood restaurant, but Noogie wasn't so sure he much trusted the idea of a seafood restaurant, so that was out. Another was a Chinese takeout place with three tables. He wasn't so sure about that, either. His mom was always talking about how the Chinese were an inscrutable people, and even though he wasn't sure what that meant, he took it as a sign that he should steer clear of them.

He settled for a bright, pleasant place known for its fried chicken.

"They dip it in batter, then roll it in Raisin Bran before they fry it," the waitress—Sadie was her name—told Noogie when he asked what was so special about it.

"Really? With the raisins and everything?"

"No, silly," she said, lightly touching his shoulder. "They take the raisins out first."

"Wow," Noogie said. "Seems like an awful lot of work. Wouldn't it be, you know, easier to just get plain bran flakes or something, instead of having to deal with picking all the raisins out? That's what I'd do."

She shook her head. "We tried that, and I'll tell ya, it's just not the same."

Noogie took her word for it and decided he had to give it a try now, after making her explain it all like that.

The thing he liked best about the restaurant was the fact that it had those place mats with games and puzzles on them. The place wasn't too busy yet, so he asked Sadie if he could borrow a pencil.

He whipped through the five trivia questions (he'd always

been good at those) but was still struggling with the maze when his dinner arrived.

He had to admit, Sadie was right. It wouldn't've been the same with plain bran flakes.

After he'd finished, he stood and paid the bill, then swung back past the table, where he slipped a twenty-dollar tip under his plate.

He thought again that maybe he shouldn't do that—that it would only draw attention to himself. But Sadie deserved it. She'd touched his shoulder after all. He was always a sucker for waitresses who touched his shoulder or patted his arm or called him hon.

He was feeling much better having eaten. As he sorted through his keys on his way back to the van, he looked up and saw a neon sign in a window across the street. The sign out front read, "West of Dublin."

Yeah, I think I deserve it, he thought.

He wasn't so sure about the name, but as he scanned up and down the quiet block he saw no other taverns to choose from. After a quick peek in the van to make sure everything was in order, he crossed the street and went inside.

Apart from the neon beer signs on the dark paneled walls and the hanging fluorescent lights directly above the bar, it was completely dark. The air was thick with smoke and some traditional Irish folk song was playing on the jukebox.

Noogie hoisted himself onto a stool at the end of the bar and reached for his pack of cigarettes to find he had only two left.

The bartender, a lean, dark-haired man in a black T-shirt, was talking with the three other men at the bar. When he noticed Noogie, he excused himself and turned to him.

"What'll it be?" he asked, his Irish accent subdued but noticeable.

"Well," Noogie said, "being as this is an Irish bar I guess I'll have a Guinness."

"No Guinness, friend."

"Oh," Noogie said. "That's surprising. I mean it's okay and everything, but I thought all Irish bars had to carry Guinness by law or something."

"What'll it be?" the bartender repeated, clearly wanting to get back to his friends.

"Oh, " Noogie nodded at the other three at the bar. "Whatever they're having."

The bartender nodded, grabbed an empty glass, tilted it beneath a tap, and pulled the handle. From where he sat, Noogie couldn't see what it was.

When the beer arrived, Noogie laid a twenty on the bar. "Also," he said, "you sell smokes here? I'm about fresh out."

The bartender glanced at the pack and nodded once. "Yeah." He retrieved a pack and tossed it down next to Noogie's glass. "Four bucks," he said.

"And how much for the beer?"

"It's for everything."

"Wow, huh? Cheap."

The bartender said nothing, took the bill, and returned his change. Noogie left a five on the bar and pocketed the rest. He lit a cigarette, feeling pretty damn good about everything.

"Don't much expect to find an Irish bar in a place like this, huh?" he said to no one in particular. One of the men glanced at him, then looked away.

Everyone sitting at the bar, he determined from the gist of their conversation, was a bartender. One of the men was about the same age as the actual bartender, the two others much older and tougher looking. One of the older ones, from what Noogie could glean from the conversation, seemed to be visiting from Chicago.

Noogie wanted to bring up the fact that he was from Jersey but couldn't figure out any way to do that. His not being a bartender seemed to preclude him from joining the conversation in any way.

That was okay. He drank his beer, smoked the second cigarette, and listened. When he finished the beer he ordered another.

Noogie had never been quite the drinker he wanted to be—and certainly not the kind his dad had been—so when he did drink, it tended to reach his brain very quickly. Soon he began dropping comments into the bartenders' conversation from his end of the bar. Nothing major—a "yeah, what an asshole," after one man told everyone what an asshole a former boss of his had been, or a "that's really funny," after another told an off-color yarn about a prostitute who used to ply her trade in the alley behind his bar.

So what if these guys were all bartenders and he wasn't? Even if he didn't know what a speed rack was, he'd had asshole bosses before. He knew a few dirty jokes, too. *Yeah,* he thought, as the second beer took hold, *I could tell them a few stories, all right.*

The conversation at the other end of the bar now focused on the worst, most obnoxious ways they've seen people try to get a bartender's attention when things were busy.

"I love those people who wave money in the air," one said. "Like I'll immediately go running for it."

"Then there are the ones—you ever get this?" said one of the older men. "Who find out your name from somebody, and they think that'll do it. You know, 'Hey Lou! I'm pretty dry over here,' that sorta shit, when you don't know these people from Adam."

"Yeah I seen that," added the gentleman from Chicago. "Obnoxious fuckers. College kids mostly, or guys in suits. That sorta shit always guarantees I *won't* notice them for a while."

"Worst way I've ever seen," Noogie began, loud enough to be heard clearly. Four sets of eyes turned slowly to look at him. "Worst way I've ever seen was in *The Killing.* You guys ever see it? Stanley Kubrick film?" Nobody said anything but they continued looking at him, waiting.

"Well, it's a long story that I won't get into. But in one scene, there's this big wrestler at a bar. He finishes his beer and wants another, but he thinks the bartender's ignoring him. So what he does, see, is he slams his bottle down on the bar and screams"— Noogie adopted a bad Russian accent—*"How 'bout some service, ya stupid-lookin' Irish pig!"*

A silence fell over the bar as solidly as a bag of damp concrete. Even the music had stopped. Although it was something Noogie would never recognize in himself, sometimes he simply wasn't very good at gauging an audience.

All four sets of eyes were now staring at the floor, the bar, their hands—anywhere but at Noogie. Pretending he was suddenly quite fascinated with the glass he was holding, the bartender finally broke the silence. "Yeah, now, that's real good there, boyo, but I think it's best right now that you get yourself on out of here before you get in any more trouble, eh?"

Back at the motel Noogie found himself pacing around the circular bed, muttering and smoking furiously.

Didn't they know he was a wanted fugitive from justice? Throw *him* out? One of the greatest bandits ever in this whole damn country's history? Didn't they know he was dangerous? Idiots. Fuckin' Irish. What the hell did they know? So what if they weren't talking about it in the papers or on tv? Couldn't they see it in his eyes? Dummies. He'd show them. He was Steve fuckin' McQueen. And Cagney and Edward G. Robinson. All of them. Better than all of them, because he got away with it.

He flopped himself on the bed, still fully clothed, grabbed the remote from the bedside table, and clicked it at the television (which, for the record, was not round).

He flipped through one hundred twenty-seven channels, pausing briefly at *America's Most Wanted*. They were profiling a serial window smasher who was working his way around east Texas and Arkansas, throwing rocks through garage windows. He'd smashed over a dozen so far, they said.

Where he lay, Noogie threw up his hands in disgust and turned his eyes to the ceiling. "What does a guy have to do?" he asked the ceiling. "Stealing a gazillion bucks ain't enough, obviously."

He punched the remote a few more times, settling on *Badlands*. Something that normally would have made him very happy only pissed him off further that night.

Sitting there in the woods all bored. Lookatem, sitting there bored. Charlie and Caril Ann were never bored. Not for those four days anyway. Ten people in four days, not counting that guy from the gas station. That was different. They had a thousand fucking cops after them. National Guard, even. Jesus, imagine that. They just kept moving and kept at it. What're these two doing? Fishing, for godsakes. I'll show those fucking bartenders.

Noogie passed out soon afterward, the television still on.

He was feeling much better, if a little foggy, the next morning. That was all right. When he climbed back into the van after checking out, he reached for the pill bottle, glad that he'd had the good sense to pick up the economy size.

He wasn't nearly as angry as he had been the previous night. He'd been tired and, god, drunk. He should never have gotten so upset at *Badlands*. He felt kind of bad about that. Great film. He remembered what he'd been thinking, though. He hadn't let go of that. He was calmer about it now, and that was good.

The road he was driving on twisted through low brush and dry farmland. Flat and empty to all sides, just like in the movie. He began seeing signs for a town named Killman. He liked the sound of that, and so he followed them. He'd be needing gas soon. Maybe he'd get something to eat.

Some five miles outside of Killman he saw a building off the road to his right. It was the first building he'd seen in some time that wasn't a dilapidated barn or a tarpaper shack, and, so far as he could tell, it was probably the last one he'd be seeing until he got to town. There was nothing else around.

He wouldn't call the place "ramshackle." Not yet at least. Not to say it couldn't use a little sprucing up. It was a single-story wooden structure. An old blue Chevy was parked out front. Huge sections of shingles looked like they had been peeled off the roof, almost as if a tornado had ripped past not too long ago. Not a direct hit, but close enough. Noogie wasn't real sure if they had tornadoes down here or not. Maybe it was a hurricane—he knew they had those sometimes.

It wasn't the shingles—or lack thereof—that first caught his attention. What caught his attention was the hand-lettered sign. White letters three feet tall, painted across what appeared to be tarpaper, the whole thing stretched along the length of the roof, to ensure that no passerby could miss it.

Before logic or reason could kick in Noogie had turned the wheel, directing the van into the dirt driveway. He parked along-side the Chevy, pocketed the keys, and reached for the suitcase.

11

THE KILLMAN REGISTER

Saturday, December 8, p. 1

Armed Bandit Strikes Local Store

Local police today are investigating yesterday's daring daylight armed robbery of Iggy's Guns & Liquor, on County Trunk B, which left store owner Angus "Iggy" Hansen bruised and upset.

According to Hansen, the gunman entered the store at approximately 11:45 yesterday morning, shortly after it had opened.

"This big fella came in the front door holding a gun," says Hansen, 67, "which is the sort of thing you'd almost expect at a place like this that sells firearms."

He knew the man was not a customer, however, when he aimed the gun at Hansen's chest. "I kind of laughed at first," said the owner, "because it was such a puny thing. A .22 pistol. But he said that he meant business, and that this was a stickup."

Instead of demanding cash from the register, the gunman proceeded to grab several bottles of liquor.

"It's all he wanted, I guess," said Hansen, who first opened Iggy's Guns & Liquor in 1975. "Weird thing is, he didn't even go for the top shelf stuff. He went for the rye and gin and those big plastic jugs of cheap vodka we got down there."

Things took an even stranger turn when the gunman then demanded that Hansen ring everything up, as he would a normal purchase,

"He paid for everything," Hansen said. "So I guess you can't exactly call it a robbery. I don't know what you'd call it."

After receiving his change, the gunman struck Hansen once in the head with the handgun. "Just like that, he hits me," Hansen recalled, pointing at the bruise on his forehead. "After I'd been real cooperative. Then he called me a 'dummy,' which I didn't think was very nice at all."

When asked if he considered using one of his store's many available firearms to stop the man, he replied, "That would have made sense, I guess."

Hansen was able to write down the fleeing assailant's license plate number, which he then reported to the sheriff's office.

The bandit was said to be a white or Hispanic male, six feet tall, approximately 225 pounds, with dark hair and a small mustache. Hansen describes him as "sort of greasy-looking." He was last seen driving a white Ford van.

Sheriff Mitch Kowalski, who called yesterday's events "really nuts," says he hopes to make an arrest soon, and that the suspect will be facing assault and weapons charges.

"If there's any consolation," Hansen added, "it's knowing that he's going to have one heck of a hangover."

Justice might have moved a bit more swiftly had Sheriff Kowalski bothered to run a check on the plates, rather than simply telling his deputies to keep an eye out for "a fat, drunken spic in a white van." It might also have helped had Iggy Hansen properly identified the tags on the van or gotten all the numbers right.

Not knowing these things, Noogie might have panicked had he seen the story. Or he might've been thrilled by it, to finally be getting some of the attention he deserved. Had he seen the story, he might not have decided to stop and take that walking tour of New Holland. But given the circulation of the *Killman Register* (2,418) he heard nothing about it, or the fact that the old coot had, in theory at least, gotten his license plate number.

Dummy, Noogie was thinking about the events of the previous morning. *Stupid old dummy.*

He hadn't meant to pistol-whip the old man. It was an accident. The guy had made a move while Noogie was scooping his change off the counter, his arm had twitched, and the old man's head had been in the way. He sort of felt bad about it, but not *too* bad. The guy shouldn't've made a move—Christ, he worked in a gun shop—didn't he know the thing was loaded? Besides, he should never have laughed when Noogie first walked in. Nobody was going to laugh at him anymore. Nobody.

No, dammit, he thought. *I'm glad I hit him. Just for that.*

All in all, things had gone pretty smoothly for a practice run. Not perfect, maybe, but pretty well, nervous as he'd been. He wasn't exactly sure why he'd gone for the booze instead of the guns. Probably because it was right there. The guns had been in those locked cases. It would've taken too much time.

And why'd he pay for everything? He was the man holding the gun. He could've taken whatever he wanted. But once he got into the store, he felt bad. There he was with all this money, and there that old guy was, just trying to make a go of it selling guns and booze. It looked like business had been slow lately.

He was a dummy anyway. He felt the flash of anger return. That had been happening more often these past two days. The pills, he figured. They made him kind of crazy after a few hours, if he kept taking them. He'd pull over in a bit, try and get some sleep someplace. At least he could use the booze he had in the back to bring him down, and he wouldn't have to worry about offending any touchy Irishmen.

Show them next time, too. Can't take a fuckin' joke. If he ever found himself there again, he'd give 'em a fuckin' joke.

Stewing as he was, Noogie didn't even notice when he drove past the sign for Cape Fear. He stewed all the way through South Carolina to the Georgia border. He wasn't sure anymore if maybe he wanted to go to Florida, or if he should take a right somewhere and go to Vegas. Or El Paso. Wherever he ended up first, he figured, and the way he was going it could be any of the three.

He rarely thought of the police anymore. It had been over a week, and if they hadn't caught up with him by now what were the chances they ever would? Not so long as he kept moving.

At about five o'clock in the afternoon, some twenty miles north of Hasty, a billboard grabbed his attention: a big picture of a Ferris wheel, a clown, and a smiling family, each member clutching what was either cotton candy or an impossibly large ice cream cone.

"Serpentine Bros. Fair," it read across the top. "Fun for the Whole Family!"

He slowed the van enough to take in the directions at the bottom of the billboard. All he had to do, it looked like, was take the next exit and he'd be there.

He was about due a nice break, he thought.

Noogie loved county fairs. He'd been to only one in his life, but it was enough to let him know that he loved them.

This was surprising, given how that one turned out. He was seven and his dad had taken him. They hadn't been there for an hour and a half before his dad, drunk off his ass, tried to strangle one of the horses in the pony ride. That pretty much put an end to the day.

Before that, however, Noogie had been in awe. All the lights and smells. All the bells and music and laughter. Every which way he looked, some new fun thing was waiting for him. Rides and games and animals he'd never seen up close before.

As the exit ramp approached, Noogie flicked on his turn signal.

12

It was the last night the Serpentine Bros. were in town and the fairgrounds were packed. The landscape being as barren as it was as he approached, Noogie found it hard to believe that this many people lived within, hell, a hundred miles. He hadn't seen that many people in one place since he fled Jersey.

He felt a twinge of panic the first few times he passed one of the several policemen strolling the midway, but when they paid him no attention whatsoever he relaxed. Cops aside, it felt good to be around humanity again. Better still, most of the folks he saw were almost as big as he was.

Maybe this is the best idea of all, he thought. *Hide in plain sight*. Working up his courage, he tested this theory by stopping a policeman and asking him for directions to the bathroom. The cop never looked at him twice—gave him directions and moved along.

Perfect.

Noogie bought himself a corn dog and a small beer. The lack of sleep and food, as well as all that driving, had skewed his perceptions. Sounds were sharper, the lights so intense he was forced to squint and look away from them initially. That corn dog was really something, too.

He didn't go on any rides—that would've been a bad idea in his state—but he liked watching them. He stopped at one of the booths and tried, without anything even approaching success, to toss some plastic rings around any of a dozen plastic ducks bobbing in a pool of brackish water. He stopped at another booth and attempted, with an equal lack of dexterity, to toss Ping-Pong balls into one of eight goldfish bowls.

"Aw, hell," he told the unshaven, dark-eyed skell behind the counter when the last ball bounced lightly off the rim of one of the bowls. "I guess this just ain't my game, huh?"

"Yeah, guess not, chum," the man said, retrieving the ball. He looked over Noogie's shoulder and shouted, "*Next! Who's next here? A game anyone can win!*"

Noogie wandered aimlessly around the grounds, mingling with the crowd. Most of these people, it struck him, seemed to be very happy. Families, young couples, even old couples, several of them carrying oversized stuffed animals, novelty mirrors with advertisements on them, or goldfish in plastic bags.

He paid fifty cents to a cheerful microcephalic before going inside the tent that promised "Rancid, the Devil Horse." The banner outside the tent featured a giant, jet-black horse on its hind legs, a wicked snarl on its lips, and flames shooting from its nostrils. Near the bottom of the banner, a crowd of tiny human figures was fleeing in terror.

Understandable, Noogie thought as he stared up at the picture, *given that this Rancid must be almost fifty feet tall. Awfully small tent for that, though.*

Once inside the tent, however, he found himself presented with a regular brown horse in a pen, just standing there. Even though someone had tied a black Zorro-type mask around its head, the horse didn't appear to be particularly devilish. Noogie looked a good fifty cents worth anyway, then left.

He glanced at his watch. It was eight p.m. If he was going to get some sleep, he'd better start looking for a place soon. He began slowly weaving his way through the thick crowds in the general direction of the exit—or at least where he thought he remembered the exit to be.

. . .

"*Hey, fat boy!*" Despite all the noise—the rides, the music, the bells, the thousands of voices all around him—this one voice sliced through them all like a dirty scalpel. Although half a dozen heads around him turned in response, Noogie knew instinctively somehow that he was the intended target. He began to look around nervously for the source.

"*Hey, ya big tubba guts. I can tell you're guilty of something—*"

What? Noogie felt the sweat begin to gather under his arms. It wasn't just in his head, was it? He'd heard about that happening to people. Voices in the head.

"*—like stealing dessert!*" This was followed by a low, evil cackle and the toot of a bicycle horn.

Looking up and to his right, Noogie relaxed again when he saw the clown with the bullhorn, perched on a narrow platform above a pool of water.

"Drippy the Clown," the sign behind him read, amid splashes of red and blue paint. "Three Tries—$1."

"Now I got your attention, huh?" the white-faced clown sneered into the bullhorn. "Was it because I mentioned dessert?"

Noogie could understand why they put a chain link fence in front of him and made people throw softballs at a target off to the right. He smiled and chuckled at the clown, knowing it was all a game and that he didn't really mean any of those things. He began moving away again.

"*Hey, hold on there a second, tubby,*" the clown shouted after him. "*Aren't ya gonna give it a go? Or ain't you got the guts? Lookin' at you it looks like you got plenty—but maybe they're all in the wrong place.*"

Noogie shrugged and turned back. What the heck? He'd give it a shot. Then he'd be on his way. He approached the woman standing next to the fence. There was no telling how old she was, anywhere between twenty-five and fifty-five, with dirty-blonde hair and a cigarette dangling from the corner of her lipstick-smeared mouth. She was wearing an aging blue baseball jersey with double zeroes on the front. In her hands she held three softballs.

"That'll be a buck for three," she told him. She didn't seem to enjoy her job very much.

"Better give him at least two balls, sweetie," Drippy shouted at her. "It looks like he could use a pair."

Noogie reached beneath his untucked shirt and into his right pocket but stopped when his fingertips touched the butt of the pistol. He'd shoved it in there after he'd left the gun shop and had since forgotten about it. "Whoops," he told the woman with the cigarette as he withdrew his hand. "Wrong pocket."

He sorted through the few bills he found in his left pocket, found a single, and handed it to her. She gave him the three softballs in return, pointed at the sawhorse he was required to stand behind, and stepped to the side.

"High and dry," Drippy said from his perch, swinging his legs. "High and dry."

The round bull's-eye he was to aim for was thirty feet away and approximately one foot across. It was attached to a long arm, which jutted out from beneath the platform upon which Drippy sat. Hit the bull's-eye and that rotten-mouthed Drippy gets dumped into the pool.

Noogie tried to measure things out. It was hard to concentrate with all the distractions. There was a shooting gallery to the right of him and a Whack-A-Mole game to his left. From up the midway, he could still hear a looped, recorded message detailing all of Rancid's fiendish exploits.

"Don't just stand there scratching your balls," Drippy shouted.

"*Do* something!" He let loose again with that annoying evil chuckle of his. "Show us all how to fail."

Noogie drew his arm back and threw the first softball. It sailed sadly through the air, bouncing in the dirt ten feet short of the target.

"*Ha!*" Drippy belched. "For a fat guy, you sure are *fat*."

A small crowd had gathered behind Noogie, most of them hoping to see someone dunk that damn smart-alecky clown. Then a beefy blond kid wearing a Georgia State Football sweatshirt jerked a thumb toward Noogie's back. "Hey, get a loada this guy," he said. He laughed, and a few others joined in.

Unaware of any of this, Noogie drew the second softball back and let it fly, harder this time. This time it fell only five feet short of the target, but far to the right.

"Oh, you *are* pathetic, aren't you?" Drippy said. "You're every bit the loser you look."

Noogie heard the titters behind him for the first time and squeezed the remaining softball until his knuckles turned white. Why had he done this? Why had he stopped? Fucking clown. He felt every muscle begin to tighten. He knew he was no good at things like this. And now people were laughing at him because of it.

"Hey lemme guess fat boy," Drippy howled. "Did your *momma* teach you to throw, 'cause it sure wasn't your daddy. You throw like a little girl!" The crowd laughed again.

"He's so right. Watch this," a voice behind Noogie whispered.

What Drippy the Clown didn't realize was that Noogie's mother *had* taught him to throw. Lord knows his dad wasn't going to do it. As a result, he had always thrown like a girl, which led to endless schoolyard tauntings.

The arm went back a third time, his face burning, fully aware that everyone behind him was just waiting for him to fail, waiting to laugh at him again.

He let go of the softball too early, felt it roll off his fingertips before he could do anything to stop it. The ball sailed six feet straight up, plunking into the dirt three feet in front of the saw-horse. The crowd erupted into cheers and whistles.

"You are one *fat, pathetic loser,*" Drippy said through his own laughter. "Why don't you go home to momma?"

As the crowd behind Noogie dispersed and continued on down the midway, and the haggard blonde weaved her way a bit unsteadily toward the bull's-eye to retrieve the other two soft-balls, a small, blinding-hot explosion erupted deep in Noogie's brain. His vision went white as he jammed a hand into his right pocket, whipped out the pistol, pointed it without seeing or think-ing, and pulled the trigger three times. He slammed the gun back into his pocket and turned away.

The three small *pops* had been lost under the cacophony from the Whack-A-Mole and the shooting gallery, the screams from the rides, and the clamor of a million other noises. The blonde was bent over, still trying to pick up the softballs, which kept getting away from her. The crowd kept walking. The only one who had seen him holding the gun was Drippy himself—and there's some question as to whether or not he even registered what he thought he was seeing.

That's what it would've been like, anyway, had Noogie actually pulled the gun from his pocket and fired it. It would've been just like in the movies. No—it would've been cleaner than that, even. It would've been like it was on tv, as if Drippy had been noth-ing more than a misplaced target from the shooting gallery next door. There would've been no screams, no thrashing around, no blood. He'd see the look on Drippy's face, that look of abrupt sur-prise you find in every clown painting, except this time the clown would have three holes in his forehead. At least no one would've been able to say he shot like a girl.

Yeah, he thought as he walked away, tears burning in his eyes, the sound of Drippy's laughter following him for a minute before the son of a bitch singled out another poor innocent from the crowd.

Within a few minutes Noogie calmed down and had the exit in sight. His steps were brisk but relaxed. He was better than all these assholes, and he knew it. Better than that stupid clown and all those stupid dummies behind him. If they only knew, they'd wish they were him.

He felt so calm, so relaxed by the time he reached the gate that he even asked the pimply-faced sixteen-year-old standing there if he could get his hand stamped for reentry.

"Naw, uh-uh," the kid drawled, " 'less you're comin' back right away, like, now. We close up and start tearing down in an hour."

"Oh," Noogie told him, "that's too bad. I had a real fine time."

"Maybe I'm invincible," Noogie was telling Dillinger, who once again was sitting in the passenger seat. "Maybe that's it. Whadda you think?" The cat offered no response.

For the past few days Noogie had been thinking of picking himself up a police scanner for the van, but now he wasn't even sure it would be necessary.

Then once more he thought, *What in the hell do I have to do? Shoulda shot that clown. Who'd miss a clown, for godsakes?*

He drove for another three hours before checking into the Galveston Motor Inn (as "Steve Andrews" in honor of the day's accomplishments, even if they were only imaginary). When he first saw the signs for the motel, he was thrilled, convinced that he was suddenly making remarkable time without realizing it. Then the clerk at the front desk informed him that no, indeed, he was still in Georgia, that "Galveston" was just the name of the motel's owner.

"Oh," Noogie said. "I knew that."

Before going to sleep that night, Noogie turned on the television and cracked one of his new bottles of gin. He unwrapped a plastic cup from the bathroom and poured himself a splash.

"Ah," he said, raising a toast to himself, "here's to ill-gotten gin." Then he corrected himself. "No, I paid for it. It's perfectly legitimate gin." It was much less interesting that way, he felt, so he went back to "ill-gotten."

He took a sip. It tasted to him like weak motor oil or fermented inner tubes. He winced, then swallowed. He was a tough guy, he thought. Tough guys always drink gin, and he was starting to see why. Except for Ray Milland—he drank rye. And look what happened. He took another sip, winced again, but got it down.

He found it strange that he still felt a few pangs of guilt when it came to that gun shop, and regret for not having shot the clown. If he'd gone ahead and done it, he knew he would've felt about as bad for shooting that clown as he did for robbing PiggyBank. That clown wasn't human.

He flipped through the channels. They didn't have so many here but he found, much to his surprise, that one of the channels was showing *The Squeeze*, starring Lee Van Cleef. He knew all about it, of course—recognized it immediately—but for some reason he'd never gotten around to seeing the whole thing before. Noogie adjusted his pillow and settled back.

"That's what you get for working with *mugs!*" Noogie yelled at the screen half an hour later when the bullets started to fly. "*Shot!*"

Soon enough, though, the gin did its work. He found the end of the film absolutely baffling, and soon after he was asleep. He awoke the next morning with a shrieking headache. It hurt to open his eyes.

He swung his feet to the floor, sat up, placed his fingertips on his temples, and pressed. It helped a little, but the moment he relaxed the pressure the shrill pain came rushing back.

He dragged himself into the small shower (which, he noticed, could've used a good cleaning) and found the same thing. While standing under the hot water there was some relief. When he turned the water off it was back.

Damn.

As he got dressed, he noticed the sound of rain slapping against the windows of his room. He replaced the gun in the suitcase and opened the door.

The low clouds ranged from smoke gray to black and back again. And him without a raincoat. Scrunching up his shoulders and ducking his head (as if that would do anything at all), he made a slow, galumphing dash for the van with his suitcase under one arm and an extremely unhappy Dillinger under the other. After some complex maneuvering, he opened the back door, dropped both inside, slammed it shut, then trotted slowly toward the office.

Inside, Noogie asked the woman at the desk if she could tell him where he might pick up a bottle of aspirin.

"Guess I overdid it a little last night," he explained.

"This weather can't help much," she added. She pulled a bottle from beneath the counter, opened it, and handed it to him.

"Well that's convenient," he said.

"In this job, believe me, it's best to keep them handy."

He thought of asking her if she also happened to have a spare bag of cat litter and a few cans of food handy, but reconsidered. Instead, he thanked her kindly, returned his room key, and stepped back out into the rain. As he drew closer to the van, he began to notice that something wasn't quite right.

"Aww *crap*," he said and began jogging toward the van.

He yanked open the door on the passenger side, made sure

Dillinger wasn't waiting to jump out, and frantically began rolling up the window. He ran around the front of the van and repeated the operation on the driver's side before climbing in. His seat was soaked. The passenger seat was soaked, too.

Next place I get out, he thought, *I'm gonna look like I had an accident.* Then he snapped around and looked in the back of the van, his eyes wide. Dillinger, his fur dripping, was sitting way to the back, yelling at him.

He reached for the nearest laundry bag (the one he'd been making withdrawals from), yanked it toward him, tugged it open, and stuck a hand inside.

It was only slightly damp, hardly soaked the way he'd feared. Good. He couldn't believe he'd left the windows down all night. Not just because of the rain—that was the least of his worries. He was getting cocky. And he couldn't afford to be cocky, not with the money at least, until he found a safe place to stash it. But where in the hell was that gonna be? He began to wonder—also for the first time—if he was now doomed to drive this godforsaken van around stupid back roads, staying at cheap motels and eating at lousy diners for the rest of his life.

He sure hoped not. He was getting bored, and his head hurt. Plus his butt was soaked.

He checked the other two bags, found them in the same condition as the first, turned the key in the ignition, and headed back out on the road, the damp on the seat fast soaking through his trousers.

Trying to keep his eyes on the road as much as possible, he flipped open the box of tapes next to him and began feeling around for a good one.

13

Some things are destined to slip beneath the radar—even the radar of the Federal Bureau of Investigation. Things like the following small item, which would appear in the December tenth issue of the *Fooslinton Weekly Gazette*, a community newspaper out of Fooslinton, Florida.

ROADSIDE ROBBER ADDS INSULT TO INJURY

Grover Crosslin's roadside vegetable and pie stand out on Hwy. 17 has been popular with Fooslinton area residents and passersby for years now. Known for his wide selection of fresh, homegrown vegetables and wife Betty's delicious homemade pies, Crosslin says that all he wanted to do was "provide people with the best vegetables and pies at a reasonable price."

So imagine his shock Saturday afternoon when a man pulled a gun on him and demanded money.

"He said, 'I don't want to hurt anybody, so give me all your money.' What was I supposed to do?"

The man, described as a Mexican of medium height with a little mustache and weighing close to 300 pounds, took everything in Crosslin's cash box and fled.

"He also took a cherry pie," Betty Crosslin added.

"He got thirteen dollars and change," Crosslin said. "And a pie. I mean, how much did he think I made here, anyway?"

Crosslin said that before the man drove away, he called

them both "dummies." "That just wasn't very gentlemanly, if you ask me," Crosslin said. "It hurt my wife's feelings. Some people are just wrong."

Neither Crosslin nor his wife were injured in the incident. Fooslinton sheriff Foam Carter, who is conducting the investigation, says he does not believe the suspect is from the area.

Noogie was feeling bad about taking that old couple's money. They certainly needed it more than he did. He could've at least paid for that pie (which had been really good—he was glad he took it along). At least they had each other. That was more than a lot of people had. They'd get by just fine. And hell, now they had a story to tell. That's worth a lot, too. That's what Dillinger (the real one) told people when he robbed them.

Imagine when the movie comes out, Noogie thought. *Hell, I could make it myself—even finance it—maybe starring...well, all the good actors are dead. But when it comes out, they'll know that they were a part of history. That's worth more than thirteen bucks and a pie.*

He considered for a moment turning around and giving them their money back and paying for the pie, perhaps even buying another, but before he could his mind wandered again.

Maybe if I found somebody, he thought, *I could settle down and stop all this. Somebody who could keep a secret.*

He wouldn't tell her about the money right away. He'd keep it hidden until he was sure she really loved him for him, and not just because he had a lot of dough.

Speaking of which, first chance he got, he needed to sit down with it and figure out exactly how much he had. The papers weren't telling him, and he didn't have any idea. There'd been about ten thousand in the shoe box, he knew that. Out here on the road, he'd been going through it like water. Meals, motel rooms, cigarettes, gas. You wouldn't think so but it can really add up.

He passed a sign that told him he was entering New Holland.

New Holland? he thought as he drove on. Hadn't he been through New Holland already, a couple days ago? Could he possibly have doubled back somewhere along the way? Left a motel and headed back the way he'd come by mistake? Or, driving the way he was, had he just taken a series of turns that had brought him around in a big circle?

No, a few days back he'd finally remembered that he could use the sun—keeping it to his left in the morning and his right in the afternoon. Maybe after a while people ran out of town names and so started reusing old ones. Maybe they should've called it New New Holland. Or Newer Holland.

Or maybe it's just like everything else. Everything else out here has been repeating. The sandwich shops and the coffee shops and the drugstores and the motels and the fast-food places and the gas stations. All the same. All just copies of the one you passed fifty miles back. And if you miss it, don't worry, there'll be another one ten miles up ahead, you can't miss it. Go wherever you want, head in whatever direction you want, you'll find all the same things.

Like Point Doom. What was that line from *Messiah of Evil*? "Entirely normal, quiet…because of the shared horror in common."

Shit, he thought. *I got nothing to worry about. They'll never find me in a country like this. The ole shell game. Am I in this New Holland or that New Holland or that one down there?*

He continued driving long after sundown, from nowhere to some other nowhere. It was a warm and humid December night. Then, from the corner of his eye, he noticed a light.

In the distance, across the fields. A light that was somehow familiar. He slowed the van, squinted, and slowly what he was seeing resolved itself into focus as it registered. He pulled the van off the road, stopped, cut the engine, and got out.

"It can't be," he whispered.

The light in the distance was coming from a drive-in movie screen. Maybe the last one in the country, who knows? On the screen, Laurel and Hardy were trying to fly an airplane. They seemed upset about something.

Noogie was beside himself. He had no idea how to get around to the drive-in theater proper, or how much time was left in the show. Was this a short subject or the feature? He didn't want to miss it, whatever it was, and whatever might or might not come afterward. If he got back in the van and tried to find it, he'd miss it all for sure.

Dammit, why didn't I bring binoculars? It didn't matter that he couldn't hear it—he just wanted to see it better. He looked back at the van in frustration.

The hood was too small to try and sit there. The roof was out of the question. He opened the passenger door and hopped in, letting his legs dangle outside. From there he watched a tiny, distant, silent Laurel and Hardy and felt the giddy, effervescent joy bubble up through his chest, while a few lonely cars roared past behind him. He didn't notice them at all.

He didn't notice the car that pulled off the road fifty feet in front of the van, either, until the driver of the car appeared next to him and asked, "You need any help there, buddy?"

Noogie's head snapped around, his eyes wide, to glare at the interloper. "I'm *trying* to watch a *movie*," he snarled. "Do you mind?" He turned his eyes back toward the screen, then added, "Stay and watch it if you like, but if you do you're gonna have to shut the hell up."

The would-be Samaritan squinted in the same direction as Noogie, shrugged, and returned to his car.

. . .

The screen went dark shortly after midnight, having shown two kung fu features Noogie had never seen. At least with those you don't have to worry about dialogue much. You can make all the sound effects right there in your car.

Noogie got back behind the wheel and drove on, feeling blessed somehow, and realizing now how very tired he was.

After spending the night in the oddly named Boda's Well Inn, apparently somewhere in central Florida, Noogie took another random turn. Though all the turns he had taken up to this point had pretty much balanced each other out, leaving him headed in a due southerly direction, this turn sent him rolling eastward.

He saw the signs for Miami, Sarasota, Fort Lauderdale, and West Palm Beach but paid no attention to them. He'd considered Fort Lauderdale briefly early on because that was where Piggy-Bank was located. But that might be pushing it a little too much and, besides, he'd told that cop he was heading there, which put it out of the question immediately.

Shortly after one p.m. on what he guessed to be Sunday afternoon (though he'd kind of lost track), the engine light on his dashboard began glowing.

That thing had been going on and off ever since he'd driven the van out of the lot. Not like his old van—that one had never given him a lick of trouble. Not that this was trouble, really. Just irksome.

He had never driven it too hard and always had the guys at the gas stations check the oil for him when he stopped. The engine didn't sound weird—no clanks or rattling or anything. Just that damn light. He shrugged and kept on driving. It would go out eventually. And if anything happened? He'd just buy himself a new van.

"Plain, Florida," he read aloud off another sign. "Hey, if you're looking for excitement, you're sure to find it in *Plain*."

It sounded tempting for a moment. Who would ever think to look for a wanted criminal in a place called Plain? Not in a million years. *Hell, I could probably buy Plain and turn it into my own little kingdom. Like that what's-her-name tried to do. But what would I do with it?*

He drove on. The land and the trees were a lush and almost phosphorescent green. Suddenly things seemed as beautiful as anything he had ever seen. Maybe Florida wasn't such a stinkhole, though he could do without the humidity.

He thought of Velda briefly. Maybe she could've loved him. He bet she would have, too, if she'd known what was really in those laundry bags. He shook his head. He didn't want it to be that way. No, Velda wasn't it. Someone named Velda sounds like someone who would be nothing but trouble in the end.

The only unconditional love he'd ever received had been from Dillinger, but that didn't really count, Dillinger being a cat and all. Every once in a while he'd felt it from his mother, but most of those moments had been in the distant past, like the afternoon she taught him how to throw a baseball.

Maybe he should call her anyway, if only to make sure she'd found the money. She could be a little batty sometimes. He should've at least left a note about that.

He wasn't sure about calling her, though. He missed her some, and he worried about her. He was sure the police must've been there, asking her all sorts of questions about him, and that couldn't've been very much fun. They better not have hurt her in any way. He felt a flash of anger. *If they had…*

He hoped she'd had the good sense to hide the money and not say a word about it to anyone. That was the important thing. Don't let anyone know.

God, maybe he should call her. He could send her more money, certainly, with a note telling her to keep it a secret and to make sure she burned up the envelope in the toilet or something, so they wouldn't have any postmarks to look at. But what did post-marks matter so long as he kept moving? Still, what if they're opening her mail before she even gets it?

At two o'clock that afternoon, Mildred Krapczak's telephone rang. She shuffled into the kitchen from the living room and picked it up.

"Yeah," she said.

"Ma, it's me."

"You son of a bitch, why aren't you dead? That woulda been your only excuse at this point."

He knew he should've expected as much. "I'm real happy to hear from you, too, Ma. So how are you?"

"Oh, couldn't be better," she barked into the phone. "My shit-for-brains son buys me slippers then abandons me. Yeah, I'm beautiful."

"Ma, I'm sorry about all that—"

"Yeah, I bet you're sorry."

At least she was still alive, he figured.

"Ma, did you get the money I left you on the table?"

"You didn't leave me any money."

"Yeah, I did, Ma, it was in a shoe box. Right there on the table."

"Why, so I could buy more *slippers*?"

"Ma, Christ, shut up about that a minute, would ya? I just wanted to see how you were doing?"

"Your damn cat ran away."

"No he didn't Ma. He's with me."

"Figures. You pick up and run away and even take the damn cat. Some son I got."

"I didn't have time to leave a note, I'm sorry. It was kinda—"

"You're a dummy."

"Ma, would you shut up a second? I was just calling to—"

"That's it? Ya call me after being away how long just to tell me to shut up? *Twice* now? You're useless. You're a useless shit for brains... And you're *fat*."

She slammed the phone back into the cradle.

Noogie held the pay phone against his ear for a moment, finding it hard to believe that she'd called him fat. She'd never gone that far before. He shrugged and replaced the receiver. As he climbed back into the van, he decided that, yes, he really was happier where he was.

Billboards along the side of the road began pointing him toward resorts and theme parks and the Everglades.

Yeah, maybe, he thought. As he looked around, it struck him that most of the towns he was driving through here seemed to consist of three bars and a church.

Then Noogie noticed a little cheese shop and pulled over. South of Wisconsin Cheese, it was called. He checked his wallet, figured he had enough cash, slipped the pistol inside his belt, loosened the shirt around it, and went inside.

The tiny bells above the screen door tinkled as it swung shut behind him.

"Hello there," someone said. The shop was unusually chilly and smelled like cheese. Sour and off-putting at first, but when you remembered where you were it was okay.

"Hi to you," said Noogie, raising a hand in a quick greeting. The proprietress was a small woman in her sixties, he'd guess, with a round, wizened face and curled white hair piled atop her head. She wore a blue apron that read "Real Wisconsin Cheese" and sported a Green Bay Packers lapel pin.

"What can I do you for?" she asked with a friendly smile.

"Well," said Noogie, placing his hands on the counter and looking about the shop, fully conscious of the gun in his waistband. Other than the old lady and himself, the shop was empty. "I was just passing through and thought I might buy myself some cheese."

"Passing through, eh?" she asked. "We don't get that many out-of-town visitors here. Where you coming from?"

"Up north," he said.

"Jersey, eh?"

He started, considered going for the gun, but stopped. No point in lying here. Not too much at least. "Yeah," he said. "Seaside Heights. How'd you know?"

"Oh, I'm a pretty clever old gal." She gave him a calculated wink. "Where you headed?"

That he couldn't really lie about, given that he wasn't all that sure where he was, apart from Florida. "Don't know yet," he said with a shrug. "Guess I'll know when I get there. I'm thinking of visiting the Everglades or Key West. Maybe even Key Largo."

"All those places are nice," she said. Then she added, "Trouble with the missus, eh?"

He started again. What's with this broad? Pretty personal question from an old lady at a cheese shop.

"You are pretty clever, aren't you?" He played along. Hell, it had been one of his cover stories, after all. He turned away from the counter and scanned the store again.

"Oh, I know, it's none of my business. I'm a nosy neighbor. Just curious, is all… Like I said, we don't get many folks from out of town. I'll just hush my mouth now and give you what you came here for. Cheese we got plenty of," she said, coming out from behind the counter. "Are ya lookin' for anything special?"

He shook his head. "Not really. Something good."

"Well, everything here's good," she said. " 'Specially the Gouda." (She always liked to tell that one. Working in a cheese shop made it especially easy.) "How 'bout something special, though. Let me show you. Something to remember us by."

She led him around the stacked white boxes, each of which contained a selection of cheese and sausages packed in among a pile of plastic grass, along a wall of refrigerator cases loaded with cheese in every imaginable form—blocks, slices, discs, cold pack spreads—to the back, where she had a display table set up.

"Look at these," she said, gesturing. "They're real art. I'll never get over what people come up with sometimes."

What Noogie found himself looking at was a collection of cheese sculptures. Four- and five-pound blocks of cheddar and Swiss and Colby, hand-carved into various shapes—the state of Wisconsin, a football player, a sailboat.

"Wow, those are really something," Noogie said, genuinely impressed.

"See, I'm from Wisconsin originally, Kenosha. Came down here to get away from the cold and decided to bring a little bit of home with me."

"Good for you," Noogie said. "I see the football players even have numbers and everything. Is that part of it?"

"Oh, I did that myself. Just used a Magic Marker. That one there?" She pointed at a cheese football player with a black number 4 scrawled across his chest. "That one there's my favorite. That's Brett."

"I could tell right away," Noogie said, having absolutely no idea what she was talking about, or why she would name her cheese.

"But don't worry, though," she assured him. "It doesn't hurt the cheese any. I made sure."

"Well that's good, huh?" Noogie said. "Tell you what…"

He left the store twenty minutes later with a bag of cheese

curds, some string cheese, a pound of cheddar, and Brett. He was also eating an ice cream cone and wearing a bright yellow foam rubber Cheesehead hat.

She'd been quite the saleswoman.

Some people are all right. He was glad that he'd never gone for the gun. She didn't deserve anything like that. Of course none of those others did, either, except for the clown. And those clowns at PiggyBank. But this lady was nice. Those others, even the nice ones, well...there they were. It just worked out badly.

He wasn't really sure why he had brought the gun in some places and not others, why he threatened some people and took things from them but not from others. It was all just a whim. He did what struck him at the time. That had to stop.

She'd been very good and he was glad to learn some new things about cheese. Good ice cream, too.

Noogie was tired. He could tell Dillinger was tired. He just wanted to stop. For a short while at least. A few weeks when he didn't have to drive anywhere. Someplace where he could just sit. Someplace where the folks were decent and not too nosy. Someplace with cable.

He pulled the van back out onto the road and cut the wheel to the right at the next corner, following a road that veered east.

Just in case anyone happens to ask her where I might be headed, he thought. *Man, she may be clever, but this creature is sly.*

14

Noogie tried to ignore the increasingly troublesome sounds coming from his engine. It had been easier to ignore the red light on the dashboard. This wasn't good. He put on his Molly Hatchet tape and cranked it up in an effort to drown out the grinding and clanking. When that was over he turned on the radio. He also tried to ignore the fact that the van was moving slower, no matter how much gas he gave it.

He knew he'd have to stop soon. It wasn't a matter of choice anymore, and the options were running thin. He just hoped he was someplace when he did. It seemed likely. From what little he knew of geography (and of where, exactly, he might be), he was getting closer to the coast. Those long, barren stretches of roadway were far behind him. He could, logically, stop at any point he wanted now and be in decent shape, yet he pushed onward, hoping something would make itself obvious.

It was another warm day, and he drove with the windows down. The sun was high and the sky was clear.

An hour later, after passing a road sign that told him he was fifteen miles from Miami Beach, he began to notice an odd smell.

He glanced in the rearview mirror to see that his tailpipe was belching a thin gray trail of smoke.

Christ, now what? It wasn't like he could just pull over to the side of the road, whip out the tool box, flip up the hood, and fix whatever was wrong himself.

"Dillinger!" he shouted over his shoulder to the sleeping cat, who raised his head only slightly, his eyes slitted. "How are you with motors?"

The cat offered only a contemptuous grunt before lowering his head down to his paws again.

"Okay, forget I asked," Noogie muttered. "Jeeze."

He didn't even dare shut off the engine at this point, out of fear he'd never be able to start it again. All he could do was hope that the thing kept rolling until he found a repair shop.

Goddamn used car, he thought.

The smell began to get worse. He sniffed and grimaced. It didn't smell like something was burning. Not exactly, anyway. But what the hell did he know? The smoke coming out of the tailpipe was growing thicker and darker with each added mile. More red lights were appearing on the dashboard. Even after rolling up the windows, he couldn't get away from that smell.

Noogie's heart lightened somewhat as he began to see more billboards, and then more buildings along the side of the road. Most of them seemed like warehouses or corporate offices, but even in that they promised greater things ahead. *Only a bit farther,* he nudged the van along silently. *C'mon, you need to hold on for just a bit farther.*

Noogie's prayers were answered ten minutes later, as the roadside—just as it had on a fairly regular basis ever since he'd left the cheese shop—erupted in a strip of fast-food joints and discount furniture stores and, thank goodness, gas stations.

The creak and the groan and the wheeze from beneath the hood became a distinct, spasmodic coughing, the smoke from the tailpipe as black and impenetrable as night.

Noogie had been aiming the van toward a gas station whose sign promised expert auto repair when the engine gagged, then died completely. He had nothing left but momentum. All the lights on the dash had gone out. There was no more power. He coasted into the station, urging the van toward a parking spot with body language alone. Then it stopped.

"All *right!*" he shouted joyously. "*Whoo!*"

As Noogie stepped out of the dead van, a tall man wearing oil-stained gray coveralls and a crumpled baseball cap strolled out from the garage and ambled toward him, offering Noogie a suspicious eye. He was wiping his hands on a filthy towel. His face was thin and sharp.

"Help you?" he asked, once he was within earshot.

"You betcha," Noogie told him, noticing the name patch on the man's left breast. "...Gus. Got some big problems with the van here." He jerked his thumb over his shoulder. "I'm surprised I made it here."

"Where you coming from?" the man asked, looking over Noogie's shoulder at the still-smoldering vehicle. He didn't seem terribly interested in where Noogie came from or what his troubles were.

"Canada," Noogie told him.

"You don't sound Canadian," said Gus, who did. "And you got Jersey plates there."

"It's a long story," Noogie said, too excited still at having actually found his way to a gas station to worry much about being interrogated. He did, however, make a mental note that it was about time to drop the Canada story. Nothing but trouble. "Look," he asked, "can you check it out? See what's wrong?"

Gus considered Noogie. Didn't much like the looks of him. Gus didn't much like the looks of anybody.

"Yeah, I'll get one of my boys to take a look," he said, still wiping his hands on the grimy towel.

"That's great," Noogie said.

"Be a while, though."

Noogie didn't much like the sound of that. He didn't much like the notion of leaving the money, let alone Dillinger, unattended for long. In a motel parking lot or outside a diner was one thing. But not when somebody's going to be crawling around the van. "How long?" he asked, a thread of anxiety creeping into his voice.

"Well," Gus said, tilting his cap back and swiping a greasy forearm across his smudged forehead. He looked at his watch. "It's four-thirty now. 'Bout that anyway. Garage shuts down at four-thirty, so it'd be tomorrow morning at the earliest."

Noogie began to say something but Gus cut him off.

"*But*—I got four other jobs lined up in front of you. Gotta do those first. My guess is the earliest one of my boys'll be able to get to it is Tuesday afternoon, if things go well on those others, Wednesday if it don't."

Shit, Noogie thought. So now what does he do, walk around the block for three days while these guys—?

"Look," he protested. "Could you at least take a peek under the hood right now? You haven't even done that yet. It might be nothing at all, right? A loose wire?" Then he thought of something. "I'll pay you. Cash."

"You bet you'll pay me," Gus said, surprised that such a thing was even a question. "You pay me sixty bucks, I'll look under the hood. Can't do anything about what I see but I'll look."

Noogie smiled, relieved. "No problem there, Gus." He reached for his wallet.

Gus didn't much appreciate strangers calling him "Gus." He felt it was awfully presumptuous. He snatched the three bills from Noogie, folded them, and slipped them under his cap. Then he strolled over to the van and lifted the hood.

"Smell that?" Noogie said, sniffing. "I've been smelling that for the last fifteen, twenty miles. I have no idea what it is."

Gus leaned in and sniffed. "I don't smell nothin' but scorched oil," he said, scanning the engine.

"Nah, it's not oil. I know that oil smell. This is more like... You don't smell that? Christ, it almost makes my eyes water."

"Nope," Gus said, "but I will tell you this. I hope you weren't in any hurry gettin' nowheres. You're gonna be here awhile. 'Lessen you want to just buy yourself a new van." Still scanning the engine, he said, "Might be cheaper in the end that way. I can't give you a dollar amount, but with parts and labor...it'll cost you a hell of a lot more'n that sixty bucks."

Noogie's heart sank. "You're kidding."

"Nope."

"Shit...pardon my French." He sighed heavily and looked around. It wasn't the money that bothered him so much as his immediate circumstances. What was he supposed to do? Buy himself a wagon and drag the laundry bags over to a car dealer? He sure as hell wasn't gonna leave it here, that's for damn certain.

"There's a hotel back out on the highway, just outside town," Gus offered. "Looks like a castle or some such. I hear it's real nice. 'Bout ten minutes away...but that's by car."

"Uh-huh," Noogie said. "Isn't there anything closer? Something in town? There's gotta be."

"S'pose there is," Gus said. "None of 'em look like castles, though."

"I don't—" Noogie began, then reconsidered. "It's just that...I have a lot of things with me in the back of the van." He tilted his head in that direction. "A cat an' everything."

"Well," Gus said slowly and evenly. "It looks like you are in a bit of a pickle, don't it?"

INTERMISSION

Beneath the Charlie Feathers blaring through the stereo speakers, Kenny heard the phone ringing in the kitchen. He turned the music down and went into the next room.

"Yeah?" he asked, after picking up the receiver.

"Hey you," a woman's voice said. "Guess what?"

"Hey, baby. What?"

"I think I found you a roommate."

He knew he could count on Liz, especially given that she was in the real estate business. She was the one who'd found him this apartment in the first place, about a year earlier. It had been perfect for a while—enough space, nice building—but now with the rent going up and him on worker's comp, he needed some help to cover the bills, even if it was only for a few months.

"One thing, though," she said. "It's a little weird."

"Uh-huh?" he said. "Weird" usually didn't scare him off too easily. "How so?"

"Well..." she said, her voice going up a notch.

"C'mon, what's weird about it? He an albino or a midget or something?"

"No, it's...well, I don't know, exactly. He might be. I haven't met him yet. Just talked to him on the phone."

"So what's weird?"

"Okay, so he calls up the agency today looking for an apartment. Thing is, he wants an apartment like right away, someplace he can move into in a day or two. I guess he's from out of town."

"Know where from?"

"New York, I think? New Jersey? Something like that? So I give him the spiel, ask him about price ranges, neighborhoods, and he says he doesn't really care. Then I tell him what we need from him—social security number, ID, all that—before I can start showing him anything. But then he tells me he can't show me any identification because he lost it all and that he can't give me his social security number."

"He *can't*?"

"He wouldn't say why. Just that he can't."

"Great. And you immediately thought of me, right?"

"No, of course not. I mean, he told me that, and I told him there wasn't anything I could do for him, 'cause the agency requires these things from everybody. No ID, no apartment."

"And *that's* when you thought of me"—he was joking with her, but some dark corner of his brain was getting annoyed—"because you figure since I—"

"*No*." She cut him off, knowing where he was headed. "It wasn't like that. So then he starts getting really pushy. Saying he really needed a place *right away*, saying he'd pay in cash, anything, just that he needed something immediately."

"And that's when you thought of me."

"Well...yeah, I guess. C'mon, Kenny, I can't do it through the office, but I can hook the two of you up. He needs a place and you need a roommate. I told him that I'd ask you and that maybe we could all meet someplace, have a drink, see what you think. It's your decision."

He did need a roommate, there was no denying that. But this guy sounded like trouble already. Christ, he hated all this. He'd had enough trouble. But he needed a goddamn roommate, and soon. *Damn.*

"What else do you know about him?" Kenny asked.

"Not too much," she admitted. "His name's Mike something, he's from New York I think, he sounds like he's in his thirties, but I'm not sure. Don't know what he does."

Kenny thought about it for a moment. New York. That meant he could be an asshole. He sounded kind of pushy already. And the ID business sounds like the guy's bringing trouble behind him.

"Shit," he finally sighed into the phone. "Guess it can't hurt to meet him."

He knew it wasn't his place to judge a man before meeting him. Anyone looking at him, Kenny, from the outside might be a little wary, too.

"Great," Liz said. "I'll give him a call back. Okay if we meet him at Fitzgerald's later? After I get off work? It seems pretty neutral."

"Sure. And Liz?"

"Yes?"

"Thanks. Fingers crossed, huh? Who knows? It might be okay."

After hanging up the phone, he went into the bathroom, opened the cabinet above the sink, and grabbed a small amber bottle. He popped one of the pills, praying that it kicked in and held on until he had to leave.

Kenneth Swanson was thirty-four years old. In the late eighties he'd been working as a plumber in Butte, Montana. But by the early nineties, for reasons nobody could quite figure, plumbing jobs in the area had become very difficult to come by. At least for freelancers like himself. His folks down in Florida told him there were plenty of plumbing problems to be found in Miami Beach, so he packed his bags and moved south. Nothing had him tied down to Montana, that's for damn sure. Not at that point. You go where the work is.

Things were great for a while. He was working plenty, making decent money. Had a nice place, was meeting plenty of girls. But then there was that misunderstanding with the rental tools place. And right after he'd done his time he'd fucked his back and couldn't work anymore. Things headed further south than he'd planned—everything went to shit, to be perfectly honest, and fast. So here he was, not working, getting by however he could, looking for a roommate. At least he had Liz. That was the one bright spot in all of it.

He turned up the music again, lay down on the couch, and waited for the pills to start doing their job.

Yeah, that could be a problem, he thought. He'd need to stash the pills. He'd learned his lesson.

He let his eyes close.

Fitzgerald's was an okay place, if you didn't mind that kind of crowd. They weren't exactly Kenny's type—young, pretty, well dressed. They had money and they let everyone know it. They played golf and tennis and packed the place every night drinking martinis and piña coladas. They crowded into the velvet-lined booths and laughed too loud. They sang along with the Fleetwood Mac and Eurythmics on the jukebox. All of them trying desperately to prove just how carefree they were, and how much fun they were having. Assholes.

He wasn't an uptight guy, Kenny. He thought he was pretty laid back, actually. This just wasn't his crowd. Sometimes he had to wonder why Liz liked it so much here. Half the time they went out they ended up here. Okay. It was still early so things hadn't gotten too bad in the place yet. Wouldn't get bad for another couple hours. He sat at the bar in his T-shirt and jeans. His light brown hair stuck out in ragged tufts from beneath his baseball cap as he kept an eye on the door. Liz said this guy was gonna come over to her office first and that she'd bring him over here.

He glanced at his watch. The Percocet was starting to wear off and his back was starting to ache again. He didn't dare pop another one at that point, so he was trying to balance things out with beer. He'd just started his second when he saw Liz walk through the door. She was one of those petite women whose face and voice had changed little since the age of twelve. He had never seen pictures of her from back then, but he could imagine. Now, at twenty-nine, she still had eyes like a Japanese cartoon and a voice tending toward squeaky (though she adopted an artificial raspy creak when she wanted to be taken more seriously). Her hair was a wild mass of blond curls, which she tried to tie back for work, usually without much luck.

Tonight she was being followed by—what? Kenny tried to size him up from a distance, given what little Liz was able to pass along.

Big guy, over two hundred pounds, maybe two-fifty. Thin mustache, dark hair. Could be Italian, or maybe Puerto Rican. What else would you expect from New York? Liz had probably guessed right about the age. Wasn't dressed too fancy, that was good. Unbuttoned shirt over a gray T-shirt that stretched over his belly and Bermuda shorts. What was his name again? Mark? Mike? The one thing that made Kenny a little nervous was the fact that the guy was wearing a pair of those heavy, wraparound amber goggles, like all the prehistorics down here wore. That was weird.

Liz spotted Kenny immediately, waved, and angled in his direction with the big guy in tow. As they approached, the guy pushed the goggles up on his forehead and stuck his hand out. Kenny slid off the stool and extended his own.

"Kenny?" Liz said. "This is Mike...oh, God, I'm so sorry—"

"Delaney," the man said, smiling broadly. "Mike Delaney. Hey, it's great to meet you, Kenny."

"Yeah, same here." Kenny looked around. "Ahh...so should we grab a table or something?"

"Sure," Liz agreed. "Should we get something to drink first?"

"Man, I could sure use it," Mike said. He yanked the goggles from his head and scanned the beer list posted behind the bar. He squinted. There must've been forty brands listed there and he didn't recognize a single one.

"Hootenanny Porter?" he read aloud. "Jupiter Saffron Stout? Braunschweiger Coffin Nail IPA? What the hell's all that? Jesus, can a guy just get a *beer* here?" Then he pointed to Kenny's glass. "What's that you're drinking?"

"Bud," Kenny said.

"Thank God," Mike said. "A man after my own heart. I'll have one of those."

"And for you?" Kenny said to Liz. "Screwdriver?"

"Please."

"Oh, hey," Mike interjected, "let me get these." He was already reaching into his pocket. "I really appreciate you meeting me here. Short notice and all. If things work out, you'll really be helping me out of a jam."

He put down a twenty-dollar bill, and when the bartender brought the drinks over the three of them found an open semi-circular booth in the back. Mike sat across from Kenny, while Liz sat in the middle, to mediate.

"Here's to getting to know you," Mike said, raising his glass. The others followed.

Kenny took a sip and set the glass down. "So Liz tells me you had a little ID trouble." He didn't want to ask about the goggles. A man's eyewear's his own business, he figured.

"Oh, yeah," Mike said, shaking his head. "Really stupid. I took the train down here from New York and my wallet must've fallen out of my pocket at some point. Unbelievable."

"Did you call, what, Amtrak, see if anyone turned it in?"

Mike laughed. "Turned it in? Are you nuts? Like anyone would do that. And even if they did, you think Amtrak would tell me about it? They'd keep it, same as anybody."

"But you still have some money."

"I had traveler's checks. Karl Malden had a profound impact on me when I was a kid."

Kenny glanced at Liz.

"Look," Mike continued, "I know it's a little crazy. Who is this guy, right? How do you know I'm not some serial killer or wanted fugitive? Some window smasher you saw on *America's Most Wanted*?"

"It's...just a little weird is all, yeah," Kenny admitted. "I mean, it doesn't bother me, but I'm just curious."

"Yeah, I can understand that. I really can. It was just a stupid thing. I'll get everything replaced. But I'll tell you whatever you want to know. Oh—hey—before we get too far along, Liz told me a little bit about the place...but what's the rent?"

Kenny took another drink. This guy was getting a little ahead of the game. "The full rent is twelve hundred a month," he said, "for a two-bedroom place. Nice place, though. You'd have your own room. I figured we'd split the rent down the middle, just like everything else. Keep it simple that way."

Mike nodded. "All right. That's cool. Better than rents in New York, I'll tell you that. Hoo-boy. And to make up for the lack of proper identification, I'll give you three months' rent, in advance. In cash. That okay?"

Kenny looked at him. "Cash?"

"All I got," he said. "I could give it to you right now, if you want it." He leaned to the side and reached into his pocket again. "I don't exactly have a checkbook with me."

"That's...really not necessary," Kenny said.

"Why don't we talk a bit first," Liz interjected. "See how well you both think this thing'll work out?"

"I think that's smart," Kenny said.

"Hey, you mind cats?" Mike asked. "Liz said cats are okay in the building and I have one. You allergic or anything?"

"Cats are fine, but no dogs. Building rule. And I'm cool with it."

"Great. Six hundred a month from me, and I got a cat. What else would you like to know?" He drained his glass. "Wait," he said, setting the empty pint glass down. "I need another. It's been a hell of a day. Are either of you ready for another?"

They shook their heads, having barely touched their own drinks. Mike headed for the bar. Kenny noted that the guy was talking almost like he was on meth, but he didn't seem to have any of the other usual speedfreak tics. Not yet anyway.

"What do you think?" Liz asked once he was far enough away.

Kenny looked over his shoulder. "A little anxious, don't you think?"

"Oh, I don't know," she said. "Maybe it makes sense to be a little anxious. I see people like that every day when they're trying to find a place. Once they do, they relax again. Become normal."

"Yeah, maybe. We'll see."

"Besides, it sounds like he's had a hell of a time, from what he was telling me on the way over here." She glanced past Kenny. "Okay, hush, he's coming back."

Mike set another three glasses on the table. "Here. I figured you'd be needing another eventually, so I saved you the trip." He smiled and squeezed himself back into the booth. The bar was starting to fill up. Somebody had punched up a string of Phil Collins hits on the jukebox. Kenny winced.

"Thanks, uh, Mike."

"Yeah, thanks."

"No problem," he said. "Pleasure's all mine. Hey, lemme ask you. You guys like movies?"

"Sure," Liz said.

"I guess, yeah," Kenny added.

" 'Cause I love them. Really, really love them. And I'm of the opinion that you can tell a lot about people by what their favorite movies are." He took a swallow of his beer. "So what about it?"

Liz blinked at him. "What about what?"

Mike looked at Liz, then to Kenny, a half-smirk on his face. "*Movies*, ya goof. What's your favorite?"

"Oh," Liz said. "Sure. Gee." Her eyes rolled skyward. "Let me think about this..."

Mike looked disappointed and turned back to Kenny. "Well, while she's thinking, what about you?"

Kenny had little use for this kind of shit. He hated "lists" and "bests" and questions about his taste in things. "Oh, hell, I dunno," he said. "Guess I like the Freddy and Jason movies okay."

"Yeah?" Mike asked, eyes sparkling. "Which ones?"

"Whaddya mean?"

"I mean which *ones*? The originals? Part Four? Part Six? There's eight of one and eleven of the other, and they're all different."

Kenny exhaled quietly through his nose. "I've only seen a couple of 'em. Not real sure which ones."

"All right," Mike said, the sparkle fading from his eyes. He was suddenly looking bored and unimpressed when he turned his attention back to Liz. "You come up with anything yet?"

"Oh," she said, smiling with recognition "God. *Titanic*. I really loved *Titanic* so much. Made me cry."

"Yeah," Mike said. "Lotta people cried at that, I guess." This clearly wasn't going the way he'd hoped.

"Well, what about you?" Liz asked. "What are your favorites?"

"Oh," he said, leaning back and smiling again and fingering the glass in front of him. "That's a tricky one, see, because I got it all broken down by decade and genre, so you'd have to ask me my favorite horror film from the forties, see? Or...or my favorite comedy of the sixties, like that."

"What's your favorite of the ones that are out now?"

"Oh," Mike said, cutting his eyes to the left. "Well, I gotta say I don't really have one. I think movies these days are crap. Mostly, anyway. Last decent year for movies was nineteen ninety-five. Don't know why, it just was."

Kenny leaned forward, figuring it was long past time to change the subject. "So Liz tells me you've been having a hell of a time. Apart from the wallet."

Mike looked off toward the far wall. His mood shifted almost physically—you could see it in his face and his posture. Almost as if being pulled away from movies and back into real life was a painful shift. But it was visible only for a moment before he was Mike again.

"Oh, man, don't get me started," he said. "So I was living in New York, right? And I don't know if Liz told you but I was in the film business."

"No, she didn't. But I guess it makes sense, given how much you love movies and everything."

"Yeah, see?" Mike went on. "And I'd just finished up this cable special with Dennis Weaver. Now, you can't *believe* how stressful this business can be, especially when you're directing. All the time, there's no getting away from it. Everybody wants something, everything needs to be taken care of right away, and you're the only one who can do it."

He took another long swallow. "Now, at the same time, while all that's going on, see, I was selling my business."

"What was that?" Liz asked.

"What was what?" Mike asked, turning to her.

She stared at him for a moment. "Your business."

"Oh," he said. "Cripes, yeah. Toothbrushes."

"Toothbrushes?" Kenny asked, almost coughing.

"Yeah, toothbrushes. Believe me, there's more money to be made in toothbrushes than in making movies with Dennis Weaver. See, I started this little company a few years back, maybe you heard of it. Toothbrushes for Life?" He looked from one to the other, hopefully. They both shook their heads.

"Sorry."

" 'S'okay. What it was was this—it was online and people would get a subscription sort of. And what we did was send them a new toothbrush every month. You could get a lifetime subscription and we'd send you a new toothbrush for the rest of your life."

Liz and Kenny were both silent, until Kenny said, "That's really a pretty good idea, I gotta admit."

"Yeah," Mike said, smiling. "See? I thought so. And so did plenty of other people. We did really well with it. Made a ton. But I figured, hey, I'm young still, right? Time to try other things. So I sold off my part of the company to my two partners. Now that was happening, and the movie was happening...and then, to top it all off, there were the attacks."

Much to Kenny's relief the Phil Collins set ended, and Fitzgerald's was quiet for a blessed instant. Then the ELO kicked in.

"You were there?" Liz was asking.

"*Christ* yeah. Of *course* I was. Saw the whole thing. What you could see, anyway, through all the dust. That's what I remember most, really, this cloud of dust that just hung there where the buildings used to be. Three days it was there, like the fog bank in Guillermin's *King Kong*. If you didn't know they'd come down, you coulda thought they were still hidden back there."

"My God."

"Yeah, it was bad. So after that, and just being exhausted from work, I decided it was time for a break, right? So I make arrangements with a friend who has a place down here. She says I can stay for six months, a year, whatever. She never uses it. I pack up, get on the train, lose my wallet, and get down here to find out my friend's place had burned down two weeks ago. Straight to the ground. Electrical problem of some kind, I guess. Nothing left. Just an empty lot."

"Shit," Kenny said. "That really sucks."

"Yeah, that's what I said, pretty much. Big time suckery. Try to come down here and take it easy, relax, and all this shit happens. Had to call her and tell her about it. She hadn't even heard about it." He coughed a brief, bitter chuckle. "That's why I'm in such a pickle right now."

There was an uncomfortable silence.

"So," Liz asked finally, "where are you staying now? Where's your cat?"

Mike took another long swallow. "Ahh, I found a little motel that takes cash and doesn't care much about identification or animals, if you catch my drift. Got a coin-operated bed. Beauty, huh? Place smells like Pine-Sol. But without ID and everything, I got no place else to go." He smirked sadly. "So there it is." He looked Kenny in the eye. "Help me, Obi-Wan Kenobi," he said sincerely. "You're my only hope."

Liz nudged Kenny under the table with her knee. When she caught his eye, she gave him That Look: the one that said it was now his responsibility to do something nice for someone.

"All right," Kenny sighed, even though he still had a lot of questions about this guy, and more than a few serious doubts about the wisdom of letting him move in. "Tell you what. Why don't we try it out for a couple weeks? See how things go?"

Mike grinned and picked up his glass again. "I think I'd say, here's to ya, roomie."

"Great," Liz said. "So that's settled."

The three of them tapped glasses once more.

He could easily get on my nerves really fucking fast, Kenny was thinking. *But at least it's only for a couple weeks.*

"We don't need a contract or anything, do we?" Mike asked, turning to Liz.

"Oh, I don't think so. Not in a situation like this, do you, Kenny?"

"The less hassle the better, I think."

"Yeah, I'm with you there. No hassle. Handshake does me fine. And my offer still stands. I can give you three months' advance, in cash, right here and now." He shifted over to one haunch again.

"No, look," Kenny said, "why not just give it to me when you move in?"

"Fine with me, whenever," Mike said, settling back down. "Like the man said, 'Money's nobody's favorite.' So...when can I move in?"

The green and white cab pulled into the main driveway of the Excelsior at about ten-thirty the following morning. It was a sprawling complex, its snaking blacktopped pathways lined with nearly identical three-story town houses, most of which had been divided into two or three units. It was connected to a golf course, had indoor tennis courts and a pool, and wasn't far from the ocean. It looked like it had been nice once but now was starting to get a little rough around the edges.

Kenny was waiting outside unit 1119, squinting against the sun, when the cab pulled to a stop.

The door opened and Mike Delaney heaved himself out.

"Hey!" he shouted. "Made it!" Then he reached back into the cab and pulled out a cat carrier and a small plastic bag.

Yeah, Kenny thought, *about four hours early*. When Mike called twenty minutes earlier to say he was on his way, Kenny hadn't even showered yet. "Can I help you with something?" he offered.

"Yeah…yeah…there's just one suitcase in the trunk. If you could grab that, that'd be great. I'll pay this guy off." Mike was still wearing his amber goggles.

The trunk popped and Kenny opened it to find, sure enough, one small brown suitcase inside, nestled against the spare tire.

My God, he looks like a bum, he thought, noting that Mike was wearing not just the same goggles but the same clothes he'd been wearing the day before. He seemed to be traveling awfully light for a man who intended to stay in Florida for six months.

"This is it, really?" he called over to Mike.

"Yeah, that's all."

"All right," Kenny said incredulously, though he was quietly relieved, considering his back. He carried the suitcase to the curb and set it down next to the cat carrier. The animal hadn't made a sound. "So you wanna come in and take a look around? Get into that AC?"

"Sure do," Mike said. "I'm not real good with the heat." He picked up the carrier. Kenny took a peek inside at the gray furry lump.

"I hate to say it," he said, "but I think your cat's dead."

"Dead?" Mike barked a laugh. "Him? Nah, he's not dead. He's just real fat and lazy." Kenny held the door for him as he heaved the carrier inside. The cold air felt good.

Mike walked into the entryway and set the carrier down. "So this is it, huh?"

"Home sweet, yeah."

It wasn't enormous but large enough. Two bedrooms, kitchen, living room, carpeting. Windows that looked out on a corner of the golf course. A long black leather couch faced the television in the middle of the living room.

"Nice," Mike said. "Hey, I'm gonna let this fat mother out, okay? Don't worry about him. He'll just sniff around for a few days, get the lay of the land, but he won't be a bother. Mostly sleeps all day."

"Yeah, that's cool. Why don't I put this suitcase in your room? You wanna come see it?"

"I will in a sec," he said as he unlatched the carrier door. "You got a beer?"

"Yeah, I think there are a couple left in the fridge."

The cat stuck a cautious head out of the carrier, his eyes bleary, his nose working the strange new air. Then he placed a tentative paw on the floor, as if to make sure it was solid. He cast an accusing glare up at Mike.

"Hey, it's your place now," he told the creature. "Live it up."

Keeping as low to the ground as his belly would allow, the cat made a dash for the wall and worked his way toward cover in the living room.

Mike stood with a grunt and headed for the kitchen with the plastic bag. He opened the refrigerator, placed the bag on the middle shelf, and saw that it contained four beers. He grabbed one.

"Hey!" he shouted to the other room, not realizing that Kenny had entered the kitchen behind him. "I brought cheese. But we're gonna have to do something about this beer situation before long."

"Yeah, we can do that."

"*Ah!*" Mike yelped, startled. He turned and saw Kenny.

Kenny looked into the living room at the cat, whose tail was sticking out from beneath a chair in the corner. "So...are you gonna need a, you know, litter box or something for your cat?"

"Sure, yeah, I'll take care of it," Mike said, apparently uncon-cerned. "But let's sit down a second. Work out the necessities. You wanna beer?" He was still holding the refrigerator door open.

"Nah, I'm okay. Little early yet. Thanks."

"Okay," he said as if doubting Kenny's judgment. "Let's sit down." He walked past Kenny and into the living room, where he let himself fall heavily on the couch. Kenny winced.

"So gimme the lowdown," Mike said. "What's this place like?"

"Well, shit, let's see. We got a pool and a gym. Tennis and rac-quetball courts. I could take you over there later if you like."

"Yeah, I don't think I'll really be using those much," Mike said, grabbing his belly and chuckling. "What about cable? You got cable here don'cha?"

"Of course."

"Thank God. How many channels?"

Kenny scratched his chin. "Hell, I dunno. Don't watch it much. Eighty? Ninety? They got a dish."

"Satellite? That's even better. Great. So what are the people around here like? And please stop me if I'm asking too many questions. Just curious, is all. New place and everything. Hell, new state, even."

"Nah, it's okay. I understand," Kenny said, still convinced this guy was on speed. "Ask whatever you like. As for the people, oh, I'd say it's a pretty young crowd here. Younger than me, anyway. Kids just out of college, a lot of 'em. It can get kind of loud some-times, but it's okay."

The guy had been there five minutes, and already Kenny was dreading the next few weeks. He couldn't exactly put his finger on it, but something about the guy scraped on him. Why in the hell had he said "a couple weeks"? Why not just "a couple days" or "a few hours"? It's what he got for being a nice guy. Mike drained the can he was holding.

"Great. Now, before we go any further, let me take care of that rent thing...Where's my suitcase?"

"I put it in your room. You want me to show you?"

Mike pushed himself up. "Nah, that's okay. I'll find it." He headed back toward the kitchen, and Kenny heard the refrigerator open again, followed by the *pfft* of another can opening.

A few minutes later Mike returned with a beer and a handful of folded bills. "Here you go," he said. "And again, let me just say thanks. I think things are gonna work out just fine with us."

Kenny took the bills and began counting. It had been a while since he'd held this much cash at once. It was all in twenties.

"Yeah, I think this is gonna be nice," Mike continued, kicking off his shoes and propping his feet up on the coffee table. "Relaxing. Just what I need." His eyes drifted toward the window.

PART TWO

15

Miami Beach PD Sergeant Paul Arbogast could think of at least five better ways to be spending his Christmas night other than cruising around the quiet, darkened streets waiting for someone to do something bad.

Still, shortly before ten-thirty, he was relieved when the call came in concerning a body at the Excelsior. It's always better to have something to do. He snapped on the siren and swung the wheel hard to the right.

When he arrived at the complex six minutes later, it wasn't difficult to find the apartment he was looking for. MB Fire and Rescue No. 7 was already parked out front, its lights flashing. Sergeant Arbogast pulled his cruiser in behind the rescue vehicle and got out. One of the paramedics was waiting at the apartment's open front door, smoking a cigarette.

"Hey, Jeff," Arbogast said as he approached. "Those things'll kill you, y'know. So what do we got here?"

The paramedic tossed the cigarette aside and stifled a yawn. "Unattended death of a white male, approximately thirty-eight years old, real fat. No sign of trauma. Looks like an overdose."

"You sound disappointed," Arbogast said.

The paramedic shook his head. "Just tired. Oh, and Merry Christmas to you."

"Yeah, same to you. Who called it in?"

The paramedic gestured over his shoulder. "Roommate. Says he got home a little after ten, found the body, and called nine-one-one."

The stench reached Arbogast's nostrils even before he stepped through the door. It was the one thing about the job he hadn't ever gotten used to. "Hey," he said to the paramedic, "you got any of those strips? Those Carry-On things?"

"For this?" the paramedic said, inhaling deeply. "This ain't nothin', fresh daisies and lavender. You can handle it. He ain't even started to turn yet."

Arbogast gave him a stern yet hapless look. "Thanks a million," he said, then stepped inside, trying to remember to breathe through his mouth. Two other paramedics were waiting. An overweight man in a gray T-shirt and underpants lay on the couch. He had dark hair and a mustache, and one arm held a pillow on his lap. A smear of vomit ran down the couch beside his head and puddled on the floor. The television was on and the remote was next to the body. On the television screen, Edward G. Robinson was wearing a fancy suit and smoking an improbably long cigar. He seemed very pleased with himself.

A couple of beer cans, a drinking glass, and what appeared to be an empty bottle of wine sat on the coffee table between the couch and the television. Sergeant Arbogast took out his notebook and began jotting down details.

"Where's the roommate?" he asked.

"In there," one of the paramedics said, pointing to a closed door off the kitchen.

Arbogast went to the door and knocked quietly. "Excuse me?" he said. "Police officer. I need to ask you a few questions." He heard a voice from behind the door and turned the knob.

Inside, a slim, unshaven man in his thirties was sitting on the bed. The lights were on. He looked nervous. His hands were between his knees.

"Mr.... ?" Arbogast said.

"Oh...uh, Swanson," the man said. "Kenneth Swanson, but call me Kenny."

"All right, Kenny. As you can understand, I need to ask you a few questions about what happened here." He pulled a wooden chair over from the corner and sat down in front of Swanson. The room was sparse, the bed unmade. There were some clothes piled in the corner. "First of all, what was your roommate's name?"

"Mike," he said. "Michael. Michael...*Delaney*, I think it was." He seemed a little stunned and distracted, which Arbogast thought was understandable, considering.

"You think?"

"Yeah," Kenny said. "He wasn't here that long. We didn't get to know each other real well."

"All right," Arbogast said, jotting that down. "How long was he here?"

"About two weeks, I guess," Kenny said. "Just long enough to ruin my carpet." He looked toward the open door.

"You didn't know him before that?"

"Uh-uh," Swanson said, shaking his head and looking at the floor.

"And how long have you been here?"

He looked up at the officer. "Me? 'Bout a year now, I guess."

"Uh-huh. How'd you meet him?"

Swanson took a deep breath, then told the story about meeting Mike through Liz—the lack of ID, the pushiness, his own need for a roommate.

"And Liz is...?"

"Oh, ummm...she's my girlfriend, Elizabeth Bezack."

"And when you first met this guy, he had no identification?" Arbogast asked.

"None that I ever saw," Swanson replied. "That's why he

couldn't get an apartment otherwise...and why he paid me three months' rent in advance, in cash. To try and make up for that, I guess."

"That was how much? Three months' rent?"

"Eighteen hundred," Swanson said. "Six hundred a month for his half."

"Uh-huh. Okay," Arbogast said. "Now, I have to ask you straight. Was Mike a drug user?"

Swanson started. "No... Well, it depends, I guess. I never saw him take anything. Except pot. He smoked a lot of pot. Mostly, though, he just drank. Morning to night—beer, wine, cooking sherry, whatever. That's why we didn't really talk a lot, I guess. Ever since he moved in, he spent most of his time sitting in front of the tv, smoking pot and drinking. He was what you'd call an eight o'clocker."

"Excuse me?"

"He started at eight in the morning. Or whenever he got up. One of those."

"Oh," Arbogast said, making another note.

Arbogast asked Swanson about the events of that evening, and Swanson laid it out to the best of his recollection.

He and Liz had gone to his parents house the night before for Christmas Eve. His brother Phil was there with his wife and kids, too, which was always kind of a drag. Afterward, he and Liz went back to her place, and that morning they'd gone to her folks' place. He'd come home at around seven that night and found Mike passed out on the couch, covered in puke.

"There was nothing unusual about that, let me tell you, I was used to it. But I wasn't about to clean it up this time, so I left again. Figured when he woke up, he'd clean it himself. But when I came home—about ten, a little after, I guess—he hadn't moved.

That's when I got worried and went over there. I felt for a pulse but couldn't find one. Plus he was cold, so I called nine-one-one."

"Okay," Arbogast said, flipping the notebook closed. "I think that should do it for now. I'm sorry to have bothered you. Thanks for your help."

Swanson half stood from the bed. "Is there anything else I should, you know, do?"

Arbogast shook his head. "Not now. If we have any further questions we'll ask them. But for now, this doesn't look to me like anything suspicious. There's no trauma, no sign of forced entry, no foul play. But you might want to stay in here for your own sake. We'll be around for a little while yet, and these things are never pretty."

"Yeah," Swanson said. "Okay."

At the door, Arbogast paused and turned back. "Oh, one last thing," he said.

"Yeah?"

"Did the people who live in the apartment above you know him at all?"

Swanson looked confused. "Nobody lives up there. It's empty."

"Oh," Arbogast said. "Then I guess they didn't."

16

Shortly after eleven, crime scene investigator Sergeant Sarah Egtin arrived and found Sergeant Arbogast.

"It seems pretty straightforward," he told her, nodding at the body, "but you should get some pictures before going over the scene."

"Well, *duh*," she said, nodding to the camera, which was at the ready.

As she started taking pictures of the body from various angles, Arbogast set about a cursory search of the apartment in hopes of finding some sort of ID—a wallet, a driver's license, anything that would help him positively identify the body. From what Swanson had told him, he had reason to doubt that "Michael Delaney" was this guy's real name and he needed a little proof one way or the other.

When she was finished taking pictures, Egtin put her camera away and reached into her bag for an ink pad and card. Rigor mortis had set in by that point, so it took some effort to get a print off Delaney's right thumb without disturbing the body. They were supposed to leave things as untouched as possible until the medical examiner arrived, which, by her watch, should be any minute now. She put the thumbprint in an evidence bag. Back at the lab, she'd enter it into the Automated Fingerprint Identification System to see what they could come up with.

Arbogast, meanwhile, was working his way through Delaney's

room. There wasn't much to look at. Not much that was of any help, anyway. Some clothes, a hairbrush, but no identification of any kind.

Then he opened the closet door. On the floor sat what appeared to be a black leather satchel. He snapped the metal latches and opened it. Empty. Next to the bag, however, was a small brown suitcase. Wrapped around the plastic handle was a tag.

He pulled the suitcase from the closet, placed it on the bed, and peered at the tag.

"Ned Krapczak" was written in small neat letters, together with a street address in Jersey City, New Jersey.

Arbogast knew it didn't necessarily mean a thing. Delaney could've picked this up someplace, or borrowed it. Any number of possibilities. But at least it was a beginning. It was as much as he had at this point.

Shortly before eleven-thirty, two men in white jumpsuits appeared at the front door. Across their backs in red letters was stitched "B & D Removal." The name was innocuous enough. You could paint it on the side of a van and no one would give it a second thought. Until, that is, they found out what "B & D" stood for. That little gem was a thigh slapper they kept in-house, figuring correctly that the firm stood to lose a lot of business if it ever became public that "B & D" stood for "bloody and decomposing." It wasn't a terribly funny joke but it did the job.

For the past seven years, B & D had maintained a very lucrative contract with the city, which gave it exclusive rights to deliver corpses from crime scenes to the morgue.

"Hey guys," said Egtin, who was in the midst of collecting physical evidence from around the couch. "We've still got a little ways to go yet, so if you could just hang tight?"

"Yeah, no problem, Sarah," one of them said. Then, looking

more closely at the body he added, "Oh, man, he's a fat one, ain't he? I think we should get double time for this."

"Yeah," his partner added. "It being Christmas and all, too, make it triple time."

"It's only Christmas for another half hour," Egtin reminded them. "So don't try pushing that one." She carefully collected and bagged two empty Heineken cans and an empty bottle of Harveys Bristol Cream. She then took a sample of the liquid left at the bottom of the drinking glass and bagged that before bagging the glass itself.

At eleven-forty-five, she packed up and prepared to head back to her lab at police headquarters.

On her way out the apartment door she nearly ran headlong into Thomas DeKay, the city's medical examiner.

"You done?" he asked.

"Uh-huh. All yours."

"Super," he said. DeKay, at forty, was considered by most as fairly young to be chief medical examiner, but he was good at what he did. In fact, it was after only a ten-minute examination of the corpse that he determined the large man on the couch had died between four and five that afternoon. As for cause of death, that would have to wait, but if he had to make an educated guess he would say the man died of either acute alcohol poisoning or asphyxiation after choking on his own vomit.

"All yours now," he said to the two men in white when he was finished. DeKay, it had occurred to them more than once, always seemed to be in a hurry—but that was just fine by them.

As DeKay gave Arbogast a thumbnail sketch of his conclusions, and Arbogast explained his problem with the man's identity, the two men from B & D rolled a large black body bag out onto the floor next to the couch and prepared to heave the underwear-clad, vomit-spattered body into it.

17

Later that night, back at his desk, Arbogast began typing up his preliminary report from the notes he'd taken at Swanson's apartment. It was all fairly straightforward. Guy moves in, sits around and drinks, then dies. It wasn't unheard of.

The identity question still nagged at him, though. If it was an alias, what was he hiding? Probably nothing. People use fake names for all kinds of stupid reasons. Still, it had to be checked out. In his report, he made a point of placing the name "Mike Delaney" in quotation marks.

After he was finished, he found the number for the Jersey City Police Department and dialed it. It was two a.m.

In Jersey City, desk lieutenant Jack Hustoff answered the phone. Arbogast apologized for the hour, then explained who he was.

"I was wondering if you could run a quick check on a name for me," he said. "I'm trying to confirm the identity of a deceased male."

"Not a problem," Hustoff said. "Been a quiet night, and I'm always happy to help our brothers in warmer climes."

The name "Mike Delaney" came up empty, so Arbogast gave him the name "Ned Krapczak," together with the address he'd found on the suitcase tag. Within a matter of seconds, Hustoff had confirmed both the name and address and come up with a driver's license number.

That still told Arbogast nothing, really, except that the name on the tag belonged to a person who lived in Jersey City. The next step was to try and get a picture from the DMV.

. . .

A few blocks away, at the morgue, Dr. DeKay was typing up his own report. On account of Arbogast's suspicions, the name on the report was listed as "John Doe," and most of the other spaces— age, telephone number—were listed as "unknown."

The report did, however, include a condensed version of Swanson's story and described Mr. Doe's final hours as consisting of "lying on the couch, drinking heavily."

18

On the morning of December twenty-sixth, the case was assigned to Detective Robert Stone. There wasn't much to it. This was fairly routine for Stone, a twelve-year veteran of the Miami Beach Police Department. With every case involving unusual circumstances or a cause of death that wasn't immediately apparent, the police had to run a follow-up. Most of it merely confirmed the initial report. In this case, Stone assumed, his final report would reveal that a guy drank too much and died on the couch. The end.

Still, it had to be done. He read over Arbogast's report, then headed over to Swanson's apartment.

Growing up black in Miami Beach hadn't exactly been easy, and in his teens Stone had had his share of scrapes with the police. Not that he had been doing anything wrong, apart from finding himself in the wrong neighborhood at the wrong hour of the night. He'd been stopped and searched more than a dozen times between the ages of fifteen and nineteen. They never found anything—and after the sixth or seventh stop, he had to admit, he'd started to resent it.

The funny thing about it all, he remembered too often and too bitterly, was that the "wrong neighborhood"—meaning affluent and mostly white—was his. That's where he lived. His father was a cardiologist and his mother a dancer. He had tried to explain this to the officers who stopped him but they never bought it. After a while he stopped trying.

His decision to enter the police academy after graduating from high school was, he freely admitted (if only to himself), more an act of revenge than anything else.

He was expecting, and was fully prepared for, more friction than he actually received once he joined the force. That lack of friction was due mostly to the fact that he played it cool, but deadly sober. He took his job very seriously and liked to believe that he took no shit from anybody.

Above his desk he had hung a framed quote from Frederick Douglass: "I prefer to be true to myself, even at the hazard of incurring the ridicule of others, rather than to be false, and to incur my own abhorrence." He figured that should get the point across.

In private moments, he liked to think of himself as Shaft—without the fancy clothes, the parade of women, or the street lingo. Especially the clothes. Stone wasn't exactly what you'd call a snappy dresser (the tie he'd been wearing for the previous five days sported an obvious, almost alarming, grease stain). This was partly on account of his salary, but due primarily to the fact that he felt he had more important things to be concerned about.

The fact that he had become one of the first African-Americans on the Miami Beach force to be named detective had less to do with his color than that he was a solid and thorough investigator. And routine follow-ups on simple cases like this were all part of the game.

Twenty minutes after leaving headquarters, Stone arrived at the Excelsior. The slim, light-haired man who answered the apartment door was pretty much what Detective Stone was expecting, apart from the yellow rubber gloves and the scrub brush.

"Oh," Swanson said when Stone flashed the badge and introduced himself.

"May I come in? I have a few questions for you."

"Yeah," Swanson said, uncertain but stepping back anyway.

"Sure. Forgive the smell. I hope it's okay that I'm cleaning up." He led the detective into the living room. "I thought you guys were all finished. Nobody told me otherwise, so I figured I could get this mopped up. Get on with things, y'know?"

"For the most part, yes, they're done here," Stone explained. "This is just a routine follow-up. I need to ask you a few more questions."

"Oh. Okay," Swanson said. He pulled off the gloves and draped them over the side of a blue plastic bucket filled with soapy water. He sat down on a far end of the couch, opposite the one where Delaney's head had lain. Stone considered dragging one of the easy chairs over, saw the sleeping cat, then reconsidered and sat on the couch next to Swanson.

"I'm sorry for any inconvenience," he said. "This won't take long." He removed a notebook and pen from his breast pocket. "Now, could you tell me what happened? I know you gave your story to Sergeant Arbogast last night, but if you could tell me again, please. When did you last see your roommate alive?"

"Well," Swanson said. "That would've been about five on Christmas Eve, I guess. That's about when I left to pick up Liz…" Having given the story to the other cop the night before, he was well rehearsed. He'd also gone over the story a thousand times in his head since then. "Then I came home last night about ten or so, and he was on the couch…y'know, dead. That's when I called nine-one-one."

"And before you left on Christmas Eve, was there anything… unusual about his behavior? Anything different?"

Swanson thought about it and shook his head. "Uh-uh. He was pretty much the same as every day—sitting on the couch watching a movie, smoking his weed and drinking."

"Right," Stone said. "Was he ever depressed that you know of? Or use any other drugs?"

"Mike? Naw. I mean, he was drunk all the time, whatever you want to make of that. But, I mean, he never seemed really depressed, no. And I never saw him take anything else. But we never talked much."

"Okay," Stone said. "And he'd been living here how long?"

"About two weeks, since the middle of December. Like I told the officer last night—"

"Sergeant Arbogast."

"Arbogast, right. I had been looking for a roommate, and my girlfriend, Liz, she's in the real estate business..." He went on to explain the whole story of their meeting once again, almost word for word.

"Uh-huh," Stone said. "And how was he as a roommate?"

Swanson made a face and shrugged. "Sorta like I said. Mike just sat on the couch and drank all the time. Drank everything. Smoked pot, drank, and watched tv. Pretty much all the time. So on the one hand, it kept him out of my hair, I guess. But he also threw up a lot. All over the place, but usually by the couch, 'cause that's where he was all the time. Look at what he did to the carpet." He pointed to where he'd been scrubbing. "I'm sorry— I know it's awful—the guy's dead, and it happened right here, but..."

"It's okay," Detective Stone assured him. "I understand."

Swanson relaxed a bit. He didn't like having cops around. He didn't like having people die in his apartment, either. But at least he wasn't being accused of anything.

"I know that Sergeant Arbogast had some questions about Mike's identity," Stone said. "Which could mean anything, really. Did he ever give you any hint as to why he might be using a false name? That is, was there anything unusual about him that you could tell me?"

"Unusual?" Swanson said, almost laughing. "*Hell* yeah he was unusual, I guess." Then he stopped himself. "Naw, that's not real fair of me to say. Who ain't a little unusual, right? I mean, I guess he had his quirks like all of us. Like, well, when he first showed up, I thought he looked like a hobo or something. Shabby clothes, one suitcase, and a cat. That's his cat, by the way"—he pointed— "Dillinger."

Detective Stone nodded and made a note. At the sound of his name, Dillinger rolled over on his back and stared at the both of them upside down.

"But that's no big deal, right? I mean, I'm not exactly the world's sharpest dresser myself. You get it." He nodded at Stone's own attire. Along with the grease-spotted tie, he was sporting a day-old mustard stain over the breast pocket of his shirt and his shoes were in need of a shining.

Swanson, realizing that maybe he shouldn't have called attention to this, quickly continued. "Anyway, he moves in, gives me six thousand dollars in cash to help cover the 'no ID' thing. He says that's all the cash he has, but every time he goes anyplace—liquor store, wherever, usually the liquor store—he takes a cab."

"I thought he spent all his time on the couch here, drunk and on drugs."

"Well, yeah," Swanson said. "Mostly he did."

"Mm-hmm," Stone said. "And after he paid the rent and told you it was all he had. Where do you think he got the money to buy the booze and the drugs and take cabs?"

Swanson thought about it and shrugged. "I'm not real sure," he admitted. "My guess was he was getting it from Steve."

"*Steve*," Stone said, staring at him expectantly.

"Dunno a last name," Swanson said. "He was a friend of Mike's, I guess. I only met him once. He showed up in a van one day, and then he gave Mike the van."

"I see... Did you mention Steve to Sergeant Arbogast?"

Swanson shook his head. "I don't think so. Never came up, I guess. I was kinda rattled last night. I'm not really sure what, uh…"

"Of course, I understand," Stone said. "No problem." He could sense that things here weren't quite as straightforward as he'd originally expected.

"Can you tell me anything more about Steve? What did he look like? We would probably like to talk to him."

Swanson shrugged again. "He was a thin white guy. Maybe in his thirties, early forties, I'd guess. Blond hair. Scraggly beard."

"Does he live around here? In the complex maybe?"

Swanson shook his head again. "I really have no idea. Like I said, I don't know anything about him. Can't say I ever saw him around before."

Stone wrote it all down. "And when did you last see him?"

"Steve?" Swanson scratched the back of his head. "Oh, hell, I dunno. Week ago, maybe? That was the only time, actually. Mike wanted to buy some new sheets and stuff—he'd kinda ruined his others—and he wanted me to show him where to go. That's when Steve showed up with the van. Then I didn't see him anymore."

"Mike ever mention him?"

"Not after that."

The detective sighed. "Do you know if Mike dealt with anybody else? Any other friends? A girlfriend?"

"Not that I know of—I don't even remember him ever using the phone."

"Uh-huh," Stone said. "What about family? Do you know if he had any family? Whoever he is, we're still going to need to track down next of kin."

Swanson shook his head. "He told me his parents were dead. His sister, too. He mentioned an uncle in New Jersey, but I guess he's dead, too."

Stone looked up. "What makes you say that?"

"Say what?"

"That you *guess* he's dead."

Swanson shifted in his seat. "You know, I'm not real sure. This was so damn complicated. He told me a bunch of different stories."

"Like what?"

"Well, at first—first time we met—he said he was from New York, that he was in the movie business, and that he was down here to relax. Then he said he was in some kind of online toothbrush business—or maybe his uncle was—and he sold it, or something. And that's where he got the hundred thousand dollars. From selling the company. But he couldn't keep his stories straight."

Detective Stone stopped writing. There was a brief, heavy silence. "*What* hundred thousand dollars?" he asked.

"The money he asked me to put in the bank for him." A flash of fear crossed Swanson's face, then drifted away. Stone read it as a sign that Swanson had just said something he didn't mean to say.

Stone continued staring at him. "I think you need to back up a minute."

Swanson excused himself to go to the bathroom, and when he returned he told Stone the whole story.

"His second day here, Mike asked me if I had a safe deposit box, and I told him I did. And he asked if he could keep something in it for a while. I didn't know what to think, but then he told me that the money he got when he sold his toothbrush company had just come through—a hundred thousand—and that he couldn't touch it for a while."

"Why was that?"

"Oh," Swanson said, "he told me some legal mumbo jumbo that I didn't really understand. Some business thing. But whatever it was it meant he couldn't touch the money until some paperwork was finished, so he wanted to stash it someplace."

"Why not just put it in the bank himself?" Stone asked.

"He said he hated banks," Swanson said, sounding doubtful himself. "And plus, he wouldn't be able to open an account with no ID. So anyway, this was the second or third day he was here…"

On the television screen, Steve McQueen and Ali MacGraw were standing by the side of a highway next to a wood-paneled station wagon. There was a lot of traffic speeding past and he was slapping her face repeatedly.

"Are we going or not?" Kenny asked, standing behind the couch. "I want to get this over with."

Mike looked over his shoulder. "Sure thing. I'm sorry. This movie just always gets me." He picked up the remote and, after lingering for another fifteen seconds, his eyes glued to the screen, reluctantly shut the television off. "Just need to get some pants on and grab the money."

He disappeared into his room and Kenny looked at his watch. The cat was asleep along the top of the couch, and Kenny reached out a hand to pet it. Dillinger emitted a small whirring noise, stretched his front legs, then rolled off the couch.

Mike's door opened and he emerged carrying what looked like a large doctor's bag.

"Where'd you get that?" Kenny asked. "I like it."

"What, the bag?" Mike looked down at it. "Hell, I dunno. Picked it up somewhere. Way down here, maybe."

"I thought you took the train."

"Yeah, I did, but I mean we had stopovers. No big deal anyway. C'mere, let me show you." He set the bag on the kitchen counter and Kenny joined him.

Mike snapped the bag open, and Kenny felt his throat tighten. Inside were bundles upon bundles of twenties.

"All told now, this is a hundred thou," Mike said. "And all I need you to do is put it in your safe deposit box for...well...safe-keeping. I'm gonna need it back in a couple weeks, but like I told you I just need to know it's safe between now and then."

"Right, like you said." Kenny couldn't take his eyes off the cash.

"And since I'm gonna need it all back, I can't have you sneaking any of it, understand? No itchy fingers, see?"

Kenny looked up at him, a little shocked. "I'd never—" Then he saw that Mike was smiling.

"I should think not, *dummy*. C'mon, let's get this down to the bank. We'll take your car."

While Mike waited in Kenny's '87 Pontiac, Kenny took the bag and went into the bank. Fifteen minutes later he came out again, looking worried.

He dropped the bag between them and slid into the driver's seat.

"What's wrong?" Mike asked.

Kenny turned the key in the ignition. "It wouldn't all fit."

"Whaddya mean?"

"I mean, it wouldn't all *fit* into my deposit box. It's too small."

Mike glared at him. "Well, how much *would* fit?"

"Not sure, exactly. I crammed in what I could. See how much is left in there."

Mike opened the bag and began counting the bundles.

"Okay, there's twenty-four thou here still. So you have seventy-six in there, right? Easy to remember."

"I guess so."

"Still, though, this ain't good. I mean, where the hell can I put this?" There was a hint of panic creeping into his voice.

I can think of a place or two, Kenny thought. But he said, "You know, I think I have an idea. Liz has a safe at her place."

"A *safe*?" Mike blurted, glaring at Kenny. "Why the fuck didn't you say that in the first place?" He was close to yelling.

"Because you said you wanted a *bank*! That's all you said!"

Mike took a deep breath and closed the bag. "You're right," he said. "I'm sorry I yelled. I just wanted to get this stashed safe and quick. It hadn't even occurred to me that Liz might, you know, have a fucking *safe* in her house."

"It's not exactly a big safe," Kenny clarified. "It's just for documents and stuff. Pretty small, actually."

"Will all this fit?" Mike asked, holding up the bag.

"I think so. Let's go find out."

"So that's what we did," Swanson finished. "We stashed the rest over there."

Stone couldn't believe what he was hearing. "And you didn't find this a little…strange?"

Swanson shook his head. "Not really, no. At least not after he explained everything with the business deal."

"Wait," Stone said. "A man you don't really know hands you a hundred thousand dollars in cash and asks you to stash it for him, and you don't find that strange?"

"Uh-uh," Swanson said, shaking his head again.

Stone had to admit the guy looked like he meant it. Maybe he was just a little slow.

"And all the money is still in your safe deposit box and over at Liz's?"

"Yeah, sure, we weren't gonna touch it. In fact, I'd pretty much forgotten about it until now."

Stone told Swanson not to touch the money until they could figure out who Mike really was and where it had come from. "I'm guessing," he said, "that we're going to want to talk to you again in the near future." Then he thanked him for his time and left.

Detective Stone's head was swimming on the way back to headquarters. Something was mighty screwy here.

19

Using the name that Arbogast had found on the suitcase, Detective Stone contacted the New Jersey Bureau of Criminal Identification on December twenty-seventh and asked if they had anything on a "Ned Krapczak." The search, Stone knew from experience, promised to take a few hours, if not a few days, so he asked that if anything came up to please fax over a copy of Krapczak's fingerprints to Sergeant Sarah Egtin at the Miami Beach PD. Her own check on the national database had revealed nothing. He wasn't sure if this would yield anything either but it was worth a shot.

Shortly before ten the following evening a fax arrived. According to the report attached to the fingerprints, it seemed one Nedward Krapczak (white male, 29 y.o., 5'9", 185 lbs.) had been arrested for reckless endangerment in Newark in 1994. Apparently Krapczak had tried to run down several members of a film crew with his van.

The report stated that a television show was doing some location shooting on the streets of Newark and Krapczak, on his way home from work, had plowed into the crew.

In the end there were no serious injuries, it was determined that alcohol was not a factor, and the whole ugly business was ruled an accident (Krapczak claimed he was approaching a stoplight and had stepped on the gas instead of the brake). The charges were dropped, but the fingerprints remained on file.

A cursory comparison by Sergeant Egtin showed them to be a

match with those she'd taken from their John Doe. It seemed they could finally put a name to the body in the cooler.

The next step for Detective Stone was to try and find a next of kin. It was one of the less pleasant routines he had to deal with.

Before he had a chance to call Newark and see what he could find, however, his phone rang.

"Detective Stone?" a voice on the other end asked.

"Yes?"

"This is Special Agent Jake Meyers of the Federal Bureau of Investigation, Newark Division…and I believe you have something we're looking for."

20

Two weeks earlier, on Thursday, December thirteenth, Special Agent Jacobean ("Jake") Meyers of the Federal Bureau of Investigation was sitting at his sterile, vinyl-topped desk in the Bureau's Newark office, flipping idly one more time through the initial report he'd been handed at eleven o'clock that morning.

Across from him sat Special Agent Sven Ludkvasen, who was seven years Meyers's junior, both in age (Meyers was forty-five) and in experience with the Bureau. The left side of Ludkvasen's face sagged a bit, and his speech was slow, nasal, and slurred, leaving him sounding both drunk and cynical (though he was usually neither). He claimed it was the result of a mild stroke he'd suffered when he was nine, following what he would refer to only as a "kickball-related incident."

"Okay," Meyers said, more to clarify things in his own head than to explain anything to Ludkvasen, "some low-rent schlub of a security guard has been skimming off the hundred-plus ATMs he was supposed to be stocking. It takes the accountants over a year to catch on to it and, when they do catch on, they call him from goddamn *Florida* to tell him that they've caught on. And they're surprised when he takes off with, what, five million dollars?"

"That's the gist of it, yeah," Ludkvasen droned. "And it was four-point-eight million, to be exact."

"Uh-huh," Meyers said. His dark hair was fast going gray above his ears, and his wife wondered why. Cases like this, he reasoned, were as good an explanation as any. "They finally figure it out at the end of November and it takes them another two weeks before they let us know about it."

"I guess they didn't exactly know how to handle something like this. It's the first time they've run into it."

"Idiots," Meyers sighed. "They're in the cash business and they didn't suspect that someone along the way would try and take some of it?" Then, after a moment's consideration, he added, "Well, God bless 'em for their faith in human nature, I guess, but all they need to do is watch tv or read a damn paper every once in a while. What you're dealing with is a bank robbery. A slow one, to be sure, but still a bank robbery. And that makes it our jurisdiction."

Ludkvasen's face shifted. "Need to take into account it also seems they thought he might…call them back or something."

"Yeah, that's what I'd do if I'd just stolen five million," Meyers said, scratching his temple. " 'Hi—yeah, um, it seems I made a little boo-boo here…' " He considered what lay ahead of him. "And now they've given him that much of a lead." He shook his head and looked back at the report. "At least this shouldn't take too long. We have a name, an address. We're not exactly dealing with the Zodiac here."

"How d'you mean?"

"Well, Zodiac was *smart*. We have a picture yet?"

Ludkvasen shook his head. "Not yet, but one should be on its way from Jersey DMV."

"Good." Meyers nodded. "You know, I find it hard to believe that they've never had anyone do this to them before. The fact that it took them over a year to catch on to this guy leaves me thinking they probably have."

The following day, with a warrant for Krapczak's arrest in hand, Meyers and Ludkvasen began a fairly standard white-collar investigation, which involved obtaining subpoenas for Krapczak's phone and credit card records, then gathering interviews with anyone who'd dealt with him in the previous months, in hopes of gleaning a clue as to where he might head with five million dollars.

Stop number one was Krapczak's house.

"I don't know," Ludkvasen was saying from the passenger seat as the two men drove to Jersey City. "There are easier ways to do this. Break into an ATM, I mean."

"And how would you suggest?"

"Well, if this guy had a home computer and a modem—and if he was any kind of a phreaker at all—there are at least three or four ways that I know of to get into most any ATM system, though it's better to work with the stand-alones, like this guy did. They're remarkably vulnerable—active taps, passive taps, PIN extraction—"

"From what little I know about him at this point," Meyers interrupted, "I'm guessing that our boy here isn't much of a computer whiz, though I may be proven wrong very shortly."

"Even if he wasn't," Ludkvasen went on, slowly, "there are plenty of simple cons out there. The Broken ATM con, the Lebanese Loop, the Bank Dick con. He could pull that thing the Russian mob's been pulling for years."

"Remind me," Meyers said, happy to have Ludkvasen talking. Not only was it good exercise for Sven's facial muscles, it gave Meyers time to relax a bit and think about other things.

"Well," Ludkvasen said, after wiping the corner of his mouth with the napkin he always seemed to be holding for just such a purpose, "it's not that tough, if you have a nearby Radio Shack and the slightest bit of technical know-how. You rig up a logic board and small reader strip. Then you slip the reader into the

slot where people swipe their cards, right? And it reads everything off the magnetic strip, just the way the ATM would. You
slip the logic board over the keypad, and when the suckers punch
in their PIN numbers it reads those, too. Those two things get
stored in the memory and you have everything you need.

"When the people go away, you retrieve the reader and the
logic board, take them home, and *poof*. Later that night you have
a dozen identical ATM cards and the PINs to go with them."

Ludkvasen sat back in his seat, reasonably pleased with
himself.

"Like I said"—Meyers glanced over at Ludkvasen—"I'm
guessing Krapczak here isn't quite that adept."

"So why not the Lebanese Loop, then? Simplest con in the
world—"

Meyers raised his hand to stop his partner from going any
further. "If you ask me, Sven," he said, "I think just grabbing a
bunch of cash that you're supposed to be putting in the machine
and shoving it in your pocket is much easier."

Mildred Krapczak hobbled into the living room, carrying a tray
with three cups of lifeless, tepid coffee.

"Now, Mrs. Krapczak," Special Agent Meyers said, taking a
cup off the tray, "about Ned…" He hadn't yet got a feel for what
he was going to be dealing with here.

"Oh," she sighed, straightening her soiled and faded blue robe
as she lowered herself into a far corner of the couch. She'd made
the funny-looking one sit on the broken spring. She didn't like
him, all funny-looking that way. "Oh," she sighed again. "There
was just something wrong with him."

"Wrong…how so?" Ludkvasen asked.

"Oh, you know." She sounded almost annoyed. "Just *wrong*."

"Can you recall when it started?" The last thing Meyers

wanted to do here was play shrink, but when it was called for he could do so.

"Oh, he's always been like that."

"You mean...stealing?"

"No, *not* stealing," she said, clearly annoyed now. "Noogie's never stolen a thing in his life. I mean he's just *wrong*."

"Could you be a little more specific, Mrs. Krapczak?" Ludkvasen pressed.

She rolled her eyes. "You're saying he stole how much, now?"

"Umm—about five million dollars, ma'am. Four-point-eight million, to be exact."

"Right," she said bitterly. "So he starts stealing. Steals five million dollars. And what does he buy me? His own mother? Chops and slippers. Can you imagine that shit? *That's* what's wrong with him."

"It's entirely possible, Mrs. Krapczak," Meyers interjected, "that he was trying to conceal it from you. That he didn't want to be too obvious about it."

She went on as if he hadn't said anything. "Little shit tells me he got a raise. Not a *five-million-dollar* raise, I'll tell you that. Still living in this crap hole, and he buys me *slippers*."

Meyers could tell this was going to take some time. He decided to cut straight to the basics. If they needed more details later, they could come back and get them.

"Mrs. Krapczak," he said, "the most important thing we need from you this afternoon is to know if you have any idea where your son may have headed. Any idea at all. Did he...leave a note before he left? Did he say anything that could tell us where he might have gone?"

"Oh he can go to *hell* for all I care," she said.

"I'm thinking, well, more in terms of geographically, Mrs. Krapczak. Did he have a girlfriend or any other friends he might stay with? Any idea if he'd head south or west? Might he head to another country?"

"…been goin' to hell for a long time now."

Meyers could tell he was losing her.

"Maybe she means Hell, Missouri, Jake?" Ludkvasen suggested. "Whaddya think?"

As the hours dragged on—at least that's how it felt to Meyers and Ludkvasen—the interview with Krapczak's mother revealed that her late husband had died on the *Hindenburg* or the *Edmund Fitzgerald,* or maybe had succumbed to yellow fever in the Congo. They also learned that she enjoyed a nice pastrami sandwich every now and again, "even though they stopped me up something awful," and that her neighbors—especially the ones to the right—"wouldn't know crabgrass from a goddamn hole in the ground." She claimed to have no knowledge of ever giving birth to a "slipper-buying bastard of a son named Ned."

A thorough search of Krapczak's room, with Mrs. Krapczak's permission, had unearthed some dirty magazines (one of them gay) and a bra, which may or may not have belonged to Ned. A framed diploma on the wall showed that Krapczak had graduated from NYU's film school in 1987.

"He was a film student, I see," Meyers said to Mrs. Krapczak. "He ever do anything with it?"

"Why don't you tell me?" Mildred responded, without any further explanation.

Flattened carpet fibers in the closet, indicating that something large and heavy had been stored in there, may have been connected to the missing cash. It might have been, certainly, but in reality it could've been anything—a toy box, a small dresser, a couple of empty beer kegs. Or a crate full of money. Mrs. Krapczak was very little help in clearing that up.

"He had a fat cat," she said. "Maybe it's from his fat damn cat."

"And where's the cat now?" Ludkvasen asked, more concerned about the cat's well-being, honestly, than he was about what Krapczak may have kept in his closet.

"Ain't here," she said. "Know that. Probably with fatso. He took everything. Cat was a better son than he was."

After leaving her house, the agents spoke with several neighbors, most of whom used the term "blowhard" in describing Krapczak. One of them described him as a "blubberpot," which made Ludkvasen snort. None of them remembered seeing him driving away for the last time.

By the time they headed back to Newark about six that evening, they had determined that the best way to go from here would be to concentrate the search in Manhattan, talk to the people he'd dealt with, and send word down the line to the other FBI field offices, as well as state and local law enforcement along the East Coast. Krapczak seemed like someone who would stay reasonably close to home, but who knows? Maybe he'd want to get as far away from his mom as possible.

Meyers and Ludkvasen returned to Newark with a few more photographs of the suspect, a description of his van, and an evidence bag containing a shoe box full of cash.

"I dunno, Jake," Ludkvasen began as they sat at a stoplight. "I know we're FBI, sworn to strictly uphold the laws of the land, but look at that poor old lady. The way she's living. To just walk out of there with what was probably all the money she had in the world at this point, it's just..." He squinted slightly, pained. "It's pretty cold."

"It's *evidence*, Sven. The cash was stolen," Meyers said, his eyes not moving from the road before him. "And it's our job to recover it."

"I know that, but—"

"But nothing," Meyers snapped. Then after a pause he added,

"And I'll tell you another thing. A simple truth of law enforcement is that it usually involves what we don't know as much as what we do know. Take the case of that shoe box, for instance. We don't know how much was in there when he left. And we don't know how much she's spent in the meantime."

"Well she clearly didn't spend anything on home furnishings or her wardrobe," Ludkvasen mumbled, trying to take some weight off his still-sore ass. "She could sure use a new couch."

"Ah, now, let me finish. When we found that box, it might've contained fifteen thousand dollars. Or it might've just as easily contained ten, or six thousand. We found what we found."

"Yeah. But—"

Meyers looked at him, the tiniest of conspiratorial smirks working at the corner of his mouth. "We *found* what we *found*."

"Ah," Ludkvasen said. "All right."

"Besides," Meyers added, "from what I could tell, she had at least three thousand stuffed into her bra."

Ludkvasen laughed, then wiped his mouth. "Maybe she's not so batty after all."

"I'm not so sure about that," Meyers said.

Quietly, he was becoming frustrated. They had a name and a face. They had a license number and knew what he was driving—or at least what he had been driving about two weeks earlier. That, unfortunately, was about all they had. But it was early yet.

Krapczak hadn't used his credit card since long before he'd left. He hadn't bought anything extravagant—no cars or jewelry or houses. Not under his own name, anyway. Krapczak's bank account (now frozen) showed no sign of unusual activity at any point in the past year, except that he had made precious few withdrawals. That, together with the shoe box full of cash found at the Krapczak home, might well indicate that he hadn't yet laundered

the money. *Might* indicate. If he hadn't, that meant he was traveling with about three hundred and fifty pounds worth of twenty-
dollar bills. If that was the case, it certainly would limit his
movement somewhat. It would, for what it was worth, be damn
near impossible for him to leave the country.

Meyers knew there were far too many "ifs" and "mights" and
"maybes" involved.

Interviews with the store owners Krapczak had dealt with
revealed, for the most part, a group of people who were both
relieved and annoyed that he wasn't coming around anymore.
Not that he was such a bad guy, most of them insisted. It's just
that they liked him better when he went away, for reasons they
couldn't quite put their finger on.

"Last time I see lard ass," the proprietor of the Green Many
Products Grocery told them, "was November. Late. He come in,
say something stupid, and go back to machine. But when he open
it, he take all money *out,* not put any in. I ask him why, he say
something about a light that need fixing, that he come back later.
But he never come back. I call and call and never see him again.
Lard ass."

They heard similar stories from other businesses. The owner
of Fast Eddie's Drug Hut told them about the time Ned threw
a fistful of money at a young kid. He also told them that after
Krapczak's last visit, he'd gone back to check out the machine.
There was a note taped to the screen saying it was out of order,
and that's when he noticed that the telephone line, which linked
the machine to PiggyBank's computer system, had been cut.

None of the people they spoke with had the slightest clue
where Krapczak may have headed.

"Well," Meyers said as he and Ludkvasen were leaving Fast
Eddie's and heading back to their car, "we know what we know."

.   .   .

On the morning of Tuesday, December eighteenth, Meyers's investigation was going nowhere fast.

The Bureau couldn't spare the manpower for a nationwide hunt for this chump. Not with the chief telling them they all had to be keeping their eyes open for Middle Eastern terrorists. Besides, this guy was small change. Although he'd never say so aloud, in his heart Meyers felt the ATM companies were the bigger crooks. In quiet moments, he even admitted to himself that he had a certain admiration for this Krapczak. It was, you had to admit, a pretty nifty heist. But his personal feelings on the matter couldn't get in the way of doing his job. And right now, his job entailed tracking this guy down with whatever meager resources he could muster and getting that money back.

Agents in the Southwest had so far come up empty-handed. No banks had reported any unusually large cash deposits. Meyers had been lucky enough to obtain a speedy court order to place a tap on Mrs. Krapczak's phone, figuring if Krapczak—or Noogie, as Mildred Krapczak had called him—was going to phone anyone, it would be her. And three days after the tap was installed, Meyers's hunch proved correct.

"Ma—hey—it's me again."

"Who?"

"Who do you think? It's Noogie. Now, Ma, listen—"

"Who is this?"

"Ma, please. I just want to—"

"I don't know you. Is this one of those dirty calls?"

"Please, you gotta—"

"You're some kind of masher! I'm not buying!"

"Fine. That's fine, Ma. Just don't hang—"

· · ·

The agents assigned to monitor the tap on Mildred Krapczak's phone hadn't, unfortunately, been able to trace the call. They did, however, relay word to Meyers that contact had been made and that they had a tape en route to him.

Meyers listened to the recording with his face in his hands.

"She hung up on him," he said, shaking his head, his face still covered. "I can't fucking believe this. Didn't even ask him where he was." He nevertheless forwarded the tape along to the lab to see what they could come up with. Those boys could work wonders sometimes.

Two mornings later, one of the Bureau's voice analysts called Meyers with his results.

"This Crap Sack," he said, "feels conflicted about his mother. He loves her very much, but he feels smothered by her, too."

"That's great, really. It's just not exactly what I was looking for," Meyers explained to him. "I was hoping you would be able to tell me something along the lines of *where he is*."

"Well, this is about all we were able to determine, so you'll have to try and be happy with that."

"Swell," Meyers said.

"It would've been better," the technician said, "if the old lady hadn't hung up on him."

No one had yet thought to connect the assault on a gentleman who had decided it would be a good idea to sell guns and alcohol in the same establishment with the man who had stolen four-point-eight million dollars from an ATM company. Nor had they connected the armed robbery of a roadside pie stand with the same man.

And although a twenty-six-year-old Hershey, Pennsylvania, resident named Velda Minion would later tell friends how "creeped out" she had been by the man who had given her a brief ride one night on her way to Miami, she was not so creeped out that she ever expressed her concerns to any local law enforcement officials. It was likely none of these things ever would be connected.

Then, as so often seems to happen, out of nowhere shortly before New Year's Meyers received a call from the Newark police department, informing him that a detective in Miami Beach, Florida, was trying to identify a John Doe who seemed to match the description of a fugitive the FBI was after.

21

After receiving Mildred Krapczak's phone number and address from Special Agent Meyers, Detective Stone was left with the unpleasant task of letting her know not only that her son was dead but that his body was in Florida and that she could claim it there.

"Yeah?" croaked the voice on the other end of the line after Stone dialed the number.

"Mrs. Crap Sack?" he asked tentatively.

"Yeah, what of it?" the old woman barked. "You from the electric company again? Well you can just go *fuck* yourself for all I care! I grew up without electricity, and I can *die* without it, too!"

"No—no, Mrs. Crap Sack," he interrupted. "This isn't the electric company. I'm Detective Robert Stone from the Miami Beach Police Department down in Florida, and—"

"Yeah, yeah, yeah," she droned. "I know. Noogie was a bad boy, right? And you wanna know why. The feds were here already. Go talk to them."

"No, ma'am," he said. "I'm afraid I have the sad job of informing you that your son has passed away."

There was a long silence on the other end. Then she asked, "Was he in a shoot-out with the feds?"

"No, ma'am."

"Figures."

Detective Stone was on the phone with Mrs. Krapczak much longer than he had planned, and by the end he had come to understand why Meyers was laughing when he'd wished him luck.

Stone did learn, however, that Mrs. Krapczak had never heard the names "Kenny Swanson" or "Michael Delaney" and knew of no friends her son may have had by the name of "Steve." She also told him that her son had never been involved in any way with the sale of toothbrushes.

"I'm amazed the dummy even knew how to use one," she added.

He told her that if she wanted any of Ned's personal effects back she could call Swanson and gave her the number.

"Did the feds gun down Dillinger, too?"

"Excuse me?"

"Dillinger. He still alive?"

He at first thought it was some kind of Alzheimer's moment. Then he remembered.

"Do you mean the cat?"

He heard her sigh. "Yes, of *course* I mean the cat, *dummy*. He alive?"

When he assured her that Dillinger was doing just fine, she said she wanted him back. She also demanded that her shoe box be returned.

"I'll...see what I can do," a confused Stone told her.

After hanging up, the next order of business was to call Swanson and let him know that he might well be hearing from Krapczak's mother. He debated a moment over whether or not to warn him what to expect. He decided against it. It seemed an indirect way of keeping a little pressure on this kid. Stone still wasn't sure what the story was over there, but he knew full well he hadn't heard it all yet. He picked up the phone.

"Hey," Swanson said, after Stone explained the situation, "speaking of personal effects, what's gonna happen with Mike's van?"

There was a brief silence before Stone said, "Excuse me?"

"His van. It's parked out back."

Stone closed his eyes and squeezed the bridge of his nose. *Stupid white boy.* "Why didn't you mention this earlier?"

"I did. I told you that Steve gave him the van."

"But you didn't tell me it was parked right there."

"Guess I figured that much could be implied."

"*Well,*" Stone began, then stopped himself. *Stay cool.* He was suddenly glad he'd decided against warning Swanson about Mrs. Krapczak.

Later that afternoon, a truck from Cindy's Towing arrived at the Excelsior and dragged the white Econoline back to the Miami Beach PD's Major Case storage garage.

22

On January third the story hit the papers in southeast Florida and northern Jersey but very few other places. It was the first time anyone outside of PiggyBank or the FBI realized that for the past three weeks there had been a nationwide manhunt, if a meager one, for a former NYU film student who had stolen nearly five million dollars out of ATM machines. And even though the focus of the manhunt was dead, it seemed the mystery was just beginning.

As FBI spokesman Whitley Bosco told reporters, "The big question that remains here is what happened to the money. There was no money in Mr. Krapczak's possession when we found him, and at present it's unclear what may have happened to it."

PiggyBank's Presley Buckitt was quoted as saying, "We just want our money back, okay? That's all. The guy's dead, fine, they found him, right? Now just find our damn money and I'll shut the hell up about it."

The day before, Special Agents Meyers and Ludkvasen arrived in Florida, contacted Detective Stone, and asked him to accompany them as they interviewed Swanson once again.

"I know what you may be thinking," Meyers told Stone after they shook hands. "That, hoo boy, here comes the FBI to start stepping all over the toes of local law enforcement."

"I can honestly say, Agent Meyers, that I thought no such thing," Stone replied, "for the simple reason that we're not in a movie." *And I'm not in blackface,* he thought to himself. "From what I can tell, we're working on two different investigations that just happen to intersect. I see no cause for disharmony. You're looking for stolen money, I'm investigating an as yet unexplained death."

"Good," Meyers said. "But even if we can't step on your toes, I assume we'll still be playing good cop, bad cop."

"There are no bad cops," Stone said.

Meyers sighed and gave up.

Even before boarding the plane to Florida, Meyers and Ludkvasen had had the good sense to obtain a search warrant for Swanson's apartment.

"I just filed the paperwork for a warrant myself this morning," Stone told them. "This saves us a lot of time. I could've been waiting a month."

"You run a check on this guy?" Meyers asked as Stone drove them to the Excelsior.

"Yeah," Stone said. "Nothing much worth mentioning. Was busted three years ago for renting a thousand dollars' worth of tools, then not returning them."

"So we're dealing with a real dangerous character, you're saying," Ludkvasen said from the back seat. Meyers shot him a look that seemed to say *Not with the locals* and he closed his mouth.

"Ended up serving ten months," Stone continued. "That's all. At least in Miami Beach."

"Gotcha," Meyers said. "Still on parole now?"

"Yeah."

"You have cause to suspect him of something here?"

"Don't know yet. There's something a little off, though. Few more sets of eyes can only help."

Meyers considered the detective. He wasn't sure about him yet. Of course they'd met only a few minutes ago, but after all his years in the business he found he was able to read people pretty quickly. This guy was clearly smart. Kind of a slob, but that usually goes along with it. A sharp cop, without question. There was something else, though, like he was trying too hard. There was a current of something taut and quivering just beneath the surface. Resentment? Anger? He wasn't sure yet. You always had to be careful with the people who felt they had something to prove. He'd have to keep an eye on him.

Ludkvasen, sensing a mild but growing tension in the car, piped up, "So Detective Stone, tell me, is it always sunny and warm down here, like they say? I've never been."

Stone was still trying to get used to that voice. He couldn't tell if the agent was being snide or not. He wouldn't put up with any patronizing shit. He cleared his throat. "Pretty much, yeah," he said. "Except for the occasional hurricane." Then, figuring they had more important things to talk about than the climate, he told them, "I can't tell yet whether Swanson's stupid, stoned, naive, or more clever than I realize. I can't say for certain...but he's at least one of the four."

"Well," Meyers said, "let's find out which."

As Stone and Ludkvasen searched the house, Meyers sat down on the couch with Swanson and asked him to tell his story again.

Swanson rolled his eyes and sighed heavily.

"C'mon, Kenny, do it for me," Meyers cajoled. "I haven't heard it yet, so it'll all be new."

Swanson looked at him. "All right," he said and took a deep breath. "So this guy Mike shows up in town looking for a place to live. He ends up calling my girlfriend, who's in real estate. But he tells her he doesn't have any ID. She can't rent him an apartment without ID so she thinks of me, 'cause I'm looking for a roommate. So we meet, and the next day he moves in."

"You two must've hit it off."

"Don't know that I'd go that far," Swanson said. "But he was in a spot, so I told him we could try it out for a couple weeks. His rent's six hundred a month, but as a kind of security for that ID thing, when he shows up he gives me ten thousand in cash. Fine with me, right?" He gave a small, nervous chuckle and shrugged his shoulders. "After that, he just sits on the couch, drinks himself stupid, smokes a lot of pot, watches movies. And believe me, when he was watching his movies, he didn't want anyone talking to him. Then he dies. End of story, really. Messed up my carpet a lot."

Meyers nodded. "All right, fine. But it's not exactly the end of the story, is it? Not as far as we're concerned anyway. I mean, you're aware of why we're down here now and why we were looking for him."

"Now I am," Swanson said. "But I didn't know that until yesterday."

"Detective Stone told you?"

Swanson shook his head and sneered. "No. A *reporter* called me. Some guy from New York—Bara-something. I don't remember the name. He told me the guy was wanted for stealing five million bucks. I told him I didn't know anything about it. Then he called me an idiot."

"Wha'd you tell him?"

"Didn't tell him anything," Swanson said. "I didn't know anything. I called him an asshole, 'cause he was, and hung up on him. To be honest, I thought he was joking. Then you guys show up."

"Ah, our glorious press," Meyers said. "But let me ask you. Detective Stone tells me Krapczak gave you a hundred thousand dollars to keep for him."

"Krapczak?"

Meyers understood the confusion. Swanson had known him only as Mike Delaney. "The guy we were looking for," he said.

Swanson stared at him blankly.

"The guy who died on your couch. It's his real name."

"Oh, yeah," Swanson said finally. "Sorry. Detective Stone did tell me that, I guess. I just can't get used to that name."

"Yeah, it's a mouthful. A lot of us can't get used to it," Meyers said, focusing on Swanson's eyes to see if they were dilated. They didn't seem to be. He shot a quick glance toward the other rooms to see how Ludkvasen and Stone were coming along. "So he gave you a hundred thousand to stash for him."

"Right," Swanson said, nodding.

"And you did what with it?"

"Well," Swanson said carefully, "I put what I could in my safe deposit box and gave the rest to Liz for her to keep in her safe. About twenty thousand."

"And the money's still there."

"Yeah."

"All of it?"

Swanson looked annoyed. "*Yeah.*"

"Good. We'll need to get that sometime soon." Meyers took a deep breath and leaned back. "Let me ask you, Kenny. Try to see this from my perspective. A guy comes in, a guy you don't know from Adam. He gives you ten thousand dollars in cash as a deposit on a six-hundred-dollar rent. Then he asks you to stash a hundred thousand in a safe deposit box. Don't you find it just a little peculiar?"

"Well, no," Swanson insisted. "Not at the time. See, like I told—" he stopped briefly, as if his brain were backing up. "I didn't think it was weird then. Maybe I should've. But there was a point when, yeah, I did start thinking maybe he had more money around than he was letting on."

"And when was that?"

Kenny exhaled. "I guess it was a few days, maybe a week, before Christmas. Liz and I went on a trip—two nights—over to

the Keys. Just a little vacation. And when I got back, Mike had
bought a bunch of new furniture. This couch, the table. Said he
wanted to make it up to me."

"Make what up to you?"

"I don't really know—all the puking, I guess. He used to throw
up a lot, on account of the drinking. Didn't always get to the bathroom first. Usually didn't."

Meyers looked around the room. "So you're saying this furniture was—"

Stone walked into the room. "Excuse me for interrupting,
gentlemen."

"S'okay, Detective. What's the story?"

Stone held out four prescription bottles. "What can you tell
me about these, Mr. Swanson?"

Swanson eyed the bottles nervously. "They're all legit," he
insisted. "You can call the doctor if you like. They're for my
back."

Stone read the labels aloud. "Xanax and three bottles of Percocet?" He looked at Swanson and raised an eyebrow. "This is a
lot of pills here."

"My back's in really bad shape."

Meyers saw where Stone was headed. "Kenny, now," he said.
"I gotta ask you this. You didn't, by chance, slip a few to Ned
Krapczak, did you?"

Swanson looked sincerely shocked. "What?"

"I'm just asking."

"Well...no."

Meyers smiled. "Fine. That's fine. You understand that we
just have to ask. Do you know if Krapczak ever took any of the
pills himself?"

Swanson shook his head. "Uh-huh. While he was here, I kept
them hidden in my room. He couldn't get to them."

"But he knew you had them."

Swanson nodded. "I would guess, yeah. I mean...my back's a real mess, so I take a couple a day. It wasn't a secret, and I didn't try to hide it from him. Besides, he was so out of it all the time, I don't think he noticed much of anything except his movies."

Dillinger ventured out from beneath one of the easy chairs, approached Meyers hesitantly, sniffed his ankle, then took a step back. He let loose with a wild hiss before darting past Stone and out of the room, his tail puffed to twice normal size.

"Jesus," Swanson said. "I'm real sorry. I've never seen him do that to anybody before. Didn't even know he could move that fast."

Meyers watched the retreating cat. "That's Dillinger, I'm guessing."

"Yeah. He was Mike's."

"I guess he can smell I'm a G-man, huh?"

"A what?"

"Never mind."

They left the Excelsior shortly after five, having found nothing else of interest, and headed across town to Liz's apartment. En route, they compared notes.

"Swanson mentioned to me once that Krapczak couldn't keep his stories straight," Stone said. "But if you ask me, I think he needs to do a little work toward that end himself."

"How do you mean?"

"On the night he found Krapczak's body, he told Sergeant Arbogast—he was the officer on the scene—that Krapczak had given him three months' rent, eighteen hundred dollars, to cover the lack of ID. Last time I talked to him, he said Krapczak gave him six thousand. That's when I first started getting itchy. I was fine with it until then."

"And today he tells me ten thousand," Meyers said.

"Maybe he's just been accumulating interest," Ludkvasen piped in. Meyers shot him another look.

"That may well be the problem," Stone said.

"Did he tell you about the furniture?" Meyers asked.

"I'm not sure."

"Said Krapczak bought a bunch of new furniture, and that's when he first started thinking there might be more money around."

"News to me," Stone said. "The furniture that was in there now?"

"I guess so."

"Pretty shabby for new furniture," Ludkvasen interjected.

The car was quiet again, and again Ludkvasen could sense an inexplicable tension.

"Before we go any further, Agent Meyers," Stone said, "I think we need to keep our own stories straight."

Meyers looked at him but said nothing.

"As I remember, you're looking for stolen money and I'm investigating a death."

"Right."

"Just confirming that. You were questioning Swanson about whether or not he drugged Krapczak."

Meyers smiled sheepishly. "I guess I was, wasn't I? Well, the opportunity presented itself. Seemed an obvious line of questioning."

"You're out of your jurisdiction."

Meyers scowled as a thought crept into his head he knew would be best to swallow. His face relaxed. "Point taken," he said. "But look at it this way, Detective. It strikes me that these two cases may well be—no, screw that—*are* connected. Intertwined, if you will. And that being the situation, it just seems obvious that if we're going to be working together to some degree, well, we might as well work together."

Stone, who wasn't used to working with the feds, and who preferred to work alone in any case, considered this. "I would've asked him about the pills."

"I know you would have," Meyers said. In his brain, he was sighing. Playing dad to Sven was enough, he didn't need it with this guy, too. *So fucking sensitive.* Next thing you know he's gonna be quoting lines from *Sounder* or something. "But look at it this way. With both of us there looking at him, don't you think it was a bit more...intimidating?"

"We shouldn't have to intimidate someone like him."

"We don't know that yet, do we? Besides, a little intimidation never hurts when someone's hiding something."

"That's not the way I like to work," Stone said.

"Hey!" Ludkvasen blurted from the back seat. "Does this mean we really are gonna play good cop, bad cop next time?"

Stone looked at Meyers and asked, "Why is he here?"

"Comic relief."

Stone glanced back at Ludkvasen's lopsided smile. "All right. Since we're working together, let me ask you this. What do you make of this friend Steve? The one who supposedly gave Krapczak the van?"

Relieved that this little problem had been resolved (at least momentarily), Meyers said simply, "There is no Steve. Never was."

Liz's eyes were wide when she opened the door. Kenny had called to let her know they were coming, but still the idea of having FBI agents looking around her apartment was a little unnerving.

"May we come in?" Special Agent Meyers asked.

"Oh, God—yes, of course, I'm sorry." She took a step back.

"Thanks."

"Kenny called?" Detective Stone asked.

"Uh-huh."

"He let you know why we were coming?"

"More or less, I guess. Yeah."

"Good, so you don't mind if we take a look around?"

"No…not at all. Can I—I get you anything?"

All three men declined. They didn't think they would find anything apart from the cash in the safe, but you can never be sure.

"One thing," Meyers said. "Kenny said that you were holding some money in your safe? Money that his roommate had asked him to hold?"

"Yes," she nodded. "Did you want me to get it?"

"Please," Meyers said gently.

He took a seat at the kitchen table. It was a nice apartment—soft lighting, lots of art on the walls, plants. It was comfortable and homey. Swanson's place, by comparison, was almost skeletal.

She returned to the kitchen a few minutes later, holding the bound stacks of bills in front of her as if they might stain her blouse. "Here," she said, placing it on the table. "There's some more. I'll be right back."

"Thank you," Meyers said softly, after she'd placed the second load of bundles on the table. "Have a seat."

She sat down across the table from him as he counted the bills. "Twenty-four thousand," he said aloud. A large plastic evidence bag seemed to materialize in his hand. He shook it open and dropped the bills inside. "Funny," he commented, as he dashed a note on the bag's label. "Kenny told us there was only twenty."

She shook her head. "Uh-uh," she said. "That's what he told me, too, but it was twenty-four. He said he could only fit seventy-six in his safe deposit box, and it was a hundred total."

Meyers nodded. "No big deal. He was just a little edgy. Nobody likes having us around, huh?"

She smiled nervously.

"Don't worry about them," he said, making a vague gesture toward the other rooms. "They won't make a mess."

He went on to ask her a few simple questions, most of which she couldn't answer. She confirmed everything Swanson had said about what led up to their first meeting. After that, though, she admittedly knew very little about Krapczak, having seen him only once or twice after he moved in. She told Meyers that the few times she went over to Kenny's place while he was living there, he was on the couch and didn't move. She didn't know for sure how much he'd paid as a deposit but thought it was just three months' rent. That's what they'd talked about at the bar. And she'd never heard of a Steve. It was her impression that the van was just Mike's, but she didn't know where he got it.

Agent Ludkvasen and Detective Stone entered the kitchen empty-handed. Apart from the money there was nothing of interest there.

"That wasn't so bad, was it?" Meyers asked as he stood. "I just want to thank you for all your cooperation. You've been a tremendous help to our investigation. And if you find that either of these guys made a mess, you just call me and I'll make sure they come back and clean it up, okay?" He smiled broadly in a way Stone had yet to see him smile and handed her his business card.

On their way down in the elevator Meyers, still smiling enigmatically but not looking at either of them, said, "I want a tail put on Swanson. I'd also like to subpoena his bank records."

23

"Uhhhh...Detective Stone?"

It took Stone a second to recognize the voice. "Kenny?"

"Yeah."

It had been less than twenty-four hours since he, Meyers, and Ludkvasen had searched Swanson's apartment. Stone was still waiting to hear about the tail and the subpoena that Meyers had requested.

"What can I do for you?"

"Well," Swanson said, sounding nervous, "I've been thinking. You guys are looking for that money Mike took, right?"

"That we are, yeah."

That was putting it mildly. When Stone first told Meyers over the phone that they'd found no money whatsoever with the body, it sounded like the agent was going to start crying. In their subsequent discussions, speculation over what might have happened to it ran the gamut. Five million bucks in twenty-dollar bills, after all, doesn't just vanish.

Krapczak had been on the road for at least a week and a half, and so far they had no idea where he'd been or what he'd done. Maybe he stopped in Atlantic City and lost it at the tables. Maybe he picked up a hooker who stole it from him. Maybe he drank it all away. Or maybe he buried it under a tree someplace along the road. If what Swanson said was true, he still had at least some of it left by the time he reached Florida. But so far as they knew at this point, that hundred ten, fifteen thousand Swanson had seen might have been the last of it.

They had their doubts, though.

"I had an idea," Swanson said. "I'm not real sure, of course, but I thought you might want to check it out. You know, just to see."

Forty-five minutes later, shortly after noon, Stone, Meyers, and Ludkvasen were once again in Stone's car (a gray Dodge Charger that had seen better days) looking for an abandoned building in one of Miami Beach's poorer neighborhoods.

"Let me get this straight again," Meyers was saying. "He told you that the money might be here—*might* be—because Krapczak used to hang out in this part of town?"

"That's what he said."

"That makes no sense. I thought he never got off the couch the whole two weeks," Ludkvasen asked.

"Right," Stone said. "Except for when he did, apparently."

"I see."

Meyers looked out the window at the small, dilapidated houses they were passing. Despite the sunshine the lawns were gray. "Looks like parts of Newark you don't want to visit... Maybe this is where he came to buy his marijuana."

"No," Stone said. "You're wrong." The voice was cool and even but the creeping anger was evident. "This neighborhood is not like Newark. There's almost no crime here. No drugs, no armed robbery. Nothing."

Meyers was still looking out the window. "Makes sense," he said. "Doesn't look like there's much of anything left to steal. The drugs, though, I don't get."

Stone shot him a hard look. "The point I was making, Agent Meyers," he said sharply, "is that despite the general perception some people have, these people look out for one another. They may be poor but they still have self-respect."

"Is this where you grew up?" Meyers asked.

"*No*," Stone said. "It's *not*." His hands grew tight around the steering wheel. "But I know this town. I know what happens, and where."

"I can imagine," Meyers said, more concerned about where they were headed, honestly, than the socioeconomic state of the neighborhood.

Stone glared at him again. "You know, a wise man once said, 'A gentleman will not insult me, and no man not a gentleman *can* insult me.' "

"*What* insult?" Meyers fired back. "I say I know that you're aware of what happens here, and suddenly you start spouting Frederick Douglass at me? I suggest you cool it a bit, Detective."

"Gentlemen, gentlemen," came a slow voice from the back seat. "You two really gotta come to some sort of agreement on your stereotypes. Good cop, bad cop. FBI, local police. Now black cop, white cop? Could you please just choose one and stick with it? For *my* sake?"

"There it is," Meyers said, ignoring Ludkvasen and glad to have a distraction. It was always something. Folks always looking for an excuse to be offended.

The car slowed and pulled over to the curb.

They were parked in front of a gray single-story house. It might've been white once but most of the paint had peeled away. One of the front windows was broken and the postage stamp of a front yard was overgrown. Clearly no one had lived there in years.

As the three men stepped out of the car, Ludkvasen asked, to whomever cared to listen, "You don't suppose this could just be a, you know, diversion on his part? Swanson's, I mean? Send us out here while he takes it on the heel and toe?"

Meyers shook his head. "Doubtful. Could he be that stupid?"

"He might be," Stone said.

"No matter. I arranged for two agents from the local field office to keep an eye on him until your request comes through. He won't go anywhere."

They walked across the weed-choked lawn and up the warped wooden step. Meyers tried the front door and found it open.

The place wasn't so bad once you got inside. It was dirty and the wooden floors creaked and there were a few broken windows, but it seemed solid. Nothing that couldn't be fixed up again.

"I'll try the basement," Ludkvasen said.

"You won't find one," Stone told him.

"Pardon?"

"Most of the houses down here don't have basements. We're at sea level. This is it."

"Oh," Ludkvasen said, wiping the corner of his mouth. "Okay then, that makes things easy. I'll just…look over here, I guess."

Each man headed for a different corner of the small house. Barely ten seconds had passed, however, before Stone's voice arose from what must have been the living room.

"Gentlemen? If you could come in here please?"

A moment later they had joined him, and the three men found themselves staring at three light blue laundry bags sitting in the middle of the floor.

Meyers knelt and yanked one of the bags open. It was stuffed with bundles of twenty-dollar bills.

"Well that was simple," Ludkvasen said. "Not terribly clever on his part, though."

"No, I think you're wrong there, Sven. Sometimes the best way to hide is to hide in plain sight. And that goes for when you're trying to hide something else, too." Meyers looked around the room. "Though you'd think he'd at least put it in a closet or something. Someplace without large windows." Then he looked around the room and reconsidered what he'd just said. "No, this is just pretty dumb."

. . .

"Tell me, uh, Kenny," Meyers began, "how was it, do you suppose, you happened to know the money was in that old house?"

The four men—Meyers, Stone, Ludkvasen, and a very uneasy
Kenny Swanson, dressed in a sweatshirt and jeans—were sitting
around a table in a stark interrogation room. After the three laundry bags were brought back to headquarters, they were found to
contain three-point-one million in cash, all in twenties. Meyers
and Ludkvasen had also retrieved the seventy-six thousand from
Swanson's safe deposit box. That, together with the twenty-four
they'd collected from Liz, wasn't everything but it was a damn good
start. The ten, or six, or whatever it was that Krapczak supposedly
gave Swanson as a deposit would likely just have to be written off.

"Like I told you," Swanson said. "Mike said he wanted to come
up with a new business plan while he was here. I mentioned this
neighborhood. Things are cheap there. Liz told me about it. So
we, you know, went out there one day. He thought he might want
to get into real estate. You know, fix up the place nice, maybe start
gentrifying the neighborhood?"

Stone closed his eyes, both in contempt for the idea and in
sheer dismay. "That's the first I've heard of that one, Mr. Swanson," he said.

"No, it's *true*," Swanson said. "I guess I didn't think much of
it—it was one afternoon, and then we stopped talking about it. So
I guess I forgot about it until, you know, I called you."

"Mm-hmmm," Meyers said, considering the Styrofoam cup of
lukewarm coffee in front of him. This kid was turning out to be
a real piece of work. "Let me ask you this. Since you, ah, *remembered* that *maybe* some money *might* be stashed there, have any
other possibilities come to mind? Maybe there's a cave someplace,
or maybe in someone's garage?"

Swanson shook his head. "No, uh-uh." Then he added, "You mean that wasn't all of it?"

Meyers looked at Ludkvasen, then Stone, with a smirk. "Tell you what, Kenny. We have a bunch of other work to do today, and I think it might be best for all of us if we—with Detective Stone's cooperation, of course—held you here overnight."

"That can be arranged," Stone said with no hesitation.

"*What?*" Swanson blurted, half-rising from his seat, his eyes wide. "But I'm helping you guys out, aren't it? I mean...*Christ!*"

Meyers remained calm. "Yes you are helping us. And that's just the point, you see? We'd like to have you close at hand just in case you happen to *remember* where the other two million might be. Make sense?"

"Makes sense to me," Stone said, pushing himself back from the table. "Let me go make a few arrangements."

"Hello, gentlemen," Sergeant Egtin said as Meyers and Ludkvasen entered the evidence garage at nine that evening. "You look like you've had a long day."

She'd been expecting them. They shook hands and made the formal introductions.

Egtin was in the midst of taking photographs of Krapczak's white van from every conceivable angle.

"This isn't the van he left Jersey in," Meyers noted. "He must've dumped the other one on the way down here. You dust for prints yet?"

"Nope," she said. "Got here just ten minutes ago and wasn't going to touch anything until you showed. By the way, was that a test?"

"Sort of. You passed."

"Of course I did. I'm a trained professional. Plus I've worked with you federal boys before."

She packed her camera back into her bag and reached for the fingerprint kit. "So what are you two looking for in here, anyway?"

"Two million dollars in cash," Ludkvasen said.

"Oh," Egtin replied. "Well then in that case maybe I should start with the rocker panels. I knew there was something strange going on when we weighed the vehicle and it came out two million dollars heavier than it should." She shook her head, pulled on a pair of latex gloves, opened the driver's side door, and leaned inside.

"*Gaah,*" she yelled. "It smells like cat piss in here."

The van gave them little to go on, though they'd have to wait to see if the prints revealed anything. The only things they found in the glove compartment were a receipt from a gas station in Miami Beach and a piece of stationery from the Round at Both Ends Motel, upon which someone (presumably Krapczak himself) had drawn a crude picture of what appeared to be a German soldier on a motorcycle. No registration papers, no insurance papers. Not even a map.

Still, everything was bagged and tagged, and by eleven-thirty they were done. They hadn't found any money.

Upon returning to his apartment that evening, Robert Stone removed his tie and holster, hung them both on the back of the front door, and set about making dinner.

The walls of his tiny apartment were lined with books. History, sociology, psychology, criminology, law. He didn't have time for fiction. He'd never read a novel that could top some of the things he'd seen.

"I'm working with a pair of clowns," he muttered down at a trio of frying eggs. Where were these mystical investigative skills FBI agents were supposed to have? So far as he could tell, they'd just been following him around, taking credit for things he was uncovering. Typical. Meyers scamming on Swanson's girlfriend. And that Ludkvasen? Stone couldn't figure out what he was doing there at all. Dead weight.

Worst of all, while they were here and he was leading them around by the hand, his own investigation into Krapczak's death had come to a standstill. Granted, he had to wait for the lab reports to come back, but there were other things he could be doing. He just didn't have the time while babysitting these two.

He was starting to get the old feeling again. The simmering anger. He knew he had to keep it in check. He'd lost it today with Meyers, and that wasn't good. Feeds right into it. Unprofessional.

He flipped the eggs and remembered what Meyers had said—that as long as they were working together, they might as well work together. Fair enough, though he'd love to see how they did without him. Find out what "work" and "together" meant.

Maybe it was all part of the game. Everything's a damn game.

Well, he thought decisively as he slid the eggs onto a small plate. *I won't give them what they want, whatever the fuck that is. This is my town.*

And who knows? If he shows them how a good cop works—how a *really* good cop works—he might find himself with the Bureau some time soon.

He set the eggs on the table and opened a beer. He took a swallow and spilled some down the front of his shirt.

It'll dry, he thought as he sat down to eat.

24

When he was awakened by the shrieking of the telephone in his hotel room at eight-fifteen the next morning, Jake Meyers found that he had an unexpected hangover.

He hadn't had that much to drink when he got back, had he? Then, through his dry and puffy eyes, he saw the half bottle of Jack on the nightstand. *Oh*, he thought. He remembered a solitary, unguarded, drunken moment when he realized that this case wouldn't be going anywhere if Swanson weren't such a dumbass. Worse still, if Krapczak hadn't died, there was a reasonably good chance they never would've found him.

He also recalled a fuzzy impulse, sometime around two, he thought it was, to pick up the phone and call Liz. Then he'd purged it. Way too complicated on way too many levels.

Still, vaguely hoping it was her now, he picked up the phone.

"Special Agent Meyers," he rasped into the receiver.

"Agent Meyers, Detective Stone here."

"Morning, Detective," he said. "*Early* morning, I might add."

"I apologize for that," the voice said, though he didn't sound too apologetic. "I just wanted to let you know that keeping Swanson overnight was a wise move."

Meyers quickly forgot about the hangover. "He's talking?"

"He will be, as soon as you get here."

Less than an hour later, the four of them were once again seated around the table in the interrogation room, and a pale, shaky Kenny Swanson was complaining about his back pain.

"We'll get you something for it as soon as we're done here, deal?" Stone said. "So I suggest you make it easy and just tell the truth." Then he added quietly, "Finally."

Swanson winced as he shifted in his chair. "All right." The banks of fluorescent lights above them left him looking even more sickly than he apparently felt. "I can't take another night in that cell."

The three investigators waited. Swanson took a sip of his coffee.

"This is what happened, okay?" he said. Then he paused again and took a deep breath. Ludkvasen sat next to the tape recorder. "The day after Mike died—"

"You mean Krapczak."

"Yeah, whatever. Whoever. The day after he died—this would've been the day after Christmas—I went out to his van, right? Just to see if there was anything of his in there, you know? Identification or something. Something that might...I dunno...help."

"How'd you get in?" Meyers asked. "Wasn't it locked?"

"Well, yeah," Swanson said. "But his keys were on a hook by the door. So I went back there, lifted the tarp—he had the van covered with a tarp—and opened the back doors. And there were these bags in there, like laundry bags. I looked inside, thinking, you know, it was just dirty clothes or something, even though I never saw him change his clothes much. But they were all full of money."

He stopped talking.

"So wha'd you do then?" Meyers pressed.

Swanson's eyes darted around. He winced again. "I guess I panicked, you know? The ID was one thing, but this was different. There was a hell of a lot of money there—more than I'd ever seen before in my life. I didn't know where it had come from...what he'd done. All I knew was that there was a shitload of money right in front of me, and the only other guy who knew about it was dead." He took another sip of his coffee. The investigators let him take his time. They weren't in any hurry.

"Then I got scared, see? I mean, the parking spot was rented in my name. I rented it for Mike after he moved in, on account of the ID thing. If anyone else came across it and traced it back to me, well, you know, they might think that it was mine…that I'd done something. I didn't know what Mike did but I thought I might get connected to it."

"Mmm-hmm," Stone said. "You panicked. That's understandable. But you could've just told the police. I was there that day. Saved yourself all this trouble."

Swanson looked at him like he was an idiot. "This happened after you were there—and you never mentioned anything about all this money he was supposed to have." He shook his head sharply. "Look, I'm trying to tell you what happened—what I did. Not what I *should've* done. "

Meyers raised his hands in submission. "Point taken. So what *did* you do?"

Swanson shifted in his seat again. He was evidently uncomfortable. "First thing I did was stuff them in my car—the bags, that is—and drive them over to a storage locker I have. Trusty Self-Storage, it's called, on Biscayne Boulevard. I was thinking… I dunno…that maybe if nobody else knew about the money, nobody would, you know, *ask* about it. I was thinking that maybe Liz and I could just sit on it a little while. It was like a dream. Sit on it and see if anybody said anything. And if they didn't, if nobody cared…it would've been real nice. For once, I'd've gotten lucky, and things would've been nice."

"Makes sense to me," Ludkvasen said. "Gotta say."

"How'd it end up in the house? Or maybe we should be asking why?" Stone asked.

Swanson rolled his eyes. "Lord knows what I was thinking…I

kept it in the locker for a few days, then I guess I got nervous about having it there. Cops coming around asking questions. I thought if you guys started poking around, you'd end up looking in the storage locker at some point, so I thought I'd better get it out of there, put it someplace you wouldn't look. Someplace that didn't have my name attached to it. I knew about that old house through Liz, and thought it would be safe—nothing ever happens over there."

"So Krapczak was never over there," Stone said. "Never considered 'gentrifying' the neighborhood."

Swanson shook his head. "No, he had nothing to do with it. Nobody did. That's why it seemed like a safe place."

"That makes sense, too," Ludkvasen said. "Though why leave all that money in the middle of the floor? Why not at least put it in a closet or something?"

Swanson shrugged. "I was scared. I wanted to get out of there as quick as possible. Didn't want people to see the car."

The room was quiet for a moment.

"I'm telling you all I can," Swanson said, almost pleading.

"We understand that," Stone said. He didn't sound completely convinced. "But let me ask you something we asked you earlier. Did you have anything to do with Nedward Krapczak's death?"

Swanson stared back at him. "*No*," he said firmly. "I'm telling you the truth. No, I didn't."

"Didn't slip him a few pills?"

"No."

"You see him with all this cash, it never occurred to you that maybe, you know...?"

"*No.*"

"But you did take his money after he died."

"Yes...but then I gave it back, didn't I?" He seemed near tears. "Once I found out what the story was, I gave it back."

"Took you a while, though, didn't it?" Meyers said.

25

With a sincere promise that he would stick around town and help the investigation however he could, Kenny Swanson was released into the cool, sunny early January afternoon. He had never appreciated the sun on his skin so much before. Best of all, he still had a quarter bottle of pills awaiting him at home. His back was killing him.

Meanwhile Meyers, Stone, and Ludkvasen were preparing to visit Swanson's brother, Phil.

"Think he's gonna run?" Stone asked. "On top of everything, he's still on parole."

Meyers smiled slightly. "I kind of hope he tries."

Swanson's brother Phil was forty-two, married with two kids, and lived in a modest split-level house in an affluent section of town. He was a computer engineer but didn't much look the part in his beach bum attire and scruffy beard. More than anything, he looked like a Beach Boys reject.

At first he seemed shocked to find the law at his door, but when they told him it was about Kenny he seemed to understand. He let them in.

They sat down in the comfortable living room. The children began shrieking in the next room, and Phil excused himself for a moment to quiet them down. When he returned he took a seat in an armchair opposite the couch.

"We just have a few questions for you," Meyers said.

"It's about the drugs, isn't it?"

The three investigators looked at each other briefly, then back at Phil.

"What about drugs?" Stone asked. Meyers and Ludkvasen sat back. This was definitely not their jurisdiction.

Phil, surprised to learn that this wasn't about drugs, hesitantly—and with some embarrassment for having opened his mouth—explained that his brother had been hooked on prescription painkillers for a few years.

"After he hurt his back," he said, "one of his friends sent him to this doctor who gave him anything he wanted. He's been hooked ever since. I'm surprised you didn't know that."

"We have no record of him ever being arrested on drug-related charges," Stone said. "At least not in Miami Beach."

"Well, no, I'm not aware of him ever actually being arrested, but I just figured you guys knew what was going on, even if you couldn't bring charges."

"Well, we try and—" Ludkvasen began before Stone cut him off.

"We found a few bottles at his place, but the prescriptions checked out."

"I bet they did," Phil said. "He just didn't tell you how many of those he was filling on a weekly basis. I've tried to talk to him about it but...no luck. At least he's not dealing anymore—not that I know of, anyway."

"Dealing?"

"Yeah. He used to brag that he could get whatever he wanted. Word got around, you know? Anyone needed anything, they came to Kenny."

"Prescription medications," Stone said.

"Yeah," Phil said. "Not hard stuff. No coke or heroin, nothing like that. Just pills. But like I said, he doesn't do that anymore."

Stone considered this. "Do you know if he ever gave anything to his roommate?"

Phil's mouth turned down at the corners. "You mean Mike? The one who just moved in?"

"Yeah."

He shook his head. "Not that I could say, really. I mean, Kenny hasn't said anything about it to me, not that he would... Why do you ask? Is Mike in some trouble?"

"You could say that. He's dead."

"Mike?" Phil looked shocked. "You're kidding."

Again, the three men glanced at each other, trying to read this guy. "No," Meyers said. "We're not. He died on Christmas. You hadn't heard?"

"No," Phil said. "I'm stunned. I mean, I just saw Kenny on Christmas Eve. I didn't really know the guy—his roommate—but... still, Jesus. What happened?"

"We're not exactly sure yet," Stone explained. "Kenny found him on the couch when he got home on Christmas."

Phil's face was dark. "My God, that's awful. Kenny found him?... I know on Christmas Eve, Kenny mentioned that this guy really put it away. Booze, I mean. That's all he really said about him."

Meyers exhaled. "But you never heard your brother say anything about drugs?"

Phil shook his head. "No, uh-uh. I mean, he said Mike smoked a lot of pot, too, along with the booze, but he never mentioned anything about pills. But to be honest he knows how I feel about that shit—excuse me—so I doubt he would."

They were quiet. The three investigators stared at Phil expectantly, an unspoken question hanging in the air between them.

"Are you seriously asking me," Phil finally began, with some astonishment, "if I think my brother had anything to do with it? Gave him something? What do you call that?"

"A mickey," Ludkvasen offered. "Slipped him a mickey, yes." He was quietly amused at how "shocked" and "astonished" people had been throughout this investigation. But then again they usually were. He was always relieved when they came across someone who just said, "Yeah, that doesn't really surprise me much." But people like that were rare.

"Oh, no no no," Phil insisted. "Absolutely not. That's just crazy—Kenny would never do anything like that. He's not that type. He has his problems, sure, but at heart he's a really good kid. Why would he anyway?"

"Right," an unimpressed Meyers said. "Fine. Let me ask you this." Meyers may not have been as amused as his partner, but human behavior never ceased to amaze him. "Has Kenny given you any money over the past week, week and a half?"

Phil laughed. "Kenny give *me* money? Are you nuts? I'm sorry, forgive me for laughing, but I can't say that that's ever happened. I'm always the one who gives him money. Rent, whatever. Groceries. Or so he says, you know? Besides, like I told you, I haven't seen or talked to him since Christmas Eve."

"All right, then," Meyers said. "Prior to Christmas, did you hear Kenny mention anything about...uh, Mike...having a lot of money?"

Again the corners of Phil's mouth went down. He looked confused. "No, not at all. Why? Don't tell me you're implying that Kenny killed his roommate and took his money, because that's just fucking insane. Again, forgive me. It's just...crazy. All this."

"We're not talking about fifty dollars," Stone said. "We're talking about five million."

"No," Phil was shaking his head vigorously, "not even for

something like that. Not Kenny. I can't see it." His voice began to grow distant. "Just...nuts..."

It was Ludkvasen who first noticed the thin sheen of sweat developing on Phil Swanson's forehead. Maybe he was warm, or maybe, like most people, he got a little nervous when the FBI started asking a lot of questions. Or maybe, as was usually the case in the end, he was hiding something. Best way to find out was to ask, he figured.

"Mr. Swanson," Ludkvasen asked. "You nervous about something?" Subtlety had never been one of his strong points. What's the point, he figured.

"Why? No, I just don't care for the things you're implying about my brother. It's just... Am I...?" Phil's hand went to his forehead. "Ah, sweating...sweating, yes, I see how that might...look to people in your...ummm...with the sweating." Then he dropped his damp hand to his lap. "Oh, dammit all," he said, standing abruptly and walking out of the room, leaving the three confused officers staring after him.

They heard a sound from the kitchen, like the hollow scrape of a cookie jar lid being removed. A moment later Phil stomped back into the room, looking simultaneously embarrassed and pissed.

"Here," he almost spat, slapping two stacks of twenties onto the squat table between them. "He said he was paying me back some of the money I'd loaned him. I thought getting wrapped bundles from Kenny was a little weird, so I hung on to them. *Happy* now?"

26

"Hi, it's me again," Kenny said. It was eleven-fifteen on the morning of Monday, January seventh.

"Hello, Kenny," Detective Stone said. "Let me guess. You thought of someplace else that we might just want to look, if we were interested, because we might just find a little more money."

"Well, yeah. But look, hey—I'm doing what I can to help. Sometimes my memory ain't so good. You don't need to be mean about it."

Stone sighed, his pen poised above the legal pad on his desk. He couldn't remember, for all his years on the force, ever having dealt with a character quite like Swanson before. "I understand that. But it would just be easier on everyone if you could do it all at once. Okay, shoot."

"Well," Kenny said, "there's a self-storage place. Not the one I told you about earlier but a different one. Over on Southwest Twenty-eighth. And in locker...let's see...seven-seven-four-oh, you might find a large black suitcase."

"Uh-huh," Stone said. "And how much do you think we might find if we were, by chance, to take a look in that suitcase?"

"Well my guess," Kenny said, "is that you'll find about half a million."

Two hours later, after retrieving the suitcase in question and returning it to headquarters, Meyers and Ludkvasen showed up at Kenny's apartment, informing him that he was now officially under arrest, charged with possessing and concealing stolen money that had moved across a state boundary.

"Those are federal charges, Kenny," Meyers clarified. "You could be looking at ten years."

Swanson's initial shock quickly faded into resignation. He put up no resistance when Ludkvasen produced the handcuffs.

"I'm sorry about this, Kenny," he said. "You seem like a nice kid. But you gotta realize you left us no choice here. You've been kind of a doofus. If you'd been completely straight with us from the start, things might've been different."

Meyers raised an eyebrow. For all his years with the Bureau, he'd never once heard a fellow agent call a suspect a "doofus."

"Oh," Swanson said, after his hands were cuffed in front of him. "One other thing—could you come with me? It'll just take a second."

Both agents reluctantly agreed.

"Dillinger's still around here somewhere," he said. It was the first time they'd ever heard real sadness or concern creep into Swanson's voice. "Do you suppose someone could call Liz? Ask her if she'd take care of him? I just want to make sure he's okay."

"I'll take care of it," Meyers said.

They thought he was heading for the bathroom but followed him instead into the kitchen. He bent down and pulled the cat box from beneath the sink. He thrust his cuffed hands into the litter.

Both agents instinctively reached for their guns, but then relaxed, sort of, when Swanson pulled his hands out of the minefield of cat shit and they saw that he was clutching yet another wrapped stack of twenties.

"Oh, Jesus Christ," Meyers said. "You have got to be kidding."

"Just trying to come clean," Swanson said with a weak smile as he shook the clay granules from the bills. He stood and held out the money.

Meyers looked at Ludkvasen. "You bag this one, would you, chief? And see that he washes his hands. I'll meet you in the car."

Doofus, he thought, as he walked outside.

27

For all that Kenny (and his girlfriend, and his brother, and Mildred Krapczak) had turned over, Meyers calculated that they were still over a million dollars shy of Krapczak's original haul. "Any ideas?" he asked. It was Thursday the tenth. He was seated behind a small cluttered desk in a makeshift office he'd taken at police headquarters. Stone and Ludkvasen were there with him, seated very closely together in the cramped quarters.

Typical, Stone thought, before saying, "I can think of a couple off the top of my head. According to PiggyBank, it's their guess that Krapczak was at this for well over a year—maybe two—before he fled. It's possible, don't you think, that he could've spent a chunk of it in that time. We don't have any record of any extravagant purchases, but we don't really know, do we? And we have no idea what he was doing between the time he left Jersey and his arrival here."

"Sure," Meyers said. "Possible. What else?"

"It's also possible PiggyBank is inflating the numbers a little bit for the insurance. Or, as I think you've pointed out, that Krapczak hid some of the money himself somewhere. Likewise, that Swanson spent it or has some more stashed someplace."

"My vote's with Swanson," Ludkvasen piped in. "Way he's behaved up to this point, I think that's the most likely possibility. Maybe if we put a little more pressure on him, he'll just happen to remember where he stashed the rest."

Meyers nodded. "That's the way I'm leaning. And that's why it's both a blessing and a curse to have him in custody. When he's locked up we can't follow him. But he also seems to have a tendency to weaken awfully quickly in stir. Maybe he'll come up with something else before his hearing Tuesday."

Stone leaned forward in the molded plastic chair. "What about the girlfriend? If anybody apart from Swanson knows anything, I think she would."

Meyers lightly bit his lower lip. "I've considered that. My gut feeling is she told us all she knew when we were there."

"Maybe. But there were a few days between then and when we finally picked up Swanson. Who knows what he told her? He seemed awfully calm after he learned he was looking at ten years."

"Ten years max if it goes to trial," Meyers said. "But maybe I should give Liz a call myself. I got the feeling she trusted me when we were there."

Over the next several days, Swanson would speak only to his lawyer, and when he appeared in federal court on Tuesday the fifteenth he announced that he would be pleading guilty to charges of receiving stolen property. With the plea deal, instead of ten years he was now looking at between twenty and forty months. But he was also looking at extradition to Newark for the sentencing.

Well, that's that, Stone thought as he left the courthouse. *Except for that missing million, it's another one down.* Just as well, too. He had plenty of other work to do. As for Krapczak's death, it was looking like the initial reports would hold—a simple accidental overdose. Still, something about the way it all shook out was unsatisfying.

When he arrived back at headquarters, he found two messages waiting for him. The first was from Dr. DeKay at the Medical Examiner's office, asking him to call at his earliest convenience. The second was from Meyers. He decided to call DeKay first, since he would be seeing Meyers shortly anyway.

When Dr. DeKay answered the phone, it sounded like he was in the middle of lunch. He crunched something for a few seconds, swallowed, and then apologized.

"I have some preliminary results from the toxicology tests on Krapczak," he said. "Hold on."

Stone now heard a shuffling of papers. He wasn't expecting much. At least not much of anything that would be of any use to him at this point. But then DeKay, after finally pulling out the report he was looking for, told him that, at the time of Krapczak's death, his blood alcohol level was point-one-two.

Stone, who's mind was starting to drift a bit as DeKay flopped around on the other end of the phone, snapped back to attention. "Could you repeat that?" he asked.

"Point-one-two."

"That doesn't make any sense. How does a guy his size die of alcohol poisoning with a blood alcohol level of point-one-two?"

"We don't know that he died of alcohol poisoning," the doctor said. "Right now it seems doubtful, in fact. But keep in mind that these results are just preliminary. I'll have more conclusive results in, oh, a week, week and a half. I just wanted to get these to you as soon as possible."

Stone thanked him and was about to hang up the phone when Dr. DeKay stopped him. "One other thing that was interesting," DeKay said. "Or at least I found it interesting, but who the hell am I?"

Stone waited a few beats for the doctor to come to some sort of decision, and finally asked, "Yes?"

"Oh. Sorry. No, the other thing was that I found no traces of THC in Krapczak's blood."

"None?"

"Nope."

Swanson's story from the beginning had always been that

Krapczak did nothing all day but smoke pot and drink himself stupid. Now the detective was being told that Krapczak not only had no pot in his system—THC hangs around in the bloodstream for at least a month—but he barely had enough booze in him to make him tipsy, let alone kill him.

Stone had to keep in mind, as DeKay told him, that these were just preliminary results. They could easily change after more extensive tests were run. But what if they didn't?

If it was true, though, it meant that damn near everything Swanson had told them from the beginning was a lie. They'd caught him in a few whoppers as it was, so why not everything? If that was the case where were they now?

Dammit. This whole case was supposed to be routine.

He hung up the phone and went looking for Special Agent Meyers.

28

"Ah, Detective Stone. Good. Have a seat. Everything go okay in court?" Meyers was on his feet. He looked agitated—more agitated than Stone had seen him these past two weeks. Ludkvasen, meanwhile, who was sitting in one of the cramped office's plastic chairs, was smiling his lopsided smile.

"Yeah, he pleaded," Stone said, unsure what this might be about. The FBI's job was finished. For the most part, anyway. He sat next to Ludkvasen. "But I just got off the phone with—"

Meyers raised his hand. "Hold that thought, if you please. Let me ask you. Does the name Simon Malstein mean anything to you?"

Stone's eyes cut to the right. "Well...no, not off the top of my head. But to be honest, umm, here in Florida, see..."

Meyers shook his head. "I mean in terms of the case at hand. Have you ever heard of Simon Malstein in connection with Ken Swanson?"

Stone thought about it for a moment but came up with nothing. He shook his head.

"Okay. That's understandable. There were no charges filed, no major investigation. But I'm getting ahead of myself. You once asked why Agent Ludkvasen was here. Well, this is why. He's one of the top investigators the Bureau's got, and he just did some...well ...some investigating, and—" He was pacing (as much as that was possible in the small office), gesticulating, the words flowing faster.

"Agent Meyers," Stone said, his voice calm and low. "Sit down. Please. Take a breath. You're overexcited."

Meyers relented and sat. "Sorry—maybe Sven should explain."

Stone turned to Ludkvasen. The crooked smile still hadn't left his face.

"Well," Ludkvasen said, "I'll keep it short. It seems that ten months ago, approximately two months after moving into his apartment at the Excelsior, Mr. Swanson had another visit from the paramedics. As he told it then, this guy Malstein stopped by his apartment late one night drunk on his ass. They were friends, or at least business acquaintances, and Swanson said he wasn't going to let Malstein drive home in that condition, so he offered to let him crash on his couch for the night. You know, sleep it off?"

"Okay, and this was about ten months ago, you say?"

Ludkvasen nodded. "Last March. Next morning, Swanson calls nine-one-one because, when he woke up, he found Malstein was dead. He says Malstein went into his bathroom and gobbled a few of his pills. Mixed with all the alcohol in his system—" He snapped his fingers. "They called it an accidental overdose and that was the end of it. Case closed."

Meyers stood up again. "And *that's* why he's here, Detective Stone."

Stone exhaled. "I can see where you're going with this, but I don't know."

"It doesn't matter where we're going with it," Meyers said. "We're just on a grand larceny case, that's all. Remember? Just following the money. What happened between Krapczak and Swanson is your jurisdiction. I'm just tossing this out there as something to consider. You have been invaluable to our investigation, and it's only fair that we offer you a little something in return."

"Yes, that's mighty white of you," Stone said. "Fair enough. Here's the thing—what I was coming down here to tell you in the first place. I'd just got off the phone with Dr. DeKay at the ME's

office. Preliminary reports show a blood alcohol level in Krapczak of point-one-two and no trace of THC."

The two agents stared at him.

"Those are preliminary reports, right?" Meyers finally asked.

"Yeah."

"Any sign of Percocet or Xanax?"

"That's all we found. And no, DeKay didn't mention them. But
the complete report's a couple weeks away."

Meyers looked at the ground and folded his arms. "Malstein
had Percocet and Xanax in his system." He looked back up at
Stone. "Something about this whole thing's starting to stink. But
there's no solid evidence for any of it."

"Not yet, anyway," Stone said. "And remember Swanson
pleaded today already. You're taking him to Newark in a couple
days."

"I know," Meyers said. He wished he had a window he could
look out when he thought aloud. Gazing at a bare wall wasn't
nearly as effective. "But should you come up with some evidence
that we're dealing with a homicide—" He stopped. "I'm sorry,
Detective. This isn't my case. I don't even know that it *is* a case.
But it's just that something about this whole mess is just too…"

"Messy?" Ludkvasen offered.

"Yeah, thank you, Sven. 'Messy' works. It seemed pretty damn
simple a couple weeks ago. Now everything we come across—yes,
circumstantial as it is—muddies the water."

Ludkvasen coughed to get their attention, spraying both men
in the process. "Sorry," he said, "but since we're muddying the
waters here, there's another little thing that's always bugged
me"—he looked at Meyers—"and I know this is out of our jurisdiction, and that we're not supposed to speculate. But it's one
little thing."

"Go ahead," Stone said.

"Well," he said, "I was going back through Swanson's various statements. And I don't know if you remember this or not, but in one of the first statements he gave to Sergeant..." He looked at Stone for help.

"Arbogast."

"...Sergeant Arbogast, he said that on Christmas Day he'd come home in the afternoon, found Krapczak on the couch having puked all over himself again, turned around, left, and came back six or seven hours later to find him dead."

"Right."

"But he only tells that story once. I went through everything, and on each subsequent occasion he neglects to mention that first stop home."

Neither man reacted.

"Just makes me curious about time of death," Ludkvasen said. "What also makes me curious is that if Swanson *did* come home that first time, he said he was used to Krapczak puking on himself. But chances are good Krapczak was already dead at that point. And if he was dead, he would've voided himself. So was our boy *also* used to Krapczak pissing and shitting himself in his sleep? And for a man with a supposed blood alcohol level of..." He stopped himself. "I'm just curious, is all. Can't help myself."

Ludkvasen pulled a napkin from his pocket and wiped his mouth.

29

Two weeks later, Meyers and Ludkvasen had returned home, Swanson was being held in a Newark jail awaiting his sentencing, and Dillinger had been safely and happily adopted by Liz Bezack. Detective Stone had other cases to contend with, but Swanson was still lurking in his consciousness. He was still waiting for a final autopsy report, and there was the question of that unaccounted-for million. Neither Swanson nor Krapczak was doing much talking these days, so his only option at the moment was to wait. Busy himself with other things.

He was typing up the final report on Androval Lincoln, a twenty-three-year-old who had murdered his nineteen-year-old wife, his mother-in-law, and a six-year-old neighbor child with a machete. It had been an ugly, dispiriting scene, one of the worst Stone had ever encountered on the job, and one he was having trouble shaking.

When his telephone rang, he flinched.

Del the Weasel looked the part. He was a small, wiry, nervous character with tiny, widely spaced eyes, a narrow mustache, and some questionable dental work. For one reason or another over the years, he'd become an all but permanent resident of the Miami Beach jail. And in that time, mostly because he was always on the lookout for an angle that might get him back on the streets for at least a week or two, Del had taken on the role of jailhouse snitch.

His track record had been better than most over the previous three years, so it had become almost routine for Del to be placed in a cell with someone the cops might want to know a little something more about. Hoping, of course, Del's new cellmate wasn't aware of his reputation.

The fact that he'd been placed with Swanson, however, had been a coincidence. They'd lived in close quarters for almost a week before Swanson's transfer, and in that time Del had learned a few things he thought might be of interest to Detective Stone.

He'd been brought into the interrogation room five minutes before Stone arrived. It was barely enough time to make himself comfortable.

"Hey, Detective," he said brightly when Stone walked in. "Good to see you again."

"Always a pleasure, Del," Stone replied. "But look, I'm busy. We need to make this quick. I sure hope you aren't going to be wasting my time. You know what happens when you waste my time."

"Oh, I don't think I'll be wasting your time," Del said with a grotesque grin. He had an oily, nasal voice that fit his features as well as his name did. "What do you think you can do for me?"

Stone sat across the table and sighed. He didn't like Del. He didn't like dealing with most jailhouse snitches, period, but it was part of the game. "What've they got you on this time?"

"Just possession, is all."

"Possession of what?"

"A little coke."

"That's all?"

Del smiled apologetically. "Maybe a little gun, too."

"Uh-huh. That figures. Look, did you happen to point the little gun at anybody? And remember, I can check all this out myself, and probably will. But you be straight with me now it'll make things easier."

Del shook his head. "You know I'm no killer. I ain't never hurt nobody."

Stone leaned back in his chair and tried to read Del's face. It wasn't easy. "I'll see what I can do," he said. "Depending, of course, on what you can tell me about Swanson."

He placed a small tape recorder on the table between them and pushed a button.

The story Del had to tell was a simple but damning one. Almost too simple and too damning, which was what you come to expect from a snitch.

He'd been Swanson's cellmate for six days after Swanson was picked up. In that time, Del said, the two of them talked a lot, about a lot of things.

One morning Del was leafing through a paper (he always liked to keep up with the news—it was good for business) when he saw a story about Krapczak, Swanson, and all that missing dough.

"So I get curious, right?" Del said. "And I start asking him about it. He can trust me. And he tells me about finding these bags of money, and hiding them, and getting busted. Later he tells me about this time he went on this trip—just a couple days down to the Keys with his girlfriend—and how when he came back his roommate had bought all this new furniture. He said that was the first time he got the idea that maybe this guy had more money around than he was letting on."

Stone tried to keep his face and eyes from revealing anything, but when Del mentioned the furniture story he could feel his muscles tighten. That little anecdote had never been released to the media—only in part because it was likely another of Swanson's lies. Still, it wasn't something Del could've known unless he'd been talking to Swanson about the case.

"So Kenny, see," Del was saying, "he got sort of curious after that about where this guy—Kenny called him Mike—might be keeping the scratch. He says he gave Mike some pills to put him out for a while so he could go take a look around. When Mike passed out, he says he found a hundred thousand in his room, in a little black bag. You'd think that'd be enough—I would any- way—but then he says he went and looked in the guy's van and found these duffel bags. 'More money than I ever seen in my life,' he says to me. That's an exact quote, by the way: 'more money than I ever seen in my life.' So he's real excited, right? But then when he goes back inside and tries to wake the guy up—*oops*, the fucker's dead. And that's when he tells me—and this is another exact quote—'I gave him too many pills.' "

It certainly fit the theory Stone had been toying with. "He tell you what kind of pills?" he asked.

The little rat-faced man shook his head. "Nah. He did tell me about this back of his. Talked about that a hell of a lot, com- plained about it all the time. How he'd hurt it on the job and was taking Percocet, so I'm guessing he used that. But he never told me direct, though, no. That's just a guess."

Neither Swanson's injury nor his use of Percocet had been mentioned to the press, either.

"All right, Del, you done good," Stone said as he shut off the tape recorder. "This pans out, I think we might be able to do a little something for you."

"Much obliged, Detective," Del said. "In the meantime do you suppose you might be able to arrange for a little…you know, con- jugal visit for me?"

Stone, who was reaching for the door, didn't look back. "You're not married, Del. And besides, don't you get laid enough in here as it is?"

Back in his office, Stone found a report from Sergeant Egtin waiting. It didn't offer much, just confirmation that fingerprint evidence proved Krapczak had, indeed, handled the bottle of Harveys Bristol Cream, the glass, and the beer cans.

He added it to the file, then called Special Agent Meyers in Newark to let him know about his conversation with Del the Weasel—though instead of calling him "Del the Weasel," he simply referred to him as "a past reliable informant." He knew Meyers couldn't do anything with it even if the information was accurate, but for all the bullshit and annoyance, after Meyers and Ludkvasen left, Stone actually almost missed them. And reluctantly he had to admit that they'd been a help. Now he was also hoping they might ask Swanson a few questions about Del's story before he went in front of the judge.

30

"C'mon Kenny," Special Agent Meyers said in a voice that seemed at once soothing and threatening. "This is your last chance before your sentence is handed down. You know that. If you come clean now—*completely* clean finally, on everything—chances are good he'll go a little easier on you. 'Course if you don't come clean, you could be looking at a hell of a lot more than three years."

"Shouldn't my lawyer be present for this?" Swanson asked.

He hadn't exactly been thrilled to learn that Meyers and Ludkvasen wanted to talk to him again. He knew what they were going to ask him. He'd cooperated up to this point, hadn't he? Best he could, anyway.

He didn't like the Newark prison. He didn't like the shackles, didn't like the green jumpsuit, didn't like the company. From what he'd seen of it through the grated windows of the prison van, he didn't even like Newark. But he hadn't much liked the Miami Beach jail, either.

Christ, what had he really done, anyway? He was human, wasn't he? He had seen a chance and he'd taken it. All those bags, all that cash. No one was asking about it. Who wouldn't have given it a shot? And shit, when they did ask him about it, he gave the money back to them, didn't he? As much as he could. And so had his brother, that shitheel, and so had Liz. *They* weren't being charged with anything—just him. This was bullshit. He did the same thing anybody would have done, and he admitted to it. Now look at him. Lotta good it did.

"There really isn't any more," he told them. "I gave it all back."

"You don't have another million packed away someplace that you just sorta forgot about until now?"

"No. *Christ.*"

Meyers had that smug look on his face that Swanson had come to hate. "Okay, Kenny," he said. "Let's hope so, because I have to take your word for it at this point."

Swanson relaxed slightly, thinking this might be the end of it. Compared with these guys, the psycho waiting back in his holding cell would be a relief.

"But I just can't help thinking," Meyers said, "a man, a complete stranger, walks in and offers you ten thousand dollars in cash for a six-hundred-dollar room. Aren't you gonna start thinking, '*Hmmm*...I wonder if there's any more where this came from'? I know I would."

"Well, I didn't," Swanson said, letting his anger slip out. "I told you what happened."

"Sure," Meyers said. "I know. You told us all sorts of things. That he gave you eighteen hundred, then six thousand, then ten thousand. That he had a friend named Steve who gave him the van. That he bought you all this new furniture. That he was smoking pot all the time. I don't know that you ever told us what actually happened, really."

Swanson started to speak but Meyers cut him off.

"In fact, you know what I think makes much more sense than any of the stories you told? I think that cash in your safe deposit box wasn't money he'd given you to stash. I think you got that money after he was dead, or maybe while he was dying. So wha'd you slip him?"

Swanson was furious. "*Nothing!*" he shouted. "I didn't have anything to do with it!"

"That's not what a friend of yours in Florida says."

"I don't know who told you that," Swanson said, regaining his composure but losing none of the anger. "I don't know who said that, but whoever it was is a liar."

Meyers glanced at Ludkvasen. They both looked smug. "All right," he said. "No need to get all testy. I'm just asking. Not my problem, anyway, even if you did."

"I gave the money back."

"Yeah, yeah, Kenny, I know. You keep reminding us. But that's not the problem. The problem is that you stole the money off a dead man. That he stole it first is the only reason you're not facing more charges. You stole money from a dead man. You hid evidence in a federal crime. And you gave the money back only after you knew that we knew that you had it. Does this make sense to you?"

Swanson decided now that maybe it would be best to keep his mouth shut. That's what his lawyer would've told him, and had.

31

Two days later Stone called Liz Bezack again and asked her the same questions Meyers had asked Swanson, though in a much friendlier manner. She told him again that she had never once heard Kenny talk about giving Krapczak some pills in order to look for the money, and could never imagine him doing such a thing.

"If he was killed," she told him, "there's no way I would believe that Kenny had anything to do with it. I know Kenny. It's not in him."

He thanked her for her time and told her he hoped he wouldn't have to bother her again with this.

"Speaking of which," he asked before hanging up. "Have you heard much from Agent Meyers lately?"

"Oh...yeah, he called me once last week, just to let me know how Kenny was doing. Why do you ask?"

"No real reason," he said. "That's very kind of him, keeping you updated that way. Next time you talk to him, be sure and tell him I said hello."

That'll give the old rooster something to think about, he thought after hanging up the phone.

Stone picked up the phone again and dialed Sarah Egtin at the lab.

"Sergeant Egtin, hey," he said, "I have a question for you concerning that Krapczak evidence."

"You got my report?"

"Yeah, I did, thanks—but this is about something that wasn't in the report."

"Shoot," she said. "I'll tell you what I can."

"Okay. Now, did you happen to test the glass or the bottle for any residue?"

She was quiet for a moment. "What, ah, kind of residue did you have in mind?"

"Drugs," he said.

"You got the coroner's report back?"

"No, not yet," he said. "I'm just playing a hunch. He didn't have enough alcohol in his system to kill him. He barely had enough to be drunk."

"Well," Egtin said, "I'll be curious to see the coroner's report myself. But what I can tell you straight off is this. We were dealing with a big guy here. And just as it would take a lot of alcohol to kill him, it would take a lot of drugs to kill him, too. In fact, I can safely say that if the drugs were of a sufficient dosage to kill him, there would be a visible residue in the glass, the bottle, wherever."

"Okay."

"And there wasn't. They were all clean."

That wasn't the answer Stone was hoping to hear.

"Do you suppose you could go back and test them again?" he asked. "If you have something specific to look for?"

"Detective Stone," she said patiently, "now, I'm not trying to be snarky or anything here. I'm just telling you how things look from my perspective. If there was no visible residue in the glass—and there wasn't—then there's no reason to dig it out again and bring it back to the lab. We won't find anything. Waste of time."

32

The final coroner's report on the death of Nedward Krapczak (white male, 37 y.o., 5'9", 263 lbs.) didn't reach Detective Stone until May tenth. No more of the missing cash had reappeared in the meantime and, so far as he knew, Swanson was still in Newark awaiting sentencing. The case, by then, had been all but shoved from Stone's mind by more pressing matters.

As he flipped through the report, though, it all came back to him. Under "Cause of Death," DeKay had typed "undetermined," which was par for the course whenever there were mysterious circumstances. Still, he felt a vague sense of disappointment that it couldn't be more concrete.

Then, in the summation, DeKay had reported that death had been caused by "combined drug toxicity: ethanol, methadone, oxycodone, paracetamol, and alprazolam." In layman's terms, booze, methadone, Percocet, and Xanax.

Stone almost wished he was surprised by this. He wasn't sure where the methadone had come from, but there was no question in his mind that the Percocet and Xanax in Krapczak's bloodstream had come from Swanson's medicine cabinet. Same drugs that had killed Simon Malstein.

The kicker was in the final line of DeKay's report: "Foul play cannot be definitively excluded."

The problem, Stone knew, was that it couldn't be definitively included, either. There was no physical evidence that Krapczak didn't take the drugs himself. There were no witnesses who claimed that they had seen Swanson give Krapczak the pills.

There was no evidence that the pills had been forced upon him in any way against his will or without his knowledge. In short, the only evidence he had against Swanson was a hunch and a jailhouse snitch, and neither one of those would hold up in court. As it stood, Krapczak's death could've been a suicide, an accidental overdose, or a homicide—and once again the only two people who could tell him which it was weren't talking.

As he filed the report away, Stone got to thinking about Ned Krapczak, a man he had come to know only after he was dead. There was so much he didn't know about him—what had driven him to take the money, what had happened to him on the road, how he'd ended up the way he did. He would never know.

Funny thing is, he thought, smiling to himself, *if this was an accident or a suicide, and if that Malstein business really was an accident, too, this Swanson kid has got to be the unluckiest son of a bitch I've ever known.*

The following day Detective Stone declared the case closed.

33

On August first, Kenny Swanson, looking pale and thin and frightened, was delivered to the courtroom of federal Judge Bertrand Williams for sentencing.

Agents Meyers and Ludkvasen were seated in the gallery. They didn't go to many of the sentencing hearings for the perps they'd nabbed, but there was something about the Swanson case. They liked him, the way you'd like a retarded puppy. At the same time they wanted to see the lying little twerp put away.

"Which one o' you jive turkeys is gonna move yo' ass?" a voice whispered behind them. Both men, more confused than anything, turned to find Detective Robert Stone, dressed in a sharp white shirt and neatly pressed black pants. He carried a sport jacket over one arm.

"Oh, you have got to be kidding," Meyers said.

"Figured you'd be here," Stone said. "And figured it would be worth the trip." He took the empty seat next to Ludkvasen. "You talk to him?" he asked, nodding toward Swanson, who was seated at the front of the courtroom.

"Nah," Ludkvasen said, as ever clutching a napkin. "I don't think he'd be much interested in seeing us right now. He's got it bad enough with this judge."

"What's with the fancy duds?" Meyers asked.

"I'm trying to impress you, Agent Meyers."

Meyers blinked at him. "Detective Stone, you are a good cop, an excellent cop. Really. But I gotta say…" He looked Stone up and down. "You are no John Shaft. And believe me, I know."

"Oh, shut your mouth," Stone said.

The court was called to order and the charges were read.

When the judge offered Swanson the opportunity to make a statement before the court, Kenny stood slowly and unfolded a piece of paper. He cleared his throat and, hesitantly, began to read.

"I...I would just like to say to the court...and to my family...and to Mike's family, how deeply sorry I am for what I did." His voice was trembling. Neither Stone, Meyers, nor Ludkvasen had ever heard his voice tremble this way before.

"I took what didn't belong to me, and I...I shouldn't have. I would also like to apologize for various things I said to investigators that weren't exactly true. But I also want them to know that a lot of the things I said—my behavior—can be blamed on the prescription drugs given to me by these pusher doctors. So I'd...I'd just like to say I'm sorry if I misled the investigators in any way."

"In *any* way?" Ludkvasen whispered. "How about in *every conceivable* way?"

"So I'm...I'm just real sorry," Swanson concluded, before refolding the paper and taking his seat.

"Now, Kenny," the judge began, sounding weary, "you seem like a mostly decent fellow. But as you know, there's still over a million dollars missing at the end of this whole sordid debacle. And the possibility that you still have it hidden someplace is right up here at the front of my mind today." He tapped his graying temple. "But since you are not charged with the actual theft you cannot legally be held liable for its whereabouts. Mr. Crap Sack had the money for a while," he said, raising his right hand dramatically, "and so who really knows what might have happened to it? But then you had the money for a while, too." He raised his other hand. "And it's possible you've hidden it and have every intention of retrieving it again as soon as you get out. I just want you to be aware that we'll be keeping our eyes on you. Now," he shuffled some papers, "before announcing sentence, I would also like to point out that figuring into my verdict is the fact that you lied to federal investigators not just once but repeatedly. Told crazy stories in an effort to hold on to that money. Lying to federal investigators is a crime, too, Kenny, and though you're not officially being charged with that here, in my mind you are. With that, I sentence you to no more than six years and seven months, to be served in a federal penitentiary, as well as to a fine of one hundred thousand dollars."

"Well," Ludkvasen whispered, "there goes the loot he was holding for Ned."

"What if he does have it stashed someplace?" Stone asked Meyers as the pair left the courtroom. Ludkvasen, that funny little Swede, had decided to stay behind and watch a few more trials.

"The money, I mean. Would you be able to do something about it? It sounded like the judge was saying he'd almost be scot-free."

Meyers paused when they stepped outside and squinted toward the sun. It was too hot out.

"Yeah, maybe Kenny has a little nest egg in mind for Liz and himself. It's a nice idea. Romantic."

"But should he get out and suddenly, mysteriously find himself with an extra million—is there anything to be done about it?"

Meyers looked at Stone, surprised that he wasn't content to let people hold on to their dreams once in a while. He sighed. "If we wanted to go back and charge him with lying to a federal officer, we could. Seven years from now, he finds himself with a million bucks and decides to take a nice trip with Liz outside of Florida? Whammo, we got him for transporting stolen property across state lines. Believe you me, Detective Stone, if we really want to snag him, there will be federal charges at our disposal that will sufficiently fit his activities."

Stone considered this as they approached Meyers's car.

"You in town long?" Meyers asked.

"Just overnight. Fly back tomorrow."

"Buy you a drink, then?" Meyers asked. "We never did get around to having a drink down by you."

"Never came up, I guess," Stone said. "But yeah, I'd like that."

Meyers put his car keys back in his pocket. "I know a place," he said, "c'mon," and led Stone to a small bar two blocks away. Johnny Rocco's, it was called, and the sun streaming through the dirty windows lit the heavy dust hanging in the air. It was early yet, and the place was empty and quiet. The two men took seats at the bar.

The barkeep, a bald man in his late sixties with a boxer's face and a white apron, asked them what they wanted. Stone ordered a beer, Meyers a vodka tonic.

"Is that Mr. Rocco?" Stone whispered as the old man stepped away to pour the drinks.

"Nope."

The bartender returned a few moments later and placed the drinks down on the bar. Meyers handed him a bill.

"So…you saw my report," Stone said. "Think he got away with it?"

"Murder, you mean?"

"Yeah."

Meyers looked at his glass and shook his head. "Not really. I don't know. But even if he did kill Krapczak, we still got him, and he's still doing time."

"Not for murder, though."

"No, but if the evidence ever crops up, you'll get him then." In a voice that was almost weary, he added, "Sometimes, Bob, you take what you can get in this business. Eliot Ness learned that a long time ago."

"So did Bobby Seale."

Meyers chuckled. "Point taken."

At the other end of the bar, the bartender was flipping sadly through the newspaper. Meyers took a sip, then paused. "You know," he said, turning to Stone, "the one thing about this whole case I can't help thinking. Been thinking it from the beginning."

"Yeah?"

"Something in me can't help but admire Ned Krapczak."

"And why's that?" Stone asked.

"Simple," Meyers said, with a rueful smile. "Because he pulled it off. And more than that. He got away with it. That doesn't happen too often in this life."

ACKNOWLEDGMENTS

I would once again like to humbly thank my agent, Melanie Jackson, and Virgin USA's publisher Ken Siman—as well as editor Caroline Trefler—for having good humor and faith enough to give this thing a go.

Special thanks are due the Federal Bureau of Investigation, specifically the Newark Division and Office of Public Affairs in Washington, D.C., as well as the West Palm Beach Police Department for their generous cooperation. The involved agents and officers provided cordial and invaluable assistance in putting all the pieces together.

Other special thanks are due remarkable book designer Laura Lindgren and the equally remarkable copy editor Don Kennison, both of whom helped make this much more than it was.

I would also like to thank Mom and Dad; Mary, Bob, McKenzie, and Jordan Adrians; Derek Davis; Ken Swezey; Bill Monahan; Dave Williams and Jennifer Bates; Daniel Riccuito and Marilyn Palmeri; Homer Flynn; Mike Walsh; Philip Harris; Ryan Knighton; Richard Dellifraine; Paul Lukas; John Graz; Linda Hunsaker; Dave Read; TRP; Tito Perdue; J. R. Taylor; the estate of the incomparable Edward G. Robinson—as well as the Residents and David Shire for providing the soundtracks that kept me going.

A particular debt of gratitude is due Morgan Intrieri, to whom this book is dedicated. Without her unshaking wisdom, encouragement, humor, and assistance—from library research to our endless conversations regarding this book (and everything else)—this never would have come about. I love her very much.